# january, february, june or july

## helen fogwill porter

BREAKWATER

**Canadian Cataloguing in Publication Data**

Porter, Helen Fogwill, 1930-

january, february, june or july

ISBN 0-920911-27-7

I. Title.

PS8581.077J36 1988   C813'.54   C88-098563-1
PR9199 . 3 . P67J36    1988

Second printing 1991.
Third printing 1994.

Cover illustration by Janice Udell.

The Publisher gratefully acknowledges the financial support of The Canada Council which has helped make this publication possible.

The Publisher acknowledges the financial contribution of the Cultural Affairs Division of the Department of Culture, Recreation and Youth, Government of Newfoundland and Labrador which has helped make this publication possible.

For

*John Knight Porter*

1930-1983

who grew up near Gaspar Street

# Acknowledgments

Thanks to      My family
The Canada Council
Marsha Kaplansky
Bucky King
Kevin Major
The Newfoundland & Labrador Arts Council
The Newfoundland Writers' Guild
Les Norris
Brenda Power
Shelley Tanaka
The Writers at Tamwood Retreat

Special thanks to Bernice Morgan, who read the book in manuscript and gave me her usual perceptive and helpful advice and to E.L. Doctorow who, without ever knowing it, inspired me to write this book.

*The summer moon hung full in the sky.*
*For the time being it was the great fact in the world.*

Willa Cather, 1876-1947

# *Prologue*

**The NCO Club, Pepperrell Air Force Base, St. John's, 1958**

Eileen sat down at the table and drank thirstily from the tall, frosty glass in front of her. "God, am I ever warm," she said, wiping her forehead with a tissue. "That fella really put me through my paces."

"Do you like him?" Ada asked. She took a compact out of her purse and checked her face in the mirror.

"How do I know? He never said one word." Eileen glanced quickly over her shoulder. "Tell you who I think I could go for, though. See that guy over by the door, the tall one with the light hair? I wouldn't mind getting to know him."

"Oh, yeah, him. I think his name is Gary. Brenda Larkin was dancin' with him the other night. He's a lovely dancer." Ada clicked the compact shut, and put it back in her purse. "Oh, my God, Eileen, he's comin' over here, and he's looking right at you."

Eileen fluffed up her hair and popped a wintergreen lifesaver into her mouth.

"Would you like to dance?" The tall fair-haired young man was standing beside her chair.

"Sure I would," said Eileen. He took her hand and led her toward the dance floor. The band was playing *Love Letters in the Sand.*

# *One*

---

Heather waved goodbye to Debbie and Donna, turned the corner and walked toward home. She hoped they hadn't noticed the sudden rush of colour to her cheeks. When was she going to get over this stupid habit of blushing? She thought she'd been so careful about keeping her feelings to herself. How in the world had Debbie caught on about Frank?

The sun was gone now. Heather shivered, wishing she had worn her jacket instead of just the sweater. After all, it would soon be October. Gaspar Street looked deserted; the children must still be playing in the meadow. Mr. Peddle was changing a tire on his car. Across the street, Bertie Lane was sitting on his doorstep, fast asleep, his mouth hanging open. At a quick glance he looked like an old man.

She walked faster, anxious to get inside the house before Bertie woke up. It would be nice and warm in there. She wanted to climb into a hot bath with the book she'd started reading the night before.

Shirley was sitting at the kitchen table, reading the *National Enquirer*. "I was wondering where you were to," she said, not looking up. "Is it nice out now?"

"Not too bad. The sun was lovely earlier but it's getting chilly. Like Nan would say, it's kind of fallish."

"Do you want a cup of coffee or anything? I just boiled the kettle." Shirley finally looked up from the *Enquirer.*"God, I wonder can you believe what's in this rag? Look what it says here about Teddy Kennedy. That can't be true, can it?"

Heather looked over her sister's shoulder to see the large colour photograph of Teddy with a tall redhead in a flesh-coloured bikini. She threw her sweater across the washer and sat down opposite Shirley, kicking off her shoes."All the Kennedys liked the women. I read a book once about old Joe and that movie star Carol Burnett is always imitatin', what's her name? Gloria Swanson. But you can't believe half what you reads in that thing. I wouldn't waste my money on it."

Shirley looked up again."I notice you don't mind readin' 'em when I brings 'em home. I didn't buy this one, anyhow. I was over to Lorraine's and she was finished with it. She picks them up when she gets her groceries."

Heather went to the fridge and poured herself a glass of Tang. "What's Lorraine doin' these days? I haven't seen her for a dog's age."

"Oh, she's okay, I s'pose. I was only there a few minutes this afternoon. Mike was gone off huntin', as usual."

"How is Jason?"

"Into everything. He wanted to come with me when I left but I was too tired to go chasin' after him today. Lorraine was browned off, like she always is. I hope I don't end up like her."

Heather looked across the table at Shirley, whose head was still bent over the *National Enquirer.* Shirley was the prettiest of the three of them, looking a lot like their mother must have looked when she was younger. There were snapshots of Eileen in the old album that you could only tell from those of Shirley by the different clothes and hairstyles. Shirley's hair was still very blonde; she didn't even have to put anything in it. Her body was soft and rounded. She could wear Eileen's brassieres, size 36 C. Heather looked down at her own front. She was almost as flat as a boy.

9

Shirley closed the magazine and passed it across the table."Here, you want this? That's about all I can take for now." Heather flicked open the *Enquirer*, glancing idly at the exposé pictures of Princess Caroline and Burt Reynolds, and a story about a woman whose retarded daughter only had three months to live.

Shirley went over to the sink and began to run hot water and liquid detergent into the frying pan."I s'pose I got to clean this thing up," she said, screwing up her face. With her back toward Heather she asked "Are you going out tonight, or what?"

"I don't think so. I'm invited to a party up to Donna Power's but I'm not fussy about goin'. Why?"

Shirley crouched down to look in the cupboard under the sink. "Haven't we got any pot cleaners? Cripes, this place is fousty. There's even beetles crawlin' around down here, or I s'pose they're beetles, them hard black things. I hates 'em."

"Mom says they're harmless, but I don't know," said Heather, putting down her glass of Tang."They turns my stomach. Mom is so proud of not havin' cockroaches or bedbugs. I think those things are just as bad." She swirled the Tang around in the glass, not sure she could swallow any more of it.

Shirley found a small piece of steel wool and began to scrub at the pan."Ugh, this stuff is caked right on. Randy phoned me when I was fryin' up some onions for my lunch and they burnt while I was talkin' to him." She scrubbed in silence for a little while and then said: "I was goin' to have Randy in tonight and I'd like to have the place to myself, you know what I mean."

Heather could not imagine anyone wanting to bring a boyfriend into this squalor. Squalor was a word she had recently come across in a story by J.D. Salinger; she felt it applied accurately to the usual state of the house. She had given up complaining about the mess; the last time she'd done it her mother had looked at her sharply and said,"I don't see nothing the matter with your two hands. If it all gets on your nerves so much, why don't you clean it up yourself? When I was *your* age I was scrubbin' floors for Mom and for Nan, too. Now when I gets home from work night-time all I wants to do is sit down and put my feet up. First when I started takin' my course I thought it'd be lovely to be a beautician, foolin' around with hair all day long.

Nobody ever told me what murder it was on the feet and back. And puttin' up with crabby customers, that's something else." The squalor in the Salinger story had been of quite a different kind but the word seemed appropriate just the same.

"Won't Mom be here?" Heather put her fingers to her lips, then remembered that she was trying to stop biting her nails.

"When was Mom last home on a Saturday night? Herself and Mollie are goin' down to the Sundance, they got a two-for-one steak special on down there." Shirley threw the dirty water from the frying pan down the drain."I can't get this friggin' thing clean. It's as old as Buckley's goat, anyhow. I'm just gonna wipe it out and put it down in the cupboard with the rest of the mess."

"Why aren't you and Randy goin' out somewhere yourselves?" Heather had seen Randy only twice, once when she had met him and Shirley at a movie and one morning shortly afterwards when he had given her a ride to school. He was a stocky, dark-haired fellow of about twenty who had recently come back from Fort McMurray and was still looking for work in St. John's.

"Two very good reasons." said Shirley, sitting down at the table again and lighting a cigarette."Number one, his car is broke down, number two we got no money. He shouldn't a bought that car, anyway. Ted Janes gave him a rotten deal on it. I wish I could get a job, I knows that much. I goes to Manpower every day and there's not a thing on the go."

"Maybe you should go back to school. Why don't you try to get into the Fisheries College? They got all the high-school grades up there and it's all grownups."

"I think you got to be out of school longer than I am to get into that." Shirley blew smoke across the table, right into Heather's face. "You're some lucky you don't smoke, girl. Cigarettes are after takin' almost all the money I got outa my last cheque from Kentucky Fried. Anyhow, I'm gonna take typing after Christmas, down to the Y. It's a lot easier to get a job when you got typing." Shirley leaned back in her chair, blowing smoke towards the ceiling."Well, what about it, Heather? Can't you go out and give Randy and me a bit of time to ourselves?"

Heather hesitated."I s'pose I *could* go the party," she said at last."Debbie really wants me to. She's phonin' me later on to see if I'm goin'. " All at once Frank Marshall's face appeared before her eyes. He was really handsome. His hair was dark and curly and he had dark brown eyes, kind of sad-looking. She wished now that Debbie hadn't told her he'd be at the party. He was probably bringing a girl with him, anyhow.

"Yes, girl, go on to the party. You never haves any fun. I'd go cracked if I was like you, stayin' in every night studyin' or readin' library books. It's not good for you." Shirley reached for her purse on the washer. She pulled something out and pushed it toward Heather.

Heather picked up the round plastic case and turned it over."My God, Shirl, that's birth control pills!" She had only seen pictures of them before."Where did you get them?"

"Myself and Carmel Healey went up to Planned Parenthood last week. She's goin' out with this fella, Wade Parsons, his name is, and she was six days overdue on her period last month. She nearly went up the wall. Anyway, I was talkin' to her over to Rice's one night and she persuaded me to go up with her the next day." Shirley looked at Heather, as if expecting her to say something. Heather was turning the plastic container over and over in her hand.

"We didn't even know where it was at, but we looked it up in the phone book." Shirley half-smiled, and went on,"I felt like a fool first but they're real nice up there, not stuck up and that like I thought they'd be. There was a woman doctor there and she examined us; I didn't like that too much. It would've felt more natural if it was a man, you know what I mean." She glanced across at Heather again. Heather was afraid she was going to giggle, not because any of this was funny but for the same reason that she sometimes laughed when she was telling somebody about a handicapped person, or something very tragic. Hysteria, perhaps, or maybe just embarrassment. She kept her head down, mentally counting the pills in the container.

"Look, Heather, do you really want to hear about this? You don't seem very interested." There was an edge to Shirley's voice; she seemed almost ready to cry.

Heather looked up, the threat of giggling over."Yes, I am," she insisted."Come on, tell me."

"Well, they gave Carmel a pregnancy test and it came out negative; don't say she wasn't happy! They told her she better have another one later on, just in case it was wrong. She did the next week, and everything was okay. Anyhow, while we were up there the doctor told us about all the different kinds of birth control and both of us picked the Pill. It's a lot easier than all the other stuff. She was already after askin' us if we were 'sexually active'. That's a nice way to put it, ent it? Sexually active! Anyway, I been takin' 'em ever since."

Heather passed the pills back to Shirley."Here, girl, put 'em away. If Mom saw them she'd have a fit and a half."

Shirley slipped them into her purse."What kind of a fit do you think she'd have if I got pregnant, then? I'm not gettin' caught like Lorraine did. You should go up and get some too, just to be on the safe side. You never know when you might need 'em. It's better to be sure than sorry."

Heather bent her head over the *National Enquirer*. She knew she was blushing again; she didn't want Shirley to see her face. Talk about sex, the Pill, intimate parts of her body, always made her uncomfortable. She didn't even like to look at her naked self in the mirror when she got out of the bath, or strip casually the way so many of the other girls did in the dressing room at the Aquarena. Debbie was always telling her she had a good figure but that wasn't what she was worried about. Of course her mother, in spite of her frank speech, was something like that herself. She often talked about having to wash herself "down there" so she wouldn't smell, and after she and Mollie had watched a television program about self-examination for breast cancer they had talked about how foolish they felt when they tried to feel for lumps in their own breasts.

"My God, Mollie, it's like feelin' yourself up," Eileen had said, looking down at her tightly-brassiered bosom."I'd rather for the doctor to do it, wouldn't you? After all, he got to know more about it than we do." Eileen was terrified of cancer, especially breast cancer. Her own mother had had a breast removed a few years before and Nan's sister, Eileen's Aunt Pearl, had died at fifty-one when her breast cancer spread to her lungs.

"Well, what about it?" Shirley asked now. "Are you goin' out tonight, or what?"

"I guess I might as well. I can always go to Nan's if I don't feel like goin' to the party. She's tired of askin' me in there to sleep."

"Aw girl, don't be an old woman before you're a young one. You'll be bored to death in there with Nan and Herb. He'll be talkin' about gettin' shaved before twelve o'clock, and shining his shoes for Sunday. You might meet a nice fella tonight if you goes to the party. You don't know what you're missin'. If Randy is still here when you gets home, give a loud knock and take your time comin' in, okay? Better still, wait for me to answer the door."

"What about if Mom comes home early? You better watch out."

"You know she's not gonna be home before two at the earliest on a Saturday night." Shirley held her hands out in front of her and looked at her fingernails. "Ugh, my nails are a mess. I wish I could get 'em to grow long. They always breaks off." She picked at the polish on her index finger. "Mom is funny, ent she? She's after havin' a hysterectomy now, so she can do what she like. But when she talks about us you'd think she was the Virgin Mary or someone."

Later, in the bath, Heather thought about Shirley and Lorraine and her mother. Life would be a lot simpler if she was more like them. Or would it? At least she didn't have to worry about the Pill or getting pregnant, things like that. She wondered how Debbie managed. If what she hinted at was true, Debbie was already sexually active, and had been for a long time. Yet Heather was pretty sure she wasn't on the Pill. She joked about French safes sometimes, especially after a date with one of the American sailors who came in from Argentia on weekends or with Harry, her latest boyfriend. But she had never talked directly about her own sex life to Heather.

Her thoughts shifted to Linda Stone, her friend at school. She hardly ever talked about sex either; if she did it was in a general way. She spoke of birth control and abortion the same way you'd talk about war or peace or religion. Debbie didn't like Linda. It wasn't fair; she had only met her two or three times, and then very briefly. "I don't know what you sees in that one Stone," she'd said to Heather time and time again. "Snobs like her got nothing in common with people like us."

14

"Linda is not a snob." She was tired of telling Debbie that. Just because they had lots of money and a big house and Dr. Stone was a professor at the university didn't mean they weren't nice."If she was a snob, why would she want to go around with someone like me?"

"I don't know, girl," Debbie had laughed and poked her in the ribs."P'raps she's studyin' how the other half lives. Anyway, you can be kind of nice sometimes, so why wouldn't she like you?" She had started to giggle herself then; the next thing the two of them were laughing helplessly, holding on to each other for support."Galin'," Nan called it, and "you'll cry before you goes to bed tonight," she'd warn anyone she noticed doing it. One thing for sure, Heather laughed a lot more when she was with Debbie than she did with Linda.

She sloshed water over herself, and looked at the length of her body stretched out in the bathtub. Except for her almost non-existent breasts, her body wasn't bad."I wish my legs were long and curvy, like yours," Debbie said often, especially when they went swimming at the Aquarena. They both liked swimming; it was the only athletic activity Heather was any good at. Floating around in the water she felt the way she wished she felt all the time; carefree and at ease, living entirely in the present.

"My knees are so skinny and knobby," Debbie would say, looking down at her legs before she started to dry herself."I had to give up wearin' shorts around the street in the summertime because the boys used to call me coke-bottle legs. I felt like killin' 'em."

Once, when she was thirteen, Heather had been lying on the grass in Bowring Park one hot July day after swimming. She'd been trying to get a sun tan. Debbie had gone up to the Bungalow to get them some drinks and a young man in the uniform of the Canadian Armed Forces had sat down beside her. Right away Heather sat up straight, covering her legs with a towel."Don't do that, Blondie," the young man had said softly."Your legs are beautiful. Don't cover them up." She had just sat there, feeling like a fool, not knowing what to do or say, until Debbie came back and he went away."Did I frighten him off?" Debbie asked, passing Heather her Seven-Up and beginning to sip her own Pepsi."He was some cute."

For months after that Heather had thought off and on about the young soldier. Sometimes, in bed at night, she let herself wonder what

15

would have happened if she had talked to him, got to know him better. The backs of his hands had been covered with fine, reddish-gold hairs. When she let her mind dwell too long on things like that certain parts of her body ached to be touched.

She picked up her book from the edge of the bath and held it close to her face, trying not to get it wet. It was *The Blue Castle*, by L.M. Montgomery. Valancy was really going to marry Barney. She had just found out from the doctor that, at twenty-nine, she had only a year to live. Shy, timid girl though she was, she had asked Barney to marry her so that she'd have one year of perfect happiness after the dull, narrow life that had so far been dominated by her mother and her older relatives. Heather knew from past experience with L.M. Montgomery that there'd be no actual sex in the book. On their wedding night Valancy would just close the bedroom door and the reader wouldn't learn anything else about her and Barney until the next morning when they were eating a tasty hot breakfast, cooked by Barney, of course. She preferred that kind of book to the ones Eileen brought home from the beauty parlour, where nothing was left to the imagination. She had to admit, though, that while she was reading an ancient copy of *The Carpetbaggers* she'd had that warm feeling 'down there' more than once. When she went to the bathroom she noticed that her pants were damp. It wasn't time for her period, and besides there was no colour to the moist spot. After she finished the book she vowed she wouldn't read another one like it, but she hadn't kept that vow very long. She was glad that today she could read in comfort, secure in the knowledge that L.M. Montgomery was very different from Harold Robbins.

All the same, *The Blue Castle* did have an aura about it that was different from any other Montgomery books she'd ever read. Unlike in *Anne of Windy Poplars* or *Anne's House of Dreams*, the reader definitely got the feeling that something strange and exciting was going on behind the closed doors even if the author didn't describe it. She turned to the front of the book and saw that it had been published much later than the Anne books. That explained it, then.

She stayed in the bath until the water was almost cold. After she had dried herself she sprinkled Johnson's Baby Powder all over her body and put on her yellow chenille dressing gown. She had seen a gorgeous red satin robe down at Bowring's but had almost fainted when she read the price tag. Nan had given her the chenille one for Christmas a couple of years before.

Eileen used Avon cosmetics; her friend Mollie had been selling Avon for years as well as working at Ricardo's House of Beauty. She let Eileen have everything at a reduced rate. One day at Bowring's Heather had sprayed herself with an expensive French perfume from one of the testers on the counter. When she got home her mother had sniffed hard and asked, "What in the name of the Almighty have you got plastered on yourself now? You smells like Barrett's Funeral Parlour."

"I'd rather smell like a funeral parlour than a beauty parlour," Heather had mumbled back, and then was thankful that her mother, preoccupied with an especially steamy scene between Mitch and Rachel on *Another World*, hadn't heard her. Eileen always got mad when she thought she heard Heather, or anyone else, putting on airs. "I hates anyone gatchin'," was the way she explained it; if she caught one of her daughters doing it she would return to the subject day after weary day.

When Heather found herself looking through the wardrobe in her bedroom to see if she had any clean pants and tops she realized she had made up her mind to go to the party. She was pulling out a burgundy-coloured velour top and her other pair of jeans when her eyes fell on the blue corduroy jumper that her father had sent her for her birthday several years before. As she looked at it she tried to remember how long it was since she or either of her sisters had got a present from him. "He forgets about ye now that he's married again," Eileen had told them, not without a note of triumph in her voice. "Especially now that they got their own little baby." Heather tried not to think of the years she'd spent writing to her father, and the plans they — or she — had made for her to go and visit him in Iowa. Then that summer she was thirteen, when she thought for sure he'd send her the money for the trip, he had written a short note to tell her that he'd just got married to Mary Lester, a young woman who lived on a neighbouring farm and whose first husband had died in a tractor accident. "I'd rather for you to wait awhile, Heather," the note had said. "Mary's got two little boys of her own and I'm going to have to spend some time getting used to them. I'll let you know later when it'll be a good time to come." She had only had two letters from him since then; neither had said anything about her coming to visit.

"I remember that Mary Lester," Eileen said when she heard the news."Only she wasn't Mary Lester then, she was Mary Woods. She must be a good ten years younger than your father, maybe more than that. She was a white-faced, skinny kind of a girl. I knew damn well he'd get married again as soon as the old woman kicked the bucket. That Mary got it a lot easier than I ever had it."

It had taken Heather a long time to put away her dream of going to her father for a long visit, or even living with him. She remembered how she had talked about him to Debbie who, after listening for an hour to Heather's rapt description of what life in Iowa would be like, would try to bring her back to earth by telling her that she didn't really know her father, that he'd be no more to her than any other stranger if she did go and stay with him. Heather had known better, or thought she had; she had let Debbie talk on, knowing she just didn't understand. Debbie didn't even know who her own father was; her mother, only eighteen when Debbie was born, had not told anyone. She had moved to Toronto years ago, married and had a crowd of children; Debbie had always lived with her grandparents, and was only occasionally bitter.

After the letter about her father's marriage had come — in her own mind Heather always thought of it as The Letter — she had tried not to think about him so much. She still kept a little box of pictures of him in her bureau drawer, mostly snaps he'd had taken with her mother before and just after they were married. Eileen had looked so different then, so slim and young. It was strange to see her with long hair and, in some of the pictures, wearing a hat. Her father looked like the boy he had been, a skinny young man in his USAF uniform, his light brown hair cut very short. She had one picture of him that he'd sent her when he was still writing regularly. He was standing under a hickory tree, dressed in his Sunday best; he had told her he'd been all ready for church when a friend had snapped the picture. He wore a blue suit, a pinkish-coloured shirt and a dark blue tie. His smile seemed artificial, put on for the purpose of the picture. Heather thought his eyes looked lonely; maybe she had just been reading that into them. He wouldn't be lonely any more now that he was married to Mary and they had their own little daughter as well as Mary's two young sons.

The little girl must be two years old now. Her father had sent a birth announcement card but there'd been no picture. Her name was Rosalie Dawn. When she thought about her, Heather imagined her as a pretty blue-eyed child with curly flaxen hair. She loved the word flaxen, had come across it in fairy tales and other old books. It wasn't used much any more.

Imagine, Rosalie Dawn was her half-sister, and Shirley's and Lorraine's. It was strange to have a blood relation so far away and unknown.

Heather was still holding the jeans and the top in her hands, as if she didn't know what to do with them. As she hung them across the back of a chair she noticed on the floor the white sandals that she'd been wearing all summer She'd been trying to decide whether to keep them for another year or to throw them out. An almost-frightening sensation swept over her as she recalled a pair of white, T-strap shoes she had worn when she was a tiny girl in Iowa. She had been in her father's arms and he'd been laughing about the white shoe polish rubbing off on his good dark suit. Surely she couldn't remember that happening; perhaps Eileen had told her about it. She'd been barely three when her mother had brought her and Lorraine and Shirley back to Newfoundland. It was funny. Shirley and Lorraine, who should be able to remember their father more clearly than she did, rarely spoke about him.

The phone rang as Heather was flinging the white shoes into the wardrobe. She hurried downstairs to answer it; Shirley must have gone out. She picked up the phone in mid-ring.

"Is that you, Heather? What're you doin'?" Automatically Heather held the receiver at arm's length as Eileen's voice came through loud and clear."Listen, will you put on something for tea? I'm goin' to be real hungry when I gets home. Kraft Dinner'll be okay, and you can fry up a bit of ham to go with it. I got some nice ham over to Murray's yesterday. What did you do today?"

"Nothing much. I got the little suit for Carol when I was downtown this morning."

"That's good. Did you get a shower card? I think I got some tissue paper up in my drawer. Are you goin' out anywhere tonight?"

"I might go to a party up to Donna Power's. Debbie wants me to."

"What Power is that? Was her mother an O'Keefe, I wonder?" Without waiting for an answer Eileen went on, "Look, myself and Mollie are goin' down to the Sundance tonight. You can lock the door and go on to bed when you're ready. I'll have my key." There was a short pause. "Listen, that's not gonna be one of them hard parties you're goin' to, is it? I don't want you gettin' mixed up with a tough crowd. If her mother was Sheila O'Keefe she'll be all right, though. Okay, I'll see you in about an hour, if I can hold out here that long. We were some busy today."

"Okay, see ya." After she hung up the phone Heather took the wet dish cloth from the sink and wiped down the kitchen table. Then she knelt on the floor and started to search in the cupboards for the package of Kraft Dinner.

# Two

The party had been going on for about three hours. By now, everyone who wanted to get drunk or stoned was already there, or nearly. The stereo was turned up high; there was just one dim light burning, a blue bulb that cast eerie shadows around the room. Heather was squeezed into the corner of a love seat, with Debbie next to her and Harry Soper on the other side of Debbie. Harry and Debbie were sharing a joint, and giggling. There was a lot of giggling in the room.

"Hey, be careful of that bit of weed there, Harry," said Donna, coming back from the kitchen with more beer."If you burns a hole in the carpet Mom'll have my head." She picked up the joint and took a long drag on it."That's good stuff, Harry," she said at last."Is it your own?"

*I said 'No, no, no, I don't sell it no more*
*I'm tired of wakin' up on the floor....'*

Harry's hand was inside Debbie's blouse as he sang. "I don't have nothing to do with pushin' the stuff now, Donna, girl," he said."All I does is smoke it. I got to be careful while I'm on probation. They're watchin' me like hawks. This is some stuff Tom Butler got in from Toronto. He haven't been caught yet." He held out his free hand; it was shaking just a little.

"Here, gimme back that smoke." He drew on it deeply, then held it in front of Debbie."You want some more, Deb, or am I makin' you happy enough?" Debbie didn't answer. Her mouth was pressed into the opening of Harry's shirt. Turning as far as he could toward Heather, he said,"How about you, my ducky? You're not havin' no fun at all. Why don't you let me get in the middle between you and Deb? I can handle the two of ye easy."

Heather got up and walked toward the kitchen, a beer bottle in her hand. She had only drunk a few sips; she didn't really like the taste of beer and, besides, she still remembered what a mess it had made of her the last time. The bottle was a kind of defence against the constant offers of beer and marijuana that were coming her way. And I can always brain someone with it if I got to, she thought, laughing nervously to herself as she made her way around the bodies on the floor.

So far, at least, the party had been a quiet one. Several of the boys, and a few of the girls, appeared to have been half-stoned when they arrived. Donna had warned them all about the dangers of making too much noise."The crowd around here are some nosy, " she said, pointing toward the big window across which the flowered drapes were pulled tightly."They likes to get people in trouble."

"I know," said a tall, thin boy with a long scar just above his mouth." 'Member the time we were up here the spring, first when ye moved in, and someone called the cops? I was scared shitless that night because I was after talkin' back to 'em down to the police station when they hauled me in the time Mike's Groceteria was broken into, right? I was afraid it was gonna be the same guys."

"Frank Marshall handled that some good, didn't he?" Donna smiled as she recalled what had happened."Was I ever glad he was here! When they came to the door he went right out on the gallery and said 'What seems to be the trouble, officer?' before they had a chance to get in the house. 'There's no problem here,' he told 'em, actin' right surprised when they said they were after gettin' a complaint. 'It's just a little going-away party for one of the boys.' We were watchin' him out through the window there, quietened right down, of course."

"Jesus, they got right back in the car and drove off," said the thin boy. "Frank never told them the guy goin' away was bein' sent out to Whitbourne the next day. That was poor old Bernie Lawlor, 'member him? I wonder how he's gettin' on?"

"I'd like to know where Frank is tonight," said Donna. "He told me today he was comin' for sure. I hope he brings some ale. We're soon gonna be runnin' short with a big gang like this here."

In the kitchen a boy and a girl were standing next to the refrigerator, arms tight around each other. The boy pushed the lower part of his body against hers.

The girl began to move her pelvis slowly and rhythmically against him. Heather thought she recognized her as Darlene Snelgrove, who was a grade below her in school. She crossed the kitchen and went to stand at the back door.

Didn't anyone dance at parties any more? She thought of all the books she'd read about high school girls in which dancing was so important. Movies, too, even the up-to-date ones like *Footloose* and *Flashdance.* Her Uncle Fred had taught her to dance when she was just a little girl. He was a waiter at the Newfoundland Hotel; she remembered dancing with him one night in a small room off the lobby. There'd been a formal dance in the ballroom and the music from the orchestra had poured out through the big double doors. Uncle Fred loved to dance; his wife, Bun, called him Fred Astaire.

"You're a nice little dancer," he said as he whirled her around to *Blue Spanish Eyes.* "Takes after your mother, I guess. When it comes to dancing, people either got it or they haven't."

Heather had wanted to keep on dancing forever. Moving to the music made her forget everything else; she felt like a popular American high school girl at a prom.

The music ended and men and women in formal clothes surged out of the ballroom. Uncle Fred dropped her arm and became a waiter again. How could he stand being a waiter when he could dance like that?

Now, at the party, Heather took another mouthful of beer, not knowing what else to do. Outside the almost-full moon was shining like a big silver hub cap in the sky. She opened the door and went out to stand on the back steps. Words of a song that she didn't even realize she knew came into her head:

*Shine on, shine on harvest moon*
*Up in the sky*
*I ain't had no lovin' since January, February, June or July.*

Doris Day had sung it in one of those old movies Nan loved to watch on television.

A nice dancer. That was how her mother had described Heather's father."That was one thing he could do, dance. But when we moved out to Iowa there was no place to go dancin' unless someone got married, and even then some of them were too religious to have a dance. And then his mother. That was the worst of all. She wouldn't even let us play a game of cards."

Heather had danced at Lorraine's wedding reception at Perry's Catering, after the cold turkey supper with three kinds of salad and trifle for dessert. She wore a new dress that night, a yellow silky one with a full skirt. It was one of the few times in her life that she'd been almost satisfied with her appearance. Mollie had done her hair with the curling iron, and smoothed some blush into her pale cheeks."She's not a bad-looking girl when she's done up," she said to Eileen over Heather's head."I'll just rub a bit of eye shadow into her lids now. My, Heather, your eyes are a lovely shade of green."

There'd been taped music that night, rock for Lorraine and Mike's friends, older hits and country for the others. She danced twice with a cousin of Mike's, Jerry Tucker from St. Phillips, to *Waltz Across Texas* and *Save the Last Dance for Me*. He hadn't said much, had just hummed along with the music and smiled a few times.

She shivered now, standing there on the small verandah in just her jeans and top, but she didn't want to go back inside."I ain't had no lovin' since January, February, June or July," she sang to herself. She didn't feel nearly as turned off by this party as she had been by the other one she'd gone to with Debbie. She supposed that what was going on inside the house should have disgusted her, but she wasn't disgusted at all. In spite of the coldness of the night she felt warm inside, partly from the beer and partly from— what? Just for a moment she allowed herself to wish that somebody was touching her the way Harry was touching Debbie, or holding her the way the boy in the kitchen was holding Darlene.

She looked across the yard at the house next door. Through a darkened window she could just make out the shape of a woman behind the curtain, peeping out. "Have a good look while you're at it," her mother would have shouted if she'd been there. From inside came the music of the Rolling Stones, with Mick Jagger's raunchy voice screaming about love and lust and violence. In spite of this, or perhaps as a counterpoint to it, the words of the song she'd just been singing rushed back to her: I ain't had no lovin' since January, February, June or July.

She'd *never* had any lovin', not of that kind, anyway. She thought of the birthday parties Eileen used to give for Lorraine, Shirley and herself when they were nine, ten, eleven, and into their early teens. There'd been boys as well as girls at those parties; young as they were they'd danced to the Top Forty songs, like *Let Me Be There* and *Physical*. At that time all the girls had wanted to look, act and live exactly like Olivia Newton-John. They'd also played Spin the Bottle at those parties, and Postman's Knock. The boys had kissed shyly, briefly; it was almost the same as being kissed by your mother or your aunt. Almost, but not quite.

She remembered particularly a Postman's Knock game at one of Shirley's parties. She'd been about eleven. The first time her number was called she was nervous about going outside. Shirley and the others had pushed her through the door, squealing and asking if they could watch. In the dark hall a boy she didn't know had put his arms around her and kissed her hard on the mouth. He was older than the others, perhaps fourteen or even fifteen. He'd been visiting the Peddles across the street. She could still remember the warm pressure. His lips, tightly closed and dry, lingered on hers a little longer than necessary. Then he had let her go and, without a word, turned and walked slowly back into the room. She had never seen him again.

She was still shivering. If she was going to stay out here she'd have to get her jacket. A loud burst of laughter came from the house but then, just as she opened the door to go in, a male voice shouted:

"Take that back, ya fuckin' cunt. Take that back, or I'll punch the face offa ya."

"What'd I say? I never fuckin' said nothing for you to get so mad about. All I said was you walks like a queer. Lots of people walks like fuckin' queers. That don't mean to say y'are one."

Heather stood still, the door knob in her hand. She felt the way she did when she was about to plunge into deep water, before she made her first stroke. She recognized the voice of the second speaker as that of the thin boy with the scar. Why did men and boys, when they were angry, call each other cunts? It was ridiculous, almost funny, in fact, but there was something scary about it too. Was it the worst thing they could call each other?

The necking couple in the kitchen, still standing in exactly the same place, broke apart when they heard the commotion. The boy looked over at Heather and said: "Well, come in if you're comin'. Donna and them can't afford to heat up all St. John's, you know. What's all the ructions about in there?" He turned back to Darlene and they started up again where they had left off.

Heather closed the door and stood with her back to it, not sure what to do next. There was a thump from the living room and then a voice said,"I told you I was gonna give it to ya, didn't I? You better watch what you says to me from now on. That's not half of what I'll give you if I gets my temper up."

"Aw, fuck off, will ya, Derek?" This time it was Donna's voice. "He never meant nothing by that. Ye'll have the cops here again if ye don't watch yerselves. That crowd next door wouldn't be the longest phonin' in if they thought there was a racket goin' on over here."

"Don't go grabbin' for that bottle now, ya fag," said Derek."Come outside and fight like a man if ya wants to settle this."

"Jesus, that's all we needs," said Donna."Listen, the two of ye are both after callin' the other one a fag so why don't ye just say it's a draw?"

"Le's hand around another joint," said a slurry voice that sounded like Harry's."Beer makes ya feel like fightin', grass makes you feel like takin' it easy, right?"

There was another burst of noisy music, intermixed with loud laughter. Somewhere in the room a girl laughed nervously again and again. Heather wondered if there were any real homosexuals at the party. How would they feel about what had just been going on? No wonder they had to keep it a secret.

She walked cautiously across the kitchen, trying to remember where Donna had put her jacket. Darlene and her boyfriend were sitting on a chair now. She was on his knee, with her legs stuck out sideways. He had his hand inside her jeans and was caressing her while she gave little moans of pleasure. Heather tried to avert her eyes but they pulled themselves back to what was happening. Only the dim light on the back of the stove was burning; that was enough for her to see what was going on.

"Let's go upstairs," said the boy hoarsely "C'mon, let's get up there quick."

They got up from the chair and, arms tight around each other's waists, left the kitchen. Heather waited a moment to make sure they were safely up the stairs; then she went to the hall closet to look for her coat. She'd better get home quick; she didn't like the way she was feeling. Or, to be perfectly accurate, she liked the way she was feeling too much.

As she reached the front door she heard the sound of a car stopping outside. Before she could get out of the house a tall dark-haired boy walked in through the door, carrying two six-packs of Blue Star.

"Not goin' home already, are you?" he asked, leaning against the wall to let her pass. "Sure the party is only just gettin' started, ent it?"

"I've been here for nearly three hours and that's long enough." God, why did she have to sound so prim and proper? Her heart was beating so loud she was sure he could hear it.

"Hey, haven't I seen you somewhere before?" He shifted the beer and looked straight at her.

"I think I met you up to the Arena one night. You're Frank Marshall, aren't you? You had your leg in a cast." Her voice sounded trembly in her ears. She almost smiled at herself for using the word "think." But why did she have to say that about his leg being in a cast? What did that have to do with anything?

She thought of the picture she'd cut out of the *Telegram*, the one of Frank's hockey team with him in the middle, holding the cup. It was still between the pages of the Bible Nan had given her on her twelfth birthday.

"Oh, I remember now, you were with Debbie Murphy, weren't you? What's that your name is? Kind of an uncommon name, isn't it?"

Heather's mouth went as dry as if she'd just finished eating a package of salted crackers."Heather Novak," she croaked."My father was...is...an American." She licked her lips; even her tongue felt dry.

"I figured it was something like that. There's no Novaks around here, is there?" He put the beer on the table and shook the kinks out of his arms. He was wearing a brown leather jacket just the colour of his hair."You're not goin' to walk home by yourself, are you? Someone might grab you, a nice-looking girl like you. Where do you live, anyway?"

"Oh, just down on Gaspar Street. It's only about fifteen minutes walk from here, if I'm fast."

He drummed his fingers on the table."Listen, why don't you let me drive you home? I'll just tell Donna about the beer first. I know they'd all rather see that than me, anyway."

"But I don't want to spoil your night," Even as she said the words she knew that what she wanted more than anything in the world was to get in the car with him.

"Naw, I'm not very fussy about goin' to the party, anyhow. They got too much of a headstart on me in there. Nothing worse than bein' the only sober person at a party."

"I know. That's why I was leaving." Heather was astonished that she was able to talk to him rationally, just as if he was anyone.

"You go on out in the car and wait for me," he said."I'll just say hello to Donna."

There was another burst of loud chatter from the living room. It sounded amiable enough this time.

Heather went out and walked down the steps toward the old blue Pontiac parked at the curb. She knew it was Frank's car; she had seen him in it one day. Her legs were stiff; she felt like one of the robots in *The Empire Strikes Back*. When she got to the car she hesitated for a moment, not sure if she should get in the front or the back. She could almost hear Debbie's voice: "For the love of God, Heather, get in the *front*. Now's your chance, girl. He'll think you're nuts altogether if you gets in the back."

After a few moments Frank came out of the house, whistling as he ran down the steps. His leg must be all better now. What was that he was whistling? It sounded familiar. Oh, yes, "You're sixteen, you're beautiful and you're mine." Ringo Starr.

He got into the car and started up the engine, still whistling. "That seems like quite a party in there," he said finally. He smiled at her; she tried to smile back. "They were glad to get the beer, though. I would've come earlier only for I was workin'."

"Where do you work?" I'm so original, she thought, as he drove along the street. Such a brilliant conversationalist.

"I'm just puttin' in some time workin' at the rink, doin' the clock and that, you know. I'm goin' out to Alberta in three weeks' time. Lots of jobs out there. I got a couple of buddies in Fort McMurray."

So he was going away. Even though she knew she'd probably never see him again after to night, certainly not alone, she would like to have known that he was at least going to be in the same town.

"So, what brought you to the party tonight? I don't think I ever seen you at one before." By this time they were driving along Harvey Road. She wished he'd slow down. She didn't want to get home too soon.

"I came with Debbie. She persuaded me to come." Well, that was true, wasn't it? As far as it went.

"And you weren't havin' a good time, right?"

He was driving more slowly now. She tried not to look at him too directly, but she was as aware of him as if her eyes were full on him. She knew he was wearing brown sweatpants, and a light-blue jean shirt under his jacket. She moved a little away from him, toward the window.

"What're ya afraid of me, are you? I don't hurt nice little girls like you. Come on, move over by me again."

Heather fixed her eyes on the windshield. "You're goin' past Barter's Hill," she said. "That's where you got to turn off for Gaspar Street."

"I knows all about that, curly-top." He touched her hair. Mollie had permed it the week before. Heather had washed it every day since then. She hoped the strong smell of the curling lotion was finally gone.

Frank smiled again; his teeth were white and even except for one slightly crooked one on the left side."It's only early yet. I thought we'd go for a little run."

"I got to be home by twelve, or twelve-thirty at the latest." Even as she spoke Heather knew that her mother wouldn't be home to know what time she came in, and that Shirl would be relieved if she didn't come home at all.

He looked at his watch."It's not ha' past eleven yet," he said. "I'll have you home time enough, don't worry. It's too nice a night to go home yet." He began to whistle again; to Heather's amazement the tune this time was *Shine on, Harvest Moon.* She started to speak, then thought better of it.

"What were you going to say?" His hands were long and strong-looking, the backs of them covered with fine dark hairs. His left hand held the steering wheel lightly; the fingers of his right hand rested on his leg just above the knee. She looked away quickly.

"Nothing."

"Come on, now. Tell me."

"Really, it's nothing. It's just...I was thinkin' about that song earlier tonight. At the party."

"I don't know what made me think of that old tune. My mother got the record. Must be the moon reminded me. Some nice, ain't it?" He began to whistle again, then stopped and asked,"Where would you like to go? I wants to give the car a bit of a spin tonight, to charge up the battery. I had a bit of trouble with her today."

"I don't care." Could he hear the tremor in her voice? She didn't quite know why it was there. She certainly didn't feel afraid. Maybe she should be. There'd been a lot of rapes in St. John's lately. What did she really know about Frank Marshall? That he was a hockey star, that he was good-looking, that he seemed nice, that he'd saved Donna's party from the police a few months before.

"Let's go in as far as Bowring Park. There won't be much traffic in there this hour of the night." He turned on the radio and they drove on the rest of the way without speaking. Heather almost expected to hear the disc jockey announce *Shine on, Harvest Moon* but it was a rock program, of course. After a commercial for Molson's Golden, Rod Stewart's harsh voice began to belt out *Do Ya Think I'm Sexy?* She had been reading about Rod, his wife Alanna and his ex-girl friend, Britt Eckland, earlier that day in the *National Enquirer*.

Frank parked in the western end of the park, on the lot near the swimming pool. There were several other cars around, all with their lights off. As soon as he had turned the key he moved toward her and pulled her into his arms. She was afraid she wouldn't know how to kiss him but he didn't complain. After about twenty minutes of kissing and hugging he put his tongue in her mouth. She jerked back her head.

"What's the matter, don't you like that?" he asked, laughing at her.

"It's just, I'm not used to it." She was breathing very fast.

"Okay, I'll be good, seein' who you are." He kissed her again, this time with his lips closed.

He unbuttoned her jacket and felt for her blouse. As he was about to slip his hand inside, she said, "Don't do that."

"Why not?" He sounded really surprised.

She said nothing. How could she tell him she didn't want him to find out how small her breasts were?

After a few moments he tried again. This time she didn't attempt to stop him.

"Umm, that feels good," he said, cupping her breast in his hand. She was glad she hadn't used padding, as Debbie was always urging her to do.

"Aren't they too small?" She could not believe this was happening, that she was allowing it to happen. More than anything else, she could not believe how good it felt.

"I don't like 'em too big. They're a nice shape, they'll grow. You're only young yet." He caressed her again. "How old are you, anyway?"

"Sixteen," she lied. Fifteen sounded so childish. She'd be sixteen soon. She knew he was eighteen; Debbie had told her.

"That's good. I'm glad you're sixteen. I was afraid you might be younger."

Why had he thought that? Was she acting like a baby? Perhaps he'd had enough of her already. Perhaps he wanted to take her home, to be rid of her.

But he continued to kiss her and to feel her breasts. Nothing that had ever happened to her in her whole life had felt as good as this.

"You smell nice," he murmured, his hands still stroking, stroking. She was glad she had dusted herself with Johnson's Baby Powder before she left the house.

After another few minutes Frank sat up abruptly. This is it, she thought. He's had enough, he's bored with me. He took her two hands in his. "Let's go out in the back seat where we'll be more comfortable."

The roar of her heart was like the roaring of a train.

"I can't," she said at last, holding tightly to his hands. "I really can't. Listen, I got to go home."

"No, you haven't. You don't want to go home any more than I do." He dropped her hands, reached across her and opened the door on her side. She stepped out of the car, feeling warm and deathly cold at the same time. He walked around the car to where she was waiting and took one of her hands in his. They climbed into the back seat where he lay down and pulled her down beside him.

# Three

When they reached her house Frank pulled Heather toward him and kissed her once again.

"Good night," he said at last. "I'll call you soon."

"Good night," she whispered.

She knocked on the door, remembering Shirley's earlier warning. It took a few moments for Shirl to answer it; when she did she looked as if she'd just got out of bed. She blinked as her eyes adjusted to the light.

"I thought you were gone for the night. You must've went to the party then, didja?"

"Yes."

"Who brought you home? I thought I heard a car."

"Oh, just one of the fellas."

"Randy is still here. You haven't got to go in the living room, have you?"

"No, I'll just go to the kitchen and get a drink. Mom's not home yet, is she?"

"No, girl, I told ya. Mom is good till at least two." Shirley went back into the living room, closing the door carefully behind her.

The next morning Debbie came over to ask Heather to go to the drugstore with her.

"What happened to you last night? One minute you were there and the next you were gone."

"I left a bit early, didn't think you'd miss me. I got a run home."

"Who with?"

"You'll never guess, Deb."

The weather was fine again today; unseasonably warm. People were out in their doorways, talking back and forth to each other. One man was painting his doorstep a bright blue.

"How can I guess? Why don't you tell me?" She grabbed Heather's arm and pulled her around in front of her.

"Ouch, let go! You're tearin' the arm off me."

"You don't mean...you're not tryin' to tell me it was Frank Marshall?"

Heather nodded, and rubbed her arm. "You almost hauled my elbow out of socket."

"My God, Heather, how can you be so calm? Almost any one of the girls at the party would have left their own boyfriend in a minute to go with him. I don't know but I woulda left Harry. I never even saw Frank at the party."

"He was only there for a few minutes."

"God, you didn't waste any time, didja? Did you go straight home, or what?"

"Or what," said Heather.

"Jesus, Mary and Joseph, this is like pullin' teeth. Where did you go?"

"Just in as far as Bowring Park."

"Just in as far as...I told you before, Heather, you're unreal. What happened?"

"Nothing much."

By this time they were at the drugstore. After Debbie had picked up her grandmother's pills and they were back outside she started in again.

"What do you mean, nothing much? Are you gonna see him again?"

"I don't know." Heather never talked as much as Debbie but this was getting ridiculous. "What happened at the party after I left?"

"Not too much. Were you there when Derek and Leo had the fight? Everything was pretty well normal after that. C'mon now, Heather, tell me what happened?"

Heather shrugged and said nothing. She just couldn't talk to Debbie about Frank. They walked the rest of the way in silence.

"I'll probably see you tomorrow," Debbie said when they reached the house. "I'm goin' for a run with Harry this afternoon. You better get on in the house now, girl. Frank might phone."

"Oh, don't be silly." It irritated Heather that Debbie had read her mind.

For the rest of the day every time the phone rang Heather jumped. She was afraid her mother would notice but Eileen was too busy and preoccupied to take much interest in what was going on around her.

"Did I tell you Mom is not very well?" she asked when the two of them were lingering at the table after dinner. "She been miserable lately and of course she didn't tell me nothing about it till I dragged it out of her. I got an appointment made with the doctor for her tomorrow. I s'pose she got herself persuaded that the cancer is after comin' back." Eileen swallowed another mouthful of tea. "I think I'll take a run up to see her this afternoon. You want to come with me? You haven't been up there lately and you know she thinks an awful lot about you."

"No, Mom, I don't think so. I got a lot of homework to do."

"You went out after last night, didja? To that party up to the girl Power's, was it? Did you find out if her mother was Sheila O'Keefe before she was married?" Eileen pushed back her cup and lit a cigarette.

"I don't know who her mother is, or was." Heather lifted a piece of meat from her plate and fed it to Puss who was lying at her feet.

"There's no need to be saucy. And don't go givin' that cat good meat. She already had a plate of cat food today. You got her ruined."

He, Heather mentally corrected her mother. Him. But what was the use? Eileen always said she and her for cats, just as she said he and him for dogs, whether the animals were male or female. "I knows the difference," she had explained more than once. "It just seems more natural to say it that way."

"It's only meat off my plate, Mom. You gave me too much. No one else is going to eat it." The cat finished the meat, jumped up into Heather's lap and began to purr.

"Did you walk home by yourself last night? You got to watch yourself in the nighttime now, you know. It's not like it used to be." Eileen took an Oreo from the package on the table, stared at it for a moment and then began to eat it.

Heather was tired of all the questions. First Debbie, now her mother. Even Shirley had wanted to know. Some girls liked nothing better than to go into detail about what their boyfriends had said and done, at least to their girl friends. She did not.

"Is that someone at the door? I hope it's not strangers, and us sittin' here with no dishes done." Eileen got up and began to scrape the plates into the garbage bag under the sink. "Oh, it's only Lorraine and Jason. Come over to Nanny, sweetness." Jason, dressed in blue corduroy overalls and a yellow sweater, hung back shyly, hiding his face in his mother's slacks.

"Now, Jason, don't be a sook," said Lorraine, pushing him away from her. "Sure it's only Nanny and Heather. You knows them, don't you?"

Jason, who had caught sight of the cat, ran toward him saying, "Hi, pussy, hi pussy."

"Be careful, Jason." Heather pushed the cat off her knees and pulled Jason on to them. "Puss might scrawb you. He's not used to little boys."

"And Jason is not used to cats. I'd love to have a kitten but Mike can't see past them two beagles he got over there." Lorraine leaned against the door frame.

"C'mon now, Jason, what does the cow say?" Heather asked.

"Moo," said Jason, his eyes still on the cat who had removed himself to a safe distance.

Lorraine sat down at the table and pulled off her jacket. "Got a cigarette, Mom? I left mine home."

"I only got a few left," said Eileen. "I can spare you a couple, though. Here you go. Now, Jason, what do the pussy say?"

"Meow," said Jason. Puss had settled down on top of the fridge, safe from unwanted attention.

"Where's Mike today?" Eileen flicked two cigarettes across the table to Lorraine.

"You knows where he's to, Mom. Up on the barrens with Bernie O'Toole."

"I thought you weren't allowed to hunt Sundays."

"Oh, I don't s'pose they're huntin' today." Lorraine closed her eyes as the smoke from her cigarette curled upwards. "They were at it yesterday and they stayed in Bernie's shack all night, or I s'pose they did. Mike don't tell me nothin'. God, if I sees another rabbit I'll vomit."

"It saves on the meat, though, you must admit. Jason, what do the doggie say?"

"Bow wow," said Jason.

"Got a bit of dinner left there, Mom?" Lorraine tapped the ashes off her cigarette on the plate in front of her. "I didn't bother cookin' today, with just me and Jason home."

While Eileen was making up a plate of dinner for Lorraine out of the leftovers, Heather looked at her sister over the top of Jason's head. She couldn't believe how much Lorraine had changed since she got married. She had been the smallest one of them all; now her stomach bulged under the tight jeans, the zipper broken. Her hair, which had never been as blonde as Shirley's but a nice colour of golden brown, was darker now; it looked as if it hadn't been washed for a week or more. She remembered when Lorraine wouldn't go outside the door without her hair shampooed, without mascara, eyeshadow, blush and lipstick on. Today she wore no makeup except for bright pink lipstick. Heather watched her taking short, quick puffs on her cigarette.

"Where's Shirl?" Lorraine asked.

"Still up in the bed." Eileen jerked her head toward the ceiling. "Up all hours again last night, I suppose. You know she sleeps downstairs in the front room now? As soon as I got out of the bed this morning she was up into it herself. I was out last night too but I still had to get up early this morning and get the dinner on. And that Shirl is not even workin' in the week like I am."

Lorraine stubbed out her cigarette. "I can't remember the last time I went any where in the nighttime," she said. "Ever since Jason

37

been born Mike thinks it's his place to go out and mine to stay home. We don't have no money to go out, anyway."

"Isn't he still gettin' his unemployment?" Eileen turned on the hot water tap and squirted some detergent into the sink. "Heather, let Jason go back with his mother and you start washin' the dishes, will ya? If you don't they'll be there till tea hour. I got to get ready to go up to Mom's."

"His unemployment ran out two weeks ago." Lorraine pulled Jason onto her lap, seeming hardly aware that she was doing it. "I had to go up and get welfare this week. It's the first time I ever had to do it, and it's horrible. They looks at you so funny, like you're tellin' lies or something. And the queer crowd up there, the regulars, you knows what they're like."

"I never been up there, thank God, but I can imagine," said Eileen. "I s'pose Mike wouldn't go up himself, would he?"

"He wouldn't be caught dead up there. I had to make up all kinds of excuses." Lorraine shifted Jason from one knee to the other. "God, Jason, you're a ton weight. Don't be such a sook, now. Go out in the backyard and look for the nice doggie." Jason twisted around and buried his face in his mother's blouse. "I hates youngsters when they're sookie like that. He's with me too much, that's all is wrong with him."

"Come to Nanny, my lover." Eileen held out her arms but Jason wouldn't look at her. "P'raps you should try to get a job yourself, Lorraine. Might do you and Jason the world of good to get away from each other more."

"Who in the name of Jesus am I goin' to get to mind him? You knows Mike is not gonna do it." With unsteady fingers she lit the second cigarette.

"You're smokin' too much," said her mother. "That's hard on the money, too."

"God, listen who's talkin'." Lorraine stood Jason on his feet. "Get away from me now, sookie-baby. Heather, take him out for a walk somewhere, for the love and honour of God. I never gets clear of him for five minutes. I'll do the dishes for ya." Then, to her mother: "I was wonderin' if I could take him up to Nan's if I got something to do parttime. They were looking for someone at the House of Pizza."

"Mom is sick, girl. I was just tellin' Heather. I'm worried to death about her."

Heather pulled Jason's overalls up around his waist and smoothed down his fine blond hair. It was sticky to the touch, as if he'd had his fingers in it a good many times since it was washed last. "Come on with Heather, Jason," she said. "We'll go over in the meadow on the swings. Mom, if anyone phones for me tell them I'll be back soon."

"What have ya got a boyfriend, have ya, Heather?" Lorraine screwed up her mouth. "If I had my time back again I wouldn't of had a boyfriend till I was about thirty-five. They're all right until you gets married."

"Heather haven't got no boyfriend," said Eileen. "She don't have time for stuff like that, do you, Heather?"

Without answering, Heather took Jason's hand and walked him toward the front door. She remembered when Lorraine had been going out with Mike. He'd been at their house, morning, noon and night. Eileen used to tell him she was going to charge him board. He came from a few streets away; his father was a longshoreman and his mother cleaned Water Street offices at night. There'd been ten or eleven children in the family.

"Mind the car-cars," she warned Jason as they prepared to cross the street. Molloy's Meadow was the only empty space anywhere near Gaspar Street. It didn't look much like a meadow any more; most of the grass had been worn away by the thousands of feet that had played there over the years. The MHA for the district had seen to it that a few swings and a slide were installed there shortly before the last election.

The warm weather had brought all the children out; Heather barely managed to get a swing. She sat on it and took Jason in her arms; he was too nervous to get on one of the baby swings by himself. In any case, there were none to be had. As they swung gently back and forth she said softly into the little boy's ear:

*How do you like to go up in a swing?*
*Up in the air so blue?*

39

*Oh, I do think it the pleasantest thing*
*Ever a child can do.*
*Up in the air and over the wall*
*Till I can see so wide*
*Rivers and trees and meadows and all*
*Over the countryside.*

She had learned the poem from a book called *A Child's Garden of Verses*. Her father had sent it to her years before, in the days when he was still sending them a Christmas parcel every year. The book was falling apart now, the back cover long since lost, but she still kept it in the bottom drawer of her bureau.

After a few moments she realized that Jason was asleep. He'd probably been up late the night before; Lorraine never managed to get him to bed early. Often he just ran around and around, stopping to play briefly with a toy or to watch something on television. Then he would fall asleep wherever he was, usually winding up on the chesterfield from which Lorraine would carry him to bed. The apartment was small; he slept in a crib in the same room with Lorraine and Mike.

She stilled the swing and stayed on it with Jason in her arms. There was no other place in the meadow to sit. In the part of the play area that had been roped off for a diamond some of the boys were playing softball. Bertie Lane was there, trying to get into the game.

"It's not fair, ye said I could play," he whined.

"Wait now, Bertie, we'll give you a turn after." Bertie sat down on the ground, a sulky expression on his face.

Would Frank phone while she was out? She hadn't given him her phone number; he hadn't asked for it. There were no other Novaks in the telephone book. If he did call, what would her mother say? Would she ask embarrassing questions? Heather had had very few phone calls from boys before; the ones she did get were usually about homework.

Forget about would he phone this afternoon, would he phone at all, ever? Perhaps she'd let him do too much last night. She'd often read in Ann Landers' column how boys lost interest in girls who let them do too much, too soon. If he was that kind, would he talk and laugh about her to the other boys? Shirl and Debbie and the others didn't seem to worry about letting their boyfriends go as far as they wanted to. Maybe it was different when you had an official boyfriend. "Let him do too much" was a strange way of putting it, anyway. She had liked the way Frank had touched her, hadn't wanted him to stop.

Frank certainly wasn't her boyfriend, not yet, anyway. Would he ever be? Just at this moment she thought she wanted nothing else in the world except to be Frank Marshall's girl. She was surprised at herself. She had never believed that something like this could happen so fast.

She hadn't really let him do an awful lot last night, anyhow. He hadn't tried to do more than kiss her and touch her breasts. If he had wanted more, what would she have done?

He'd told her last night that he was going to Alberta in three weeks' time. What was the sense of starting something with him, even if he wanted to? If she never saw him again, if last night was to be the one and only time, then surely she'd get over this strange feeling that she had now. Suddenly she knew she didn't care if he was going away in three *days'* time, she wanted to be with him every hour, every minute, every second that she could while he was still here.

Jason stirred in her arms and rubbed his eyes. She swung gently back and forth, back and forth. He closed his eyes again, resting his head against her breast. The pressure recalled the movement of Frank's hand there the night before.

Was she in love? Could something like that happen so fast with a boy she knew nothing about except that he was good-looking and had been nice enough to drive her home? Had that really been done out of niceness, though? "All men are alike. They're only after one thing." She'd heard her mother say that so many times, although it had never stopped Eileen from being interested in men. Was Frank like that, too? He'd certainly been insistent about not bringing her home right away. Was one girl's body the same as another to him?

Why, then, hadn't he tried to get further with her than he had? She probably wouldn't have resisted. He could have done exactly what he wanted to do. Even if she had protested, he was much bigger and stronger than she was.

Had he thought her too easy? Was he the kind of fellow who was excited by girls who put up a struggle? Had she let him do what he wanted because she was strongly attracted to him, or would she have been the same with any other boy? She didn't think she would have been, but how could she be sure?

When she'd been reading *The Blue Castle* she'd marvelled at the shy Valancy, who had reached the age of twenty-nine without ever having had a boyfriend, getting up the nerve to actually ask a man to marry her. And here was she herself, not even sixteen yet, falling hard for a guy on the first date. It hadn't even been a date, really.

She thought of a couple of lines of a poem they'd had to study in English class:

*And all my homage at thy feet I'll lay*
*And follow thee, my liege, throughout the world*

That was exactly how she felt about Frank at this moment.

Her mother despised women's libbers. Manhaters, she called them. Eileen often criticized men herself, but that was different. From the few feminist articles Heather had read, at the library and at Linda Stone's house, she'd thought that what those women were trying to do made sense. She had seen herself as a girl who would go to university when she finished school, if she could get student aid, and then move into some kind of glamorous career like journalism or broadcasting. She had visualized a future where she'd at first have her own apartment, the way women in the stories did; later she would move into the house that had been part of her dreams for years. It would be grey stone with green painted trim and frilled white curtains at all the windows, like the house right at the top of Barter's Hill, the house that looked as different from all of its neighbours as Linda Stone's house did from Heather's. There'd be flower beds in the front yard, enclosed by its low, wrought-iron fence, and there'd be a verandah at the front with green and white lawn chairs on it in the summer. Inside there'd be gleaming golden hardwood floors with thick, deep rugs scattered all over the place. The fireplace would have bricks around it; on cool days it would glow with a warm orange flame.

Her fantasy never extended to who would keep the house immaculate, or how she'd pay for everything. When she thought about a husband she had seen a shadow man, handsome and clever and devoted to her, someone who hovered around the edges of her life, watching as she watered the large, healthy green plants that were everywhere, hanging from the ceiling, on the wide window sills, trailing along the walls. Her mother had one plant, an asparagus fern that a customer had given her for Christmas. It was beginning to look yellow and dry.

The more she thought of Frank, the more the dream retreated, becoming vague and lifeless. At this moment she wanted only to be with him again. How had she changed so fast? Yesterday she'd been embarrassed by the warmth that spread over her when someone used the word sexy. Last night at the party the petting couples around her had not repelled her the way she would have expected. Rather, against her will, they had fascinated her. She could not even attempt to describe the feelings that had washed over her when she was in the parked car with Frank. In a magazine that Eileen brought home from Ricardo's Heather had read a story about a nymphomaniac. She hoped now that she wasn't one herself.

Jason was wide awake now. "Want to go on the baby swing, Jason?" she asked, smoothing down his hair. "You can't fall out." Most of the swings were empty again. The weather had turned windy and colder. Over on the softball diamond Bertie Lane was up at bat, closing his eyes as the ball rushed toward him.

"Wanna go home," said Jason, rubbing his eyes. "Want my mommy."

Back at the house, Lorraine had moved from the kitchen to the living room where she was watching an old Bette Davis movie on television.

"Mom is gone to Nan's," she said. "She asked me to go with her but it was so nice sittin' here without Jason tormentin' me every second I didn't want to move."

Jason climbed into his mother's arms.

"You big sook," she said, patting his head. "You're a real mommy's boy, ent ya?"

"Mommy's boy," he repeated.

43

Heather sat down on the chesterfield and picked up the TV Guide.

"Did anyone phone?" she asked, her eyes on the magazine.

"Not as far as I know. The phone rang a couple of times before Mom left but she didn't say who it was. Go over to the store, will ya, Heather, and get us a large Pepsi, and a big bag of chips. I found a five-dollar bill I forgot I had in the bottom of my purse. It's there on the kitchen table."

Lorraine put her arms around the little boy and hugged him to her. Over his head she stared at the flickering picture on the television, a blank look in her eyes. Heather started to say something, then changed her mind. She took the money and left the house.

# *Four*

Frank didn't phone that day, or that night either. Perhaps he'd forgotten her last name. Maybe he had a girlfriend who'd been somewhere else on Saturday night. How could a boy so good-looking, so nice, so...so *sexy*, not have a steady girlfriend? The familiar blush spread over her body as she thought the word sexy. She'd often heard her mother talk about men, and sometimes women, who were oversexed. "I mean, enough is enough, right?" she'd say to Mollie. "I mean, you got to keep a man happy to a certain extent, right? But enough is enough."

Enough is enough. When you had enough of something, did that mean you didn't want it any more? When you ate a big, heavy dinner you didn't think about food for hours afterwards, but the next day you were hungry again. As Heather walked slowly up the hill to school on Monday morning, she realized that even when she and Frank had been together on Saturday night *she* hadn't had enough. Could he tell? Had he had enough, or perhaps too much? That girl is too easy, she could imagine him saying to himself with contempt. Surely he must think that she had behaved with other boys the same as she'd behaved with him. Why would he not think that?

She hadn't heard from Debbie since the previous morning. Sometimes they walked part of the way to school together, until

Debbie had to turn east to go to Holy Heart. But Debbie hadn't come over for her this morning.

As she continued on her way up Prince of Wales Street, past Dyke's Delicatessen with its yeasty smell of baking bread, she wondered again how Debbie handled her own feelings. She talked a lot about boys, and about sex in a general kind of way. Sometimes she said about a boy or a man she liked the look of: "He can put his shoes under my bed any time." Heather had even heard her say that about Christian Brothers and priests. But she never talked much about what she actually did when she was out with a boy. It was all hints, or jokes. Only at a party with Debbie, like on Saturday night, did Heather get any idea of what really went on between her and Harry.

Debbie still went to church sometimes. She even went to confession once in a while. What did she tell the priest when she sat in one of those dark little box-like cubicles over at the Basilica? Did she tell him about everything she let boys do to her, and what she did to them? If she did, what did the priest say? Did he tell her to repeat so many Hail Marys, and warn her not to do those bad things any more? Debbie talked a lot but she never talked directly about things like that.

Heather didn't go to church very often. Technically the family belonged to George Street United but when they were younger she and Shirley and Lorraine had often gone to the Salvation Army with Nan. Heather liked the singing there. A lot of their songs (they never called them hymns) were about being washed in the Blood of the Lamb. It didn't sound very pleasant but Heather liked the feeling the words gave her. Nan often sang around the house too, when she was ironing or washing the dishes:

*Whiter than snow, ye-es whiter than snow*
*Now wash me and I shall be whiter than snow.*

That was one of her favourites.

Her husband Herb, Eileen's stepfather, sometimes played hymns on his accordion. Eileen didn't like Herb much. "He thinks it's a sin to dance, or play cards, or smoke, or drink," she would scoff. "I don't trust anyone like that. Jesus, what else is there to do? I'm even afraid to smoke in my own mother's house since she married him. I think he's only usin' her, anyway. He never had his own home, always rented or boarded. She met him up to the Army, when she started goin' there after Dad died. There he is now, nice and cosy, in the house my father killed himself to build. Dad always liked his drop of rum and his bit of tobacco but you wouldn't find a kinder man."

Heather liked Herb. She played games with him sometimes, Chinese checkers or ordinary checkers. He didn't talk much but he was easy to get along with. Sometimes he gave her a dollar when she was leaving to go home.

As Heather waited for a chance to cross the busy intersection the thought struck her that Nan actually went to bed with Herb. She had always known that, of course; she'd just never really thought about it before. And Nan had been close to sixty when she married him. Surely Herb had never made her grandmother feel the way Frank (or something) had made her feel Saturday night.

The driver of a green Chevette honked at her. She realized that she'd stepped off the curb and then stopped, thinking the car was too close. Now he was apparently angry because he had braked to let her cross. She hurried to the other side, and along the sidewalk toward the school.

Frank, of course, was no longer in school. She didn't even know where he lived, or what school he'd gone to. Debbie had told her he was a Catholic. She wondered if he'd graduated, or just left when he got tired of school, the way so many of the boys and some of the girls in her own neighbourhood did. Lorraine had gone as far as Grade Ten and then quit to take a job in a supermarket. Shirley, who'd been really smart, especially in math and science, had failed Grade Eleven English, mostly because it bored her.

"Hi, there." Linda Stone was walking toward her. Her mother's little blue Toyota was just pulling away from the curb.

"Hi, Linda. Some cold this morning, isn't it?"

Linda looked nice, as usual. Even her jeans were never shabby. Debbie always said they looked too new, but then Debbie didn't like Linda. Even as the two girls chatted Heather's mind was working in a different direction. Had Linda ever been out with a boy? If so, she never talked about it. She hardly ever talked about boys at all. Although she was taller than herself, Heather always felt that Linda looked a lot younger. For one thing, you could never tell if she had breasts or not. She always wore layers of clothes, even in the summer. Today, under her unbuttoned camel-hair jacket she was wearing a cable stitch red pullover with a white blouse inside it, the collar pulled out over. Heather remembered the thick old books she used to get from the library, boarding school stories. Nan had given her one for Christmas once, years before. Linda looked something like the girls in those stories, English girls with names like Hilary, Diana and Letitia, girls who loved to play cricket and netball and field hockey, and who didn't like boys at all. She couldn't find any of those books at the library any more; the librarian had told her that most of them were out of print.

"What'd you do on the weekend?" Linda asked as they bent over their adjoining lockers.

"Oh, nothing much." Heather felt a stab of guilt when she said that. When they were younger, trying to prove that what they were saying was the truth, she and Debbie used to tell each other: "It's as true as God can strike me down dead." Heather didn't really expect God to strike her down dead any more, even if she told a deliberate lie. But every time somebody asked her about Saturday night and she answered so casually, she recalled her and Debbie's lurid imaginings of the bizarre ways God might choose to end their lives if they told lies. "What about yourself?"

"Well, I played basketball Saturday morning. You knew we had a game, didn't you, against PWC? I thought you might come up to watch. We lost, as usual."

"That's too bad." Heather was only half-listening to Linda. Darlene Snelgrove was standing just opposite, talking to a couple of girls from her class. "What a *time* we had Saturday night," Heather heard her say. "Ya shoulda been there." Darlene was small for her age; in spite of that, she looked older than she really was. She was wearing lipstick, eye shadow and mascara, as she did every day; her jeans looked as if they'd been sprayed on her. She glanced briefly at Heather, then looked away again.

For the rest of the day everything seemed blurred, out of focus. Heather answered questions automatically, thinking all the time of how little they mattered. Mr. Harris, her English teacher, stared at her once or twice; Heather had noticed him before looking that way at students who came to school half-stoned.

Every time she heard the name Frank she jumped. "Frank, if you don't start paying attention I'll have to give you a detention," Mr. Harris shouted at Frank LeDrew, who was drawing funny faces all over the back of his exercise book. And "To be frank with you, Susan, I don't remember," Mrs. Armstrong, the history teacher, said to the school secretary who came to the door with a question.

"Did anyone phone?" she asked Shirley as soon as she got home from school. Shirley was sitting at the kitchen table reading again. This time it was a *People* magazine with Dudley Moore and Susan Anton on the cover.

"Not while I was here. I was up to Manpower this morning, and then when I got back I had to go over to Joyce's to get the loan of her hair dryer. Mine is broke again. Oh, yeah, that's right, Mom phoned. She's all upset because Nan got to go in the hospital."

"Oh, have she? I knew she was goin' to the doctor today but I didn't think it was that bad." Heather cleared a place on the kitchen table for her books, and sat down on the nearest chair. Her legs went shaky all of a sudden. Why hadn't she gone up to see Nan yesterday afternoon after she brought Jason back, or last night? Just because she thought Frank might phone she had stayed home and waited. Served her right that he hadn't phoned.

"She's sick to her stomach and that. I dropped in last night while Mom was there. She's after losin' weight too, you can see it, and her appetite is *gone*. Mom brought her up one of them Pepperidge Farm chocolate cakes and you knows how much she used to like them. She couldn't even touch it."

A series of pictures of Nan flashed through Heather's mind, like the Viewmaster slides she'd gotten for Christmas when she was a child. Nan doing the laundry that day when Heather was lost and the policeman brought her home. She'd made Heather's blouse wet from her dripping hands when she threw her arms around her. Nan showing her the little pink teapot her own grandmother had bought the day she was born, and telling Heather it would be hers some day. Nan taking her and Shirley down to Bannerman Park when they were small, pushing them on the swings and buying them chocolate bars and

Cokes at the Fountain Spray store afterwards. Nan looking after her and Shirley and Lorraine when Eileen was taking her beauty culture course at the Trades College. Nan at a Salvation Army holiness meeting on a Sunday morning, singing with obvious enjoyment and belief "Have you been to Jesus for the cleansing power?" and "He leadeth me, O blessed thought." Nan at Pop's funeral at George Street Church, looking unlike herself in a black dress and a black hat, sitting through the service not singing, not crying, not moving. Nan when they went to see her soon after she came home from hospital following the breast operation, trying to laugh as she showed them the new foam rubber breast that she'd be wearing for the rest of her life.

"You're awful quiet," Shirley said, looking up from her magazine. "Listen, it says here that Jackie Onassis's new house at Martha's Vineyard got heated towel racks. Just imagine, what a waste of money. God, we haven't even got ordinary towel racks in this house, let alone heated ones."

Heather considered telling Shirley that it was "vin-yard," not "vineyard" (she'd heard the officer read it from the Bible the last time she'd gone to church with Nan) but decided it wasn't worth the trouble. Besides, she hated it when one of the girls at school corrected her, the way Dorothy Bennett was always doing. Like telling Heather to say "Kebeck," not "Kew-beck," as she used to do. She'd felt so embarrassed, in front of a big bunch of girls, too.

"Some people got all the luck in the world," she said, going to the fridge and opening the door. "God, there's not a thing to eat in this house. Didn't Mom get any groceries?"

"How could she, she was workin' all day Saturday. There's some tin stuff there in the cupboard if you're hungry. But'll soon be teatime, anyway."

"Did Mom say what was for supper?"

"No, she never said nothing about supper. She's not even comin' home herself. She's going right on up to Nan's from work."

Heather knelt on the floor and opened the door of the bottom cupboard: a large tin of Habitant pea soup, a tin of wieners, a tin of spaghetti and two tins of milk.

"Not much to choose from here. Gee, wouldn't it be nice to come home to a cooked supper once in a while. Linda Stone's mother...."

"For the love of God, shut up about Linda Stone's mother. How d'ya expect Mom to get meals ready when she's workin' all day long? If you wants stuff like Linda Stone's mother haves you'll have to do your own cookin'. "

"I wouldn't mind cookin' if there was ever anything to cook. Anyway, what's with you, takin' up for Mom? You're usually the first one to complain."

"Aw, girl, what's the good? This is the way things are, and this is the way they're gonna be. Bitchin' about it all don't make things any better."

"If I had any cheese I'd make macaroni and cheese." Heather wiped at the fingermarks around the cupboard door with a wet dishcloth.

"Sure we had Kraft Dinner Saturday, didn't we?"

"Yes, but homemade macaroni and cheese is different altogether, you know that yourself. Especially when it's made with a white sauce." Heather threw the dishcloth into the sink and started to pack up the dirty dishes on the table and the counter.

"Well, *I* got no money, so it's no good lookin' at me. I haven't got a cent left to my name and I won't get my unemployment for another six weeks." Shirley closed the magazine, took a clip out of her hair and began to clean her nails with it.

"Wouldn't you've been better off if you had stayed at Kentucky Fried instead of walkin' out like that?" Heather's back was toward Shirley; she stooped and reached into the cupboard under the sink for the detergent.

"My Jesus, it's easy to know you never worked in a place like that. Matter of fact, you never worked anywhere in your life yet, did ya? I was workin' when I was younger than you, after school and Saturdays."

"Well, you didn't have to, you just wanted to. And besides I do work, babysittin'."

"Babysittin' is a picnic compared to what it's like in a restaurant or a take-out with a crabby boss over ya. I coulda had a job today in that Mary Brown's up there by the school but I wouldn't take it. I wants to get something into K-Mart or Woolco, somewhere nice like that."

"Well, why can't you get one, then? You got your Grade Ten, after all, and most of your Grade Eleven." Heather screwed up her face at the dark stains on the insides of the white Corelle cups Lorraine had given Eileen for Christmas. "God, these cups are shockin'. Have we got any Javex?"

"I don't think so, girl. I believe Mom used the last of it when she done the washin' Friday night. Leave the old cups alone. What odds about 'em, as long as they're washed?"

Heather pictured the thin bone china cup and saucer Eileen had won in the Lucky Cup at a shower, and how proud she'd been of it until Lloyd, the man she'd been going out with, accidentally broke it one night when he came in for a cup of coffee. It was white and gold with a design on it of a girl in ringlets and an old-fashioned hoop skirt watering her flowers. Lloyd had promised to replace it but it was shortly afterwards that he and Eileen broke up; the new cup had never appeared. Eileen had a few other china cups but they were all either chipped or had cracks in them.

"Here, gimme a cup towel," said Shirley. "I might as well dry 'em for you, I s'pose."

"Shirl," Heather asked as she handed her the towel, "Shirl, do you ever think about Dad?"

"About who?" Shirley rinsed a mug under the tap to get the soap out of it. "My God, I don't even call him that no more. When I do have to say anything about him I says 'my father.' No, girl, I don't think about him much. Why? Do you?"

"Not as much as I used to." Heather supposed Shirl knew about the letters she used to write to her father; they had never discussed it. "No, I was just thinkin', well, you're older, and that. You must be able to remember him better than I can."

"Not really. Sure I'm only two years older than you, after all. I don't remember too much, except him and Mom fightin' and his mother— you know, our Grandmother Novak— buttin' in all the time. I didn't like her. She wasn't a bit nice, not like Nan at all."

Heather could just barely remember Grandmother Novak. In the few pictures they had of her she was a tall, thin woman with big dark eyes that looked as though they never smiled. She thought she could remember sitting on her knee in a rocking chair in a strange, gloomy kitchen; Grandmother Novak's body had been bony and hard to lean against, not soft and warm like Nan's. She probably couldn't really remember it at all. Most likely it was something Eileen had told her about.

"Now they're all done, for a little while," said Shirley as she hung the last mug on its hook. "I don't know why you wastes time thinkin' about stuff that happened so long ago, Heather. Take life as it comes, girl. It's the only way."

The telephone rang shrilly; Heather's heart lurched in her chest.

"God, that ring is awful loud, ain't it?" said Shirl as she reached for the phone. "I must see if I can turn it down after. Hallo? Yeah, she's here. Just a minute now."

"Who is it?" Heather's mouth was so dry she could hardly form the words.

"You'll find out. Answer it and see."

Heather wrapped her hand tight around the receiver, afraid she might drop it.

"Hallo?"

"Oh, hi," said Debbie's voice. "It's only me. Who'd think it was gonna be, Frank Marshall?"

"No, of course I didn't." She relaxed her hold on the receiver and ran her tongue over her lips. "Where were you this morning, you didn't come over?"

"I never even went to school, girl. I had the sore throat, thought I was gettin' the flu. I feels better now, though. What're you doin'?"

"Shirl and I were just doin' the dishes. Then I s'pose we got to see what we're gonna have for supper. And after that there's homework. We got a lot tonight."

"Ma got a pot of fresh meat soup on, outa the bones from the roast. Want me to bring some over? She always makes too much."

"Yes, sure, if you got any to spare. It's only gonna be myself and Shirl, anyway. Mom is goin' to Nan's after work."

"Did you see Frank since?"

"Where do you think I was goin' to see him, in school?"

53

"Now, Heather, don't go makin' out you don't care. I knows you're nuts over him, and I wouldn't blame you."

Heather wished she could think of something to say.

"Heather? Are you still there, or what? Listen, I'll be over later on with the soup, okay? Do you want to take a walk up as far as the Arena tonight? Frank might be playin'."

"No, he's not. The doctor won't let him go back at it for another couple of weeks."

"Oh, so you do know more about him than you're lettin' on. Did he get you to rub his leg for him?"

"Debbie, I got to go." Why didn't she shut *up*?

"Okay, okay, I won't ask you no more questions about Frank. He's some cute though, ent he?" She was laughing when Heather hung up.

She glanced at Shirley, wondering if she'd heard anything. Debbie's voice was so loud on the phone. But Shirley was crouched over her magazine again, intent on another story. Heather gathered up her books and went upstairs. She sat down on the bed, still unmade as she had left it in the morning. The afternoon sun showed up all the grimy marks on the window, and the dust on the furniture. She picked up a sock from the floor and ran it over the surface of the bureau. It felt sticky, though she couldn't remember spilling anything on it. She went to the bathroom to wet the sock, came back and scrubbed vigorously at the sticky place. Then she wiped it carefully with the dry part of the sock. She'd have to remember to ask her mother to get some furniture polish.

She pulled a chair over to the window, knelt on it and looked out. In the books she read, girls were always kneeling down and looking out through the window. Most of them saw trees and meadows, lakes and flowers. The ones who lived in big cities saw skyscrapers and bright lights, fast cars and glamorous people. Sometimes the settings were exotic, with larger-than-life plants and blossoms, and jungles and wild animals nearby. When Heather looked out she saw the harbour, crowded with boats and ships today. She could see the drydock where one of the big railway ferries was being repaired. Her mother and father had spent their honeymoon on a coastal boat, the *Bar Haven*. "I was never so bored in my life,"

Eileen had told them when she was showing them some old pictures. "Going in and out of those little tiny outports all day long, same old thing, days after day. But Gary — your father — loved it. He wasn't used to the salt water, where he came from, and he couldn't get enough of it. He was always up on the bridge with the captain, or down below talkin' to the engineers. I couldn't wait to get home myself. The only good thing about it was the meals. I put on pounds while we were on that boat."

Heather had never been on a boat or a ship, except the little white rowboats in Bowring Park and the rubber dinghy Uncle Fred had taken them out in once when they'd gone up to Cochrane Pond. She wondered if Uncle Fred knew that Nan was sick. Nan had never been the same with Fred since he'd married Bernice Connolly. He was her only son, the youngest of the family, and had lived at home with her until a little while after she married Herb. "Mom is old-fashioned, see," Eileen had said at the time. "Just because Bun is an RC she holds it against her. And of course Fred goin' and turnin' over to her didn't help matters. I wouldn't change my religion for any man." Heather couldn't remember the last time her mother had been to church. "But I don't see nothing wrong with Bun. He coulda got lots worse."

Heather looked across at the South Side Hills on the other side of the harbour. She had climbed up over them a few times with Nan, right up to Soldier's Pond at the very top, where they could sit and look out over the open Atlantic. Nan had showed her how to pick berries "clean," and how to tell the good ones from the poison ones. "I had a friend once was poisoned when she was small," she'd told Heather, picking as she talked. "Or they said it was the berries. She took sick with a hard pain across her stomach, had convulsions and died. They never even had time to send for the doctor. Not many phones over here then."

Now, as she knelt, Heather could see cars and trucks, small in the distance, going up and down the South Side Road, the road where Nan had lived until she got married, and for a short time afterwards. Was she in hospital yet? What would they find when they did the tests? Nan's sister, Eileen's Aunt Pearl, had died of cancer three years before. "I wish I didn't have to go to that funeral home," Eileen had sighed. "I hates lookin' at dead people, especially when it's anyone belong to ya. Nighttime, when I'm trying to get to sleep, they comes right before my eyes. They says Aunt Pearl went down to seventy-three pounds." Heather had wondered at the time if they weighed people before they died, or afterwards.

Heather had never yet seen a dead person. When Pop Morgan died she had cried when Nan asked her if she wanted to see him one last time, and they hadn't forced her. Lorraine and Shirley both looked at him; it hadn't seemed to bother them at all. "It was like lookin' at a dummy or a statue," Shirley had told her. "I touched his face and it was right cold and hard, just like he was never alive." Lorraine hadn't talked about it at all.

The South Side Road was widened now, and paved. "You wouldn't think anyone ever lived here to look at it now," Nan said one day when Fred took them over there for a drive. "It's like a ghost town until you gets out to Fort Amherst, and I s'pose they'll be tearin' that apart one of these days." Heather's eyes moved from the distant harbour to the street below her window. There wasn't much going on there at this time of day. A couple of boys were practising ball hockey in the middle of the road. Bertie Lane lurched toward his house, drunk again by the look of him.

Her knees were stiff from kneeling. She looked at her hands and saw that they were clenched tight. She stood up, shook her hands out in front of her and turned away from the window. Then she heard the phone ring.

"It's for you, Heather," Shirley called.

"Okay, I'm coming." She hurried down the stairs, almost tripping over Puss who was sleeping on the third step from the top.

"Hallo," she said, her heart beating fast. From hurrying down over the stairs?

"Hallo, there," said a voice that she recognized instantly. "This is Frank."

# Five

"Look, Mom, I brought you up some gum, a couple of bars and two tins of Pepsi. I'll give the drinks to the nurse, okay? She can keep them nice and cold for you out in the fridge. Oh, yes, here's that nice little pink bedjacket I had when Heather was born. I never wore it since, girl. Here, put it on, that's right. It'll be nice and warm around your shoulders."

Nan was half-sitting, half-lying on the bed. Eileen had adjusted the head into an almost perpendicular position; Nan resembled a body on display in some weird kind of science fiction movie. Her dark eyes looked tired; her greyish-brown hair was combed straight back from her forehead. Heather realized that Nan must have been feeling sick indeed not to have set her hair.

"How're you tonight, Daisy?" Herb asked from the chair he had pulled up close to the bed. It always shocked Heather to hear her grandmother called by her given name. Mom, now, or Nan, or Auntie, or Mrs. Abbott, those were the names she expected to hear. Some people still called her Mrs. Morgan. But of course she was Daisy to Herb.

Heather glanced at the women in the other three beds. Next to Nan was an old, old lady, her wispy white hair falling across her face, her dull blue eyes staring straight ahead of her. The middle-aged woman sitting beside her bed was knitting steadily away on a long, navy blue sock, her eyes on her work. The woman in the bed didn't seem to know anyone was there. The other two patients had no visitors. One, an enormously fat woman with thick dark hair hanging to her shoulders, was reading *The Fletcher Inheritance* and eating grapes from a brown paper bag on the night table. The other, more girl than woman really, was sitting up in bed doing a crossword puzzle. She kept glancing toward the door.

Heather's eyes moved back to her grandmother. Under her high-necked brushed nylon nightgown, Nan was wearing a bra. Heather had seen the outline of the straps when Eileen was helping her mother with the bedjacket. Although one of her breasts had been removed in the operation two years ago, both looked artificially firm. The brassiere was of the stiff, uplift type. You couldn't even tell which breast was foam rubber and which was real.

"Which twin has the Toni?" For some absurd reason that old television commercial flashed across Heather's mind. She thought of the two identical girls with the identical blonde heads, one of which was Toni-home-permed and the other naturally curly. She began searching through her purse, afraid she might say something foolish.

"I had to take castor oil this afternoon," said Nan, pulling herself up higher on the bed. When she had raised her arms to put the bed jacket on, Heather had seen the tufts of brown hair. Eileen was always trying to persuade her mother to shave her armpits, especially in the summer when she sometimes wore sleeveless dresses. "Ouch, my back is burning off me. Why do they have to put those old rubber sheets in the bed?"

"They're afraid you're not goin' to get to the bathroom in time, maid," said Herb, pulling the white hospital blanket farther up around his wife's body. Herb was originally from a little place called Yard Cove in Bonavista Bay; Nan teased him sometimes because he dropped his aitches and said maid instead of girl.

"What'd you have for your tea, Mom?" asked Eileen, keeping her eyes away from Herb. Eileen looked worn out tonight; the makeup didn't hide the smudgy circles under her eyes. The dark roots in her hair were really noticeable now. What was it Mollie said? "Shoemaker's wives go barefoot and a beautician's hair is a mess."

"You're not sayin' too much tonight, Heather," said Nan, smiling at her. "Of course, you never do say much, do you?" And then, not waiting for an answer, she said to Eileen: "We had sandwiches and soup, girl, and a little bit of lettuce and tomato. Then they gave us tin peaches and a pot of tea. All I could get down was the soup and the tea. The soup wasn't too bad, homemade turkey soup, it was. And they gives you a nice strong drop of tea."

"I betcha it wasn't as good as your soup, Daisy," said Herb, still leaning across the bed. "She makes wonderful soup," he said to the room at large. " 'twould revive you if you was dyin'. Certainly everything this woman cooks tastes good." Heather watched her mother draw her lips together and turn her head away.

"What are you havin' done tomorrow, Nan?" Heather felt she had to say something, to justify her presence here in this stuffy hospital room. Ever since she had come, at her mother's insistence, she had been trying with all her might not to think about Frank. It didn't seem right, somehow, to be thinking about a boy when her grandmother was lying there so sick. At least Heather supposed she was very sick. Eileen certainly thought so.

"I don't know, child," Nan said in answer to Heather's question. "They never tells me nothing. Some kind of an x-ray, I s'pose."

"It's the cancer back, as sure as you're born," Eileen had said to Heather when they were walking up the hill to the hospital. "For God's sake, Heather, don't walk so *fast*. We're not goin' to a fire, are we?" Eileen puffed a lot these days when she was walking up steep steps or hills. "I know it's the smoking," she said, time and again. "I s'pose I should give it up but I enjoys it so much. Why do everything that's good have to be bad for ya?"

Heather looked across at her mother, whose face had been stiff and tight ever since Herb had made the remark about Nan's good soup. Why did Eileen dislike Herb, or 'erb as she called him behind his back, so much? He'd always been nice enough to her, as far as Heather could tell. So what if he didn't want anyone smoking in his house? It was his house, wasn't it? Or Nan's, which was practically the same thing. Anyway, he had never once complained about Eileen's smoking, or about Shirl's or Lorraine's, either. All he ever did was open a window when the room got smoky, or leave the room himself and go upstairs from where, a short time later, they'd hear him playing Salvation Army songs on his old accordion. He was never unpleasant about it or anything.

"I don't know," Eileen would say when anyone asked her what was wrong with Herb. "There's just something about that man gets right on my nerves. It's not natural for a man to be all the time praisin' up his wife the way he do with Mom. I think it makes her right embarrassed like, you know what I mean? I b'lieve he's puttin' on an act half the time. You know what that crowd that's always goin' to church are like, hypocrites, a good many of 'em. We'll find out something about him one of those days, just you wait and see."

Eileen's own father had smoked constantly. Heather remembered how his fingers used to shake when he was rolling a cigarette or drinking a cup of tea. He'd been in hospital for a long time before he died; she had been too young to visit him there. The last time she saw him alive he was sitting at the kitchen table in his own house, the house where Nan and Herb lived now. He'd had a bottle of Blue Star in front of him; Heather could still picture the way his hand shook when he poured the beer into a glass. "I don't know why you always gives me a glass, Daisy," he'd grumbled. "I'd sooner drink it right out of the bottle." He had gulped it down thirstily, and then gone to the fridge for more.

"That's enough now, Ches," Nan said. "Save the other one for byme by. Remember what Dr. O'Leary told you."

"Doctors," Pop sniffed, opening another bottle. "What in the hell do they know? If I never had to have that operation I'd probably be better off today. "

Nan had sat back in her chair, looking as if she was going to cry. She had often looked that way when Pop was around.

Eileen cried hysterically at her father's funeral. Looking back now, Heather often wondered why. Pop Morgan had been a heavy drinker, an alcoholic really, for most of Eileen's life. Heather knew that because Nan had told her, a little bit at one time, a little bit at another. He'd been rough when he was drinking, too, slapping the children around, especially Fred. Yet, ever since his death, Heather had heard Eileen say nothing but good about her father.

At the funeral, in one of her calmer moments, Eileen had run her fingers lovingly along the polished side of the casket. It surprised Heather that she could remember that so distinctly. "Mom thought she'd have to get one of them ugly old cheap coffins," Eileen told Mollie. "You know, what they calls the welfare coffins. We used to call them paupers' boxes. They got some kind of funny old cloth covering on them. I know Mom got no money to spare; Pop haven't worked for years because he was too sick. But I told her to go ahead and get a good one and I'd help her pay for it. Fred should chip in on it too, by rights. We can't expect no help from the other two, I know. Just imagine, never even came home for their own father's funeral. I'd come back from Timbuctu if I had to. Poor old Pop. It's a good thing he don't know how little they thought about him."

Lorraine had told Heather and Shirley about Eileen's relationship with her father earlier, before he got sick with the lung cancer that killed him. "She used to call him a drunk old bastard and tell him to get home out of it whenever he came to the house. Ye two'd be gone to bed but I can remember that right plain. I used to be scared myself when I'd see him almost fallin' in the door, with the smell of booze on him so strong 'twould knock you back. Mom even used to lock the door sometimes, so's he wouldn't get in. But now, the way Mom acts, you'd swear he was an angel from heaven."

"He was a good person, really, even if he was a hard man in liquor," Nan had told Heather. She had gone to her grandmother's to sleep often after Pop died, before Nan married Herb. "He only had the one fault, but that was a big one. He couldn't help it, I s'pose. They says now alcoholism is a disease."

After Pop's death, Nan went to work in the cafeteria at the university. Heather dropped in there sometimes after school for a Pepsi and a doughnut. She'd been embarrassed, but pleased too, when Nan told the women she worked with how smart Heather was, and how she'd won a prize every year since she started school. "She gets it from her grandfather," she'd say. "He was a clever man when he was young. If it hadn't been for the war he probably would have been somebody. But he was never the same after he came back from that."

"Oh, my, Eileen, I got to go the bathroom," Nan said now. "Help me down, will ya? Those beds are so darn high."

It almost amused Heather to see Herb and Eileen vying for the privilege of helping Nan to the bathroom. Eileen won. Nan got there just in time. A second after the door closed there was a sound like an explosion. Nobody in the room looked at anybody else.

Herb and Eileen settled Nan back in bed and Heather wondered what excuse she could make to leave. She hadn't told her mother yet that she wouldn't be going home with her. All evening she'd been using every trick she could think of to keep her mind off Frank. Now she could do it no longer.

She was glad she'd been sitting down when she answered the phone. She'd felt weak and useless all over, just as she had the day she took sick in school and had to go to the staff room to lie down. She and Frank hadn't talked very long, just long enough for Frank to ask if he could see her the next night. "Yes," she replied, sure she was going to start stammering badly if she said anything else.

"Will I come to your house or do you want to meet me somewhere?" Frank asked then.

"I'll meet you...oh, up by Scamper's," she'd managed to say. "Do you know where that is?"

"Oh, yeah, sure, I often goes there for fish and chips. What time?"

"About nine o'clock, okay?" When she tried to hang up the receiver it had almost slipped out of her hands, they were so clammy. She'd had to get a tissue to wipe the phone.

She didn't know why she hadn't let him pick her up at the house. Shirley had looked at her curiously when she'd hung up the phone, and asked her who it was. None of your business, Heather wanted to answer but instead she'd said shortly, "Frank Marshall," as if he phoned her every day. She was pretty sure Shirley wouldn't tell Eileen. She didn't know why it was so important to her that her mother shouldn't find out about Frank. Eileen would laugh and tease, and ask all kinds of questions. She just wouldn't be able to stand it.

Now, unexpectedly, here in the hospital room, she felt her nipples sting as they did when she came out into the cold air after swimming at the Aquarena. She didn't want to think about what was happening to her, but she didn't want the feeling to go away, either. Before, when such a sensation had come over her when she was reading about sex or for no apparent reason at all, she'd tried to abolish it, to pretend it wasn't there. Now that it was connected with Frank she didn't want to run away from it any more.

The girl patient had a visitor now, a young man wearing a shiny wine-coloured jacket with the words Centennial Dart League across the front. He looked about twenty. He was sitting beside her bed, holding her hand and talking to her in a low voice. The girl's head was as close to his as it could be without her getting out of bed altogether. It must be difficult to have a confidential talk in a stuffy, crowded room like this, with people all around who were able, and sometimes eager, to overhear.

"Will you be there when I wake up?" Heather heard the girl ask.

"I'll even be there when you goes to sleep," the boy promised, trying to move his chair even closer to the bed.

The old, old woman was still lying completely still, her eyes fixed on the crucifix on the wall above Heather's head. Could she see it? If not, what did she see? Her visitor was knitting furiously, as if she were engaged in a competition. Occasionally she glanced at the bed as though to check that the old woman was still alive. The fat woman had switched from grapes to jellybeans. A nurse came in, swept the room with her professional eyes and pounced on the candy eater.

"Oh, no, Mrs. Mercer, my love, you know you're not allowed candy. Be a good girl now, or I'll have to tell the doctor on you." She looked over at Nan and said, "I'll see *you* later, Mrs. Abbott."

"Not if I sees you first," said Nan. For a moment Heather caught a glimpse of her grandmother as she used to be, before she had her breast operation.

Heather looked at her watch. It was a quarter to nine.

"I got to go now, Mom," she said. "I promised Linda I'd run up to her place for an hour or so. She wants some help with her French."

"What about your own homework? You don't go out weeknights very often."

"I did it this afternoon. I won't be late."

"Mind you're not, now. Do you good to go out somewhere for a change. I s'pose I'll be going home myself soon, anyway." Eileen was still standing as close to Nan as she could get. Herb was on the other side of the bed, just as close.

"Don't do anything I wouldn't do," Herb called as Heather, after kissing her grandmother on her damp, powdered cheek, was leaving the room. She didn't look back at him but she knew he wasn't feeling as bright as he pretended to sound.

Outside, Heather began to run. Scamper's wasn't very far away, but perhaps her watch was slow. She'd been so stupid when she talked to Frank on the phone; maybe if she wasn't there when he arrived he'd leave again.

When she reached Scamper's, completely out of breath, it was still only seven minutes to nine. She leaned against the wall and waited. And waited.

Maybe her watch was fast, not slow. It was a Timex that Nan and Herb had given her last Christmas; Eileen had said at the time she'd be lucky if she got a year out of it. Maybe he wouldn't come at all. Maybe she'd imagined that he wanted to meet her. Maybe he'd meant last night. Perhaps she sounded so dumb on the phone that he changed his mind.

She almost didn't see him when he did come. He must have parked his car around the corner, for he came striding toward her, whistling *I Wanna Hold Your Hand*. She didn't see his face at first, for she'd been looking down at her feet, trying to avoid the interested glances of passing men and boys. What if they thought she was a prostitute? She'd seen Loretta and Elsie Sheppard standing around outside restaurants just as she was doing and, as Eileen liked to put it, "Everybody knows what *they* are."

"Hey, good lookin'," Frank whispered. "What're you thinkin' about?" She looked at her watch, and then felt like an idiot. It was ten after nine.

"Nothing." He looked handsomer than ever, in a dark-blue jean jacket with a lighter blue shirt under it. In spite of the chilly night air the shirt was open halfway down his chest, showing thick, curly dark hair. Around his neck he wore a thin gold chain with a cross on the end of it. The light from Scamper's window shone straight on him. She tried to remember what movie star he reminded her of.

They got into the car and drove away without exchanging another word. When Heather had pictured herself going out with a boy she'd expected to be transformed into someone bright and witty, like the girls in *Seventeen* magazine and on television shows like *Too Close for Comfort* and *One Day at a Time*. Perhaps she should have rehearsed what she'd say to Frank. But even if she had, she was sure she would have forgotten it all as soon as he looked at her. I'm worse than Valancy, she thought. She, at least, had something to say. He must think I'm retarded.

If he did, he didn't let on. They drove over LeMarchant Road without speaking. Frank continued to whistle. "The radio is broke," he said finally, as if in explanation. "I miss the music, don't you?"

The way he spoke, you'd think she'd been in the car with him dozens of times instead of just once before. Did he consider her his girl friend already, or was she being crazy to think that?

"Are you hungry or anything?" he asked as they passed the cluster of fast food places in beyond the Village Mall. "We could go into Tim Horton's for some doughnuts."

"No, I'm not hungry." She could hardly speak, let alone eat. She tried to remember what it was like to be the Heather she'd been last week. Was she cracking up, or what? What would Linda Stone think if she could see her now? She knew she didn't care what Linda thought, what her mother thought, what anyone thought. All she knew at this moment was that she wanted to be with Frank and that he, right now at least, wanted to be with her. She looked out through the window, away from Frank, afraid he'd read her mind. Her eyes fell on a huge billboard, brightly lit, on the righthand side of the road. It must be a new one; she had never noticed it before. The word "Ramses" was there in big letters, beside a picture of a girl and a young man holding hands and gazing into each other's eyes. They were both very good-looking, of course. In large, block letters, the words "It's better to be safe than sorry" were printed under the picture. She looked away quickly, wondering if Frank had seen it too.

He was heading for Bowring Park again. When they got there he parked in almost the same spot they'd been in on Saturday night. "Maybe you'd rather've gone to the show, or something?" he said as he turned to her.

"No, that's all right."

He put his arm around her and pulled her toward him. "Well, I told ya I'm goin' away in three weeks' time, not quite three weeks, so we haven't got much time. I wish I'd met you before."

"You must know lots of other girls." She wasn't trying to be coquettish; she didn't know how. She was simply stating a fact, a fact that she feared.

"I don't know any like you." His mouth was against her hair. "Mmmm, your hair smells nice. You don't smoke, do you?"

"No, I don't. Do you?"

"I'm tryin' to give it up. I knew you didn't smoke because girls who smoke, their hair smells funny, all smoky and stale. You don't notice it so much when you're smokin' yourself."

Heather tried not to think about all the other girls he'd had in the car with him. Had they come here, to this very spot?

"I'm glad you were at the party the other night," he said, putting both his arms around her. "I was lookin' for someone like you."

"You don't even know what I'm like." How long would it be before his hand found her breast again? She'd taken a bath before she went to the hospital, and put on the new lacy bra that Shirley had bought out of her last cheque from Kentucky Fried. It was the kind that hooked in front.

He unbuttoned her blouse and unhooked the bra while he was kissing her. He did it easily, smoothly, as if he'd had lots of practice.

For a few moments they sat with their arms around each other, their lips together, his hand cupping her breast. She wondered if she should pull away, at least pretend to resist. His arms were strong around her, but that wasn't the only reason she didn't try to break away. She wanted to be exactly where she was.

He stopped kissing her and said, "Let's go out in the back seat again."

She sat up straight and turned her head away.

"What's the matter? Don't you want to?"

"It's not that I don't want to. It's just — oh, Frank, I'm afraid."

Now she'd done it. She was sure he'd move away from her in disgust. But he didn't. He put his arms around her again and said, "You needn't be afraid of me. I wouldn't hurt you. I know you're a

66

good girl." He got out of the car, came around to her side and opened the door. He took her hand and she stepped out, shivering in the October air. She climbed into the back seat and he followed her.

# *Six*

After that Heather's life divided itself into three parts, school, the hospital and Frank. The time she spent at home, or outdoors, or at the store, or at the library, didn't count; it was as if she had put herself on automatic for those things. Even school was like school in a dream, taking out her books, answering questions when she was asked, talking to Linda and the others, playing basketball in the gym. She performed all those actions as if her real self was behind her, enduring the daily round as something that had to be got through before night came and it was time to meet Frank again. The hospital part, though, she couldn't quite put herself on automatic for that. The minutes and hours she spent in that stuffy room, with Nan growing thinner in front of her eyes, were all too real. They gave her time with Frank a hectic intensity; she felt herself fending off the years that were to come when she wouldn't be young any more.

Being young, and being with Frank, were the two most important things in the world. Of course Nan's illness was important, too, but, when she wasn't actually at the hospital, even that took on a dream-like quality. In fact, it did get into her dreams. One night, after she'd spent an hour at the hospital, a relatively peaceful hour since Eileen was working and couldn't be there to defend her position against the ever-present Herb, and then gone with Frank to park in a deserted spot overlooking the sea on the Marine Drive, she dreamed that she and Frank, Nan and Herb, were climbing a steep staircase, with two evil young men following close behind them. In the dream the young men were not much more than shadows; when Heather did see them they looked skinny and undernourished. Their hair was cut very short, like the skinheads she had seen on a television news report from England. Over the dream hung a chilly sense of menace that was somehow associated with the two boys. Frank was ahead of Heather, holding her hand, while Herb and Nan kept dropping farther behind, never quite falling into the hands of the evil ones. Just before she woke up she glanced back and saw Nan's white, terrified face as she leaned over the banister, Herb at her side. Then Frank tightened his grip on Heather's hand and pulled her on. When she woke up it took her several minutes to fully realize that she was in her bed. She felt dreadfully cold; the heavy blankets didn't warm her at all. She was almost afraid to go back to sleep after that; she wanted to run to her mother's room, to snuggle down in bed with her, as she had done when she was little. When she dropped off again her sleep was heavy and dreamless; she was still very tired when morning finally came.

She didn't see Frank every night. There was homework to do, and some nights he worked at odd jobs in garages and service stations to help toward his fare to Alberta. Heather wouldn't let herself think about the time when he'd be gone; when he talked about it she tried to change the subject. Yet it was constantly on her mind.

"Why do you have to go away?" They were driving up Signal Hill when she said that. Bowring Park was still their favourite place but Signal Hill was closer. On this particular night Frank had been working until ten-thirty. He was still in his work clothes, smelling of gasoline.

He didn't answer right away, but kept his eyes on the dark, twisting road up the hillside. "Because I can't get a decent job here, that's why. I should never have left school in Grade Ten, but it's no good worrying about that now. I thought to get into the Mechanics course at the Trade School but it's easier to get into heaven than it is into that. And, even if you do get in, there's not many jobs when you comes out of it. I'd like to be somewhere where I could make good money, buy a decent car, send a bit home to Mom, like that, you know. Don't you go leavin' school before you're finished."

"You could go to night school." Heather's mind was more on what Frank had just said than what she was saying herself. His father had died when Frank was eight. He'd been a truck driver; he and his helper were killed when their truck lost its brakes on one of the steepest hills in the city and plunged into an office building on Water Street. "Lucky it was on a Saturday," Frank had said. "Everybody who worked there was off." He smiled a strange smile when he said the word lucky. His voice held a note that Heather had never heard before. Frank's mother received very little compensation; a loophole allowed his father's employer to escape responsibility. Frank wasn't nearly as bitter about it as Heather was sure she would have been if the same thing had happened in her family. "That's life for ya," he concluded when he finished telling her about it. "It's mostly all a matter of luck, or that's what I think, anyway." His mother had gone to work at Woolworth's when the youngest of her six children started going to school all day. Before that they lived on welfare.

"That was pretty tough, let me tell you." Frank's face had tightened when he told her that. "I'd never want to go through it again. The worst part Mom hated about it was the crowd on Open Line sayin' that the ones on welfare were better off than the ones workin'. She used to get so mad. But she was always afraid to phone up and contradict them because she thought she'd get all flustered knowin' she was on the radio."

Heather had seen Mrs. Marshall once, at Woolworth's. Frank had told her what his mother looked like, and which checkout she was on; one day Heather had gone to her to pay for a pair of pantyhose. She was a small, frail-looking woman with light brown hair and pale blue eyes, about Eileen's age but of an obviously very different temperament. Frank looked like his father, he told Heather; his father had been tall and dark and... "And handsome," Heather had finished.

"I wasn't goin' to say that, sure that'd be braggin' about myself. But if you says it, well, I s'pose it got to be all right." He had reached over then, and ruffled her short hair.

Her own mother still knew nothing about Frank. Heather wasn't really sure why she hadn't told her; Eileen probably wouldn't object at all to her having a boy friend, had often encouraged her to. "You

70

wants a nice boy friend for yourself, girl," she said one Friday night, before Heather had met Frank, when she was sitting in the living room, half-reading, half-watching TV. "There's nothing like a fella to perk up a girl." Eileen had been going to the Strand after work with a man named Ron whom she'd met the week before at a party.

Heather still couldn't help feeling that if Eileen knew about Frank she'd say or do something that might cheapen the relationship. Relationship, that was a word you heard a lot these days, especially on TV talk shows. Her mother would probably laugh and hint about what men wanted from women. Eileen had never in her life talked straightforwardly about sex to Heather, any more than she had to Lorraine or Shirley. Sometimes she'd say, more to Shirley than to Heather, "I hope you don't get into it like Lorraine did. There's nothing worse than givin' a man something like that to slap back at you later on. 'I wouldn't of married you if I didn't have to,' that's the first thing comes up when you starts havin' an argument. Thank God father could never throw that up to me. His old mother tried to do it, but I soon put her straight." Heather remembered what Nan had said once about Eileen: "Your mother wasn't really wild, but she liked the boys. I was delighted when she married your father, even though she was only nineteen. He was such a nice, quiet boy, a real gentleman." Then she had sighed. "I don't know what's the matter with people today, they can't stand up to things the way we could. Her and your father coulda made a go of it, if she had tried a bit harder. She'd be no worse off than she is now, and probably a lot better." Even at the time Heather had wondered why Nan sounded as if she were blaming Eileen, her own daughter, more than her son-in-law for the breakup. And then her grandmother said: "Women can't expect to have it all sunshine in this world. I had my troubles with your grandfather but I didn't run away. Men are weaker than we are, you got to make allowances." She sighed again, and then started to talk about something else.

What would Nan and Eileen think if they knew what was going on between her and Frank, about how, each night they were together, they went a little further, giving in more and more to the feelings that were beginning to dominate both their lives? "Oh, God, Heather, it's hard to stop," Frank murmured one night when they'd been lying down together in the back seat for more than an hour. "I don't want to hurt you but it's getting harder and harder." Lying there in the darkness, feeling the warmth of Frank's body so close to her own, Heather thought about what Eileen would read into what Frank had just said. She and Mollie enjoyed telling each other jokes that had as their punch line something to do with what happened to a man when he was aroused by a woman. Why did she have to think about her mother at a time like this? She pressed herself closer against Frank, imagining what it would be like to be actually in bed with him, the two of them with all their clothes off, secure in the knowledge that they would not be disturbed, in the knowledge that she wouldn't get pregnant unless she wanted to, or, best of all, that if she did get pregnant everything would still be all right.

"What are you thinking about?" Frank's mouth was against her neck, his hands under her sweater, stroking her breasts.

"Nothing." That was what she always said, or almost always. "What're you?"

"Oh, a lot of things. I'm wishin' I didn't have to go away, for one thing. And I'm wishing I could do what I want to do with you."

"What's that?" She whispered the words.

His right hand travelled from her breast, along the skin of her abdomen, down over the soft flesh that led to...that led...Down There. She still couldn't give that most private centre of exquisite feeling a name. She knew all the scientific names, had read them in the old red "doctor's book" that Nan kept on a high shelf in her bedroom. She knew the vulgar names, too; she could not deny that, crude though they were, they carried a strange kind of fascination. But those words were too often used to convey scorn, condemnation, revulsion, to apply to what was happening between her and Frank. He never really talked about what he was doing, except in a kind of oblique way. It was as if it was somehow safer to feel and touch silently, to let their fingers, their lips, their flesh itself, take the place of words. "Let your fingers do the walking." From out of nowhere came that stupid advertisement. Surely Frank didn't have such foolish thoughts as she did.

"Oh, Heather, if you only knew how much I wanted to." His hands moved up toward her breast again and cupped them, this time squeezing until they hurt a little. Why didn't you leave your hand where it was? she asked silently, the lower part of her body aching now, and tingling. He took her hand and moved it gently down towards the bulge of his penis under the tight jeans. "Would you just...touch it?" His voice was so low she was afraid she had only imagined the words. She left her hand where he had placed it, and moved it slowly up and down, up and down, outside the worn denim. His own hand moved downward again, and came to rest where it had been before. With his other hand he pulled down his zipper and put her hand on the warm flesh inside. "Oh, yes," he said, at the same time touching her in the exact spot that she wanted to be touched. "Oh, yes, that's it. That's it." And they gave themselves up to the pure pleasure of the moment.

Afterwards, driving home in the car, they talked very little. What does he think of me now? she wondered. She looked sideways at him. His eyes were fixed on the road ahead.

"Frank?"

"Yes?" He turned briefly toward her.

"Have you had many — you know — girlfriends?"

"Oh, I've had a few. No one like you, though." He smiled at her as he spoke, that smile was the last thing she saw in her mind at night, and the first thing in the morning. "What about you?"

"Well, you know I've got lots of girl friends. All girls do." Did she sound as silly as she felt, as silly as American girls she'd seen in movies, or read about in books, who wisecracked their way through life?

He put his hand on her thigh and patted it. "Now don't you play games with me, Heather Novak." He gently stroked the inside of her thigh, and then left his hand there. "I s'pose you've had lots of boyfriends."

"What do you think?" She couldn't bring herself to tell him that there'd been no one before him, and yet she didn't want him to think that what she was doing with him was a habitual thing.

"I think you're sweet." He removed his hand from her thigh and took her hand in his. "I think you're the sweetest girl I've ever met." Heather felt the words engraving themselves on her consciousness as if her mind were made of grooves, like a record.

They were at the top of the hill now, where he always dropped her off. "Why don't you let me take you to the door? I feels foolish havin' you walk down there by yourself. You never know who might be hangin' around."

"Oh, it's not very far. Don't worry, nobody's going to grab me. You know what I told you. I don't want Mom to know about us."

"I can't see why not." He put his arms around her, and drew her close to him. "From what you're after tellin' me, I'm sure she's not the old-fashioned type."

"It's not that at all. I'd just rather for her not to know. She'd ask me all kinds of stupid questions and I...I just wouldn't be able to stand it, that's all."

"Okay then, if that's the way you want it. I'll be up by the school for you tomorrow, okay?" She got out of the car, then turned to wave after him as he honked the horn in that jazzy, special way and drove off. He often picked her up after school; she didn't want to make her mother suspicious by going out every night. In the afternoons Eileen was at work and didn't know what time Heather got home.

Shirley and Eileen were sitting in the kitchen drinking tea when Heather opened the door. She stopped for a moment in the hallway, her mother's artificially blonde hair and Shirley's pale golden curls so close together reminding her of the advertisements for Ivory Snow where the reader was supposed to guess which hands belonged to the mother and which to the daughter. Her mother's hands were red and rough from the harsh lotions she used day after day on customers' hair; even rubber gloves did not really protect them. Shirley's hands were whiter and softer; she was trying to let her nails grow. Some of them were long and nicely-shaped while others had broken off. It wasn't often she saw her mother and sister sitting compatibly together like that.

"Oh, it's you," said Eileen as she turned toward the door. "Did you walk all the way out from the library by yourself?"

"I got a ride part of the way." Heather didn't look at her mother. She sat down in the rocking chair and took off her heavy shoes. "Oh, that's better. Those shoes pinch my feet."

"You'll soon want your boots on. The forecast calls for snow tonight." Eileen went to the stove and turned on the burner under the kettle. "Imagine, snow already."

Shirley looked straight at Heather and said, "Who gave you the run, Frank Marshall?" Heather felt her face go hot. Why had she ever mentioned Frank's name to Shirley? She wished there was something, anything, she could do to keep the colour out of her face. She went to the sink and turned on the tap, her back to the other two.

"Oh, my God, I believe she's blushing. Look, Shirl, her face is as red as a beet. Don't tell me you got a boyfriend, Heather." Heather didn't want to face the knowing grins on the two faces. She leaned against the counter, as if for support. "Ye two makes me sick," she said, unable to keep the tremor out of her voice. "You're always tormentin' and makin' fun." She was afraid she was going to cry.

"Ah, girl, we're only carryin' on. Come and have a cup of tea, now. You must be frozen. It's like a winter's night out tonight." Eileen moved a newspaper and a sweater from the chair next to her, and pointed at a brown paper bag on the table. "Look, Mom sent you down some bananas. She knows how much you likes 'em. She got food goin' bad right and left up there. There was a crowd in from the Army tonight and they brought her everything you could mention. Poor Mom, she used to love eatin' so much and now she don't want none of it." Eileen blinked quickly a couple of times. Heather sat down, picked up a banana and peeled it, refused a cup of tea.

Shirley carried her cup and saucer to the sink. "I'm goin' out for a while now, Mom. Randy got the loan of his brother-in-law's car and we're gonna take a run in as far as his sister's."

"My God, you goes out when it's time to come home." Eileen sighed, reached for a banana and started to peel it.

"Frank Marshall is a nice guy," said Shirley, poking Heather in the ribs as she passed behind her chair. "Valerie Miller used to go out with him last year. She was dyin' to the world about him. She won't talk about him now, but I believe he dropped her. I never could figure out what he saw in her anyway." She looked at Heather for a moment, frowning. She's probably trying to figure out what he sees in me, thought Heather, wishing herself in bed, in school, anywhere but here in this kitchen with a mother and a sister who didn't understand or wouldn't care if they did.

"Don't you be late, now," said Eileen absentmindedly.

"Oh, Mom, don't you know it's not late till twelve o'clock and after that it's early?" And with a slam of the front door she was gone.

"That Shirl, I don't know what I'm gonna do with her." Eileen shook her head as she felt around the table for a match to light her cigarette. "I don't like the looks of that fella Randy. He's one o' them Noseworthys from down there on Walker Place. You knows what a hard crowd they are. Mollie's sister lives in by them and she told me they got the police down there nearly every weekend." She drew hard on her cigarette and then blew out a mouthful of smoke, watching as it circled above her head. "Who is this Frank Marshall Shirley is talkin' about, anyway? Did he really drive you home?"

Heather looked at the pattern on the plastic placemat until the orange and white swirls made her head spin. "He's just a boy I know, Mom," she said, keeping her head down. "He lives way down the east end."

"Marshall." Eileen repeated the name thoughtfully. "I don't think I knows any Marshalls. But what is it about the name, oh, I know who I'm thinkin' about, that man who was killed that time when his truck bumped into that insurance building down there at the foot of Queen Street. That was some sad, that was."

"He was Frank's father." Heather picked up her spoon and tapped it rhythmically against the placemat. "His mother works down to Woolworth's." She didn't know why she was telling her mother all this.

"I don't know her but I know *of* her." Why did her mother feel that she must know everybody in town? "This Frank now, is he really a nice guy, or what?"

"Yes." Heather's head felt the way it did sometimes when Mrs. Arnold, her science teacher, was explaining an experiment.

"All right then, *don't* tell me." Eileen got up quickly, almost knocking the chair over in her haste. "I don't know where I got the three of ye. Mollie's girls are like friends to her, they goes everywhere together, especially her and Carol. Ye acts like I'm poison or something." She turned her back on Heather and began to run water into the sink.

Heather had ceased being bewildered by her mother's outbursts and changes of mood, which happened for no particular reason. She couldn't imagine what she had said, or hadn't said, to make her mother so mad. "Oh, Mom, what's the matter now? There's nothing to tell. I don't know what to be sayin' to you when you gets like that." She gathered up the rest of the dishes and brought them to the sink.

"I don't know what's wrong with me tonight," said Eileen, still not looking around. "I'm worried to death about Mom, I s'pose that's half of it. The nurse told me tonight the doctor wanted to have a talk with me. And Herb is makin' such a nuisance of hisself up there, they're havin' a job to get him to leave nighttime when visiting hours are over. And oh, Heather, she looks so sick. She got the real look Aunt Pearl had, you know, right pinched and grey lookin'."

Heather wished she could hug her mother the way daughters hugged their mothers on soap operas and in the movies. Everybody was always hugging everybody else on *Another World*. Eileen had never been one to show affection; when she and Shirley and Lorraine fell and scraped their knees when they were small she'd wash the cut and put a bandaid on it but rarely would she kiss them or speak tenderly to them. She was much more likely to bawl them out for being clumsy enough to fall down. The only time Heather had seen her mother cry was when Pop Morgan had died; then it had seemed as if she was never going to stop. Linda Stone had long conversations with her mother, conversations such as Heather had never had with anyone, not her mother, her sisters, Debbie or Linda herself. They talked about books, movies, politics, the Third World, their own reactions to things, everything that came into their heads. I must be like Mom, she thought. I don't like to show my feelings.

Except to Frank. She certainly didn't hide her feelings from Frank. But even when she was with him there were many things she couldn't and didn't talk about, things like sickness and death and fear and how unfair the world was and what happened after you died. Nan, of course, believed that if you were good you went straight to heaven. Heather had heard her testify to that fact in the Army, and had heard Herb say the same thing. But did they really believe it, down deep?

How could they know for sure? If you really believed all that, you surely wouldn't mind dying. And yet she was certain Nan didn't want to die any more than Heather did herself. There were tears in her own eyes now; she even felt one running down her cheek. She went and stood beside her mother at the sink.

"Mom, Nan is not going to die, is she? Is she?"

Eileen picked up the detergent bottle, bent down and put it in the cupboard. "I don't know, Heather. I just don't know. Sure they don't even know what's wrong with her yet. What's the matter with doctors, anyway? They can't do no more about cancer now than what they could a hundred years ago. Half the time they can't even find out if you got it or not. They got all that marv'lous equipment up there and Mom woulda been just as well off if she had to stay home." She stepped back, looking at Heather for a moment as if making up her mind what to do with her. "I'm goin' to bed," she said, her face suddenly looking very old, older than Nan's. "Finish up the dishes for me, will ya? I'm dead tired tonight." She almost collided with Heather as she moved away from the sink. "Don't worry too much, girl," she said, her eyes softer than they had been before. "It don't do no good. Mom prob'ly haven't even got cancer at all." When she reached the door she turned back and said, "See if that cat wants to go out before you comes up to bed, will ya? I don't want her smellin' up the house."

Heather nodded. What did it matter if the dishes were done or not, if Puss went out or not, if Frank really liked — loved — her or not, if Nan lived or died? She felt like a very tiny puppet at the end of a very long string. As she washed the dishes her mind moved from Nan to Frank to her mother, from her mother to Nan to Frank. For an instant she could see Lorraine as she had looked that Sunday afternoon when she came over to the house with Jason, that beaten look in her eyes, that what-does-it-matter set to her shoulders. Where had the old Lorraine gone, the Lorraine who laughed at nothing and had such a winning smile that one of her teachers had nicknamed her Sunshine? She thought of Frank's mother at that Woolworth's checkout counter, with the same patient expression that Heather had seen on the faces of the very old women at the Hoyles Home that a group from her class had visited last Christmas. Why couldn't people be happier? She had felt, earlier in the evening, that if she could only be with Frank all the time she would be perfectly happy forever. All those people, her mother, her grandmother, Mrs. Marshall, Lorraine, they must all have felt like that once. And Debbie, what about Debbie? Debbie was light-hearted and jolly most of the time, never wanted to hear anything about sickness or death or dying, but what did she really feel like inside?

As she was going up the stairs she thought of something Frank had said earlier in the evening when they had been close together in the back seat. "Aren't we lucky?" he had said. "Don't you think we're lucky, Heather?" She had assumed he had meant lucky because they were together, but now she wasn't so sure. At the time she had nodded her head against his chest, wanting to agree with him no matter what he meant.

What does it matter what we do? she said to herself as she undressed and got into bed, the sensations of her body quieter now, not dominant any more as they had been when she'd been with Frank. What does it matter if we're happy or not, if someone loves us or not, if we have what we want or not? It's all the same in the end, isn't it?

She pulled the blankets tightly around her; the night was cold and the old house had no insulation. Frank's face was before her, as it always was these nights the instant she closed her eyes. It matters, she thought, feeling very sleepy. It all matters.

# *Seven*

"Hey, Heather, wait for me." Heather turned around to see Debbie hurrying toward her, her long hair flying, the plastic supermarket bag of school books swinging as she ran. "I been shoutin' out to you so much I'm gettin' a sore throat again."

Heather stopped and waited. "Whew, just let me stand still for a minute," said Debbie. "I'm winded. You're some stranger, you are. Where have you been keepin' yourself lately?"

Heather didn't answer right away. She looked at the string of cars moving slowly up over Prince of Wales Street, most of them driven by women going to pick up their daughters and sons from school. There'd been snow earlier in the afternoon, just enough to make the streets slippery. Some of the cars skidded dangerously as they tried to make the turn at the top of the street.

"Okay now?" she asked after Debbie had taken a few gulps of fresh air.

"Yeah, I'm okay. I got my lungs ruined with all them cigarettes. Ma says she haven't got a bit of sympathy for me. She won't even buy me cigarettes in the groceries."

They fell into step together, their book-bags bumping against each other until they moved them to their other hands.

"So, I hear you been doin' the rush with Frank. I got to admit, Heather, I never thought you had it in you. There's some lot of girls jealous of you."

"Like who?"

"Like Donna Power for one. Didn't you know she used to go out with him? She thinks the sun shines out of his arse."

Heather laughed, "Oh, Deb, you're the same as ever." Then she realized what Debbie had said about Donna and Frank. That made at least two girlfriends he'd had before, Donna and that girl, Valerie, Shirl had mentioned. She wondered how many others there'd been.

"When did they break up, do you know? Frank and Donna, I mean?"

"Oh, they're broke up this nice while now. I don't know what happened, Donna never said. She still won't let anyone say a word against him, though."

"I phoned you a couple of times but you were out," said Heather, trying to remember if she really had. "I been up to the hospital a lot lately, girl. You know Nan was sick, didn't you?"

"Yeah, I heard that. But you weren't up to the hospital all the time, don't give me that. I seen you myself in Frank's car two days after school, and Harry told me he saw you and Frank drivin' up Signal Hill one night. That's the place to go, Signal Hill."

Heather wondered briefly what Harry had said to Debbie about her and Frank. She was probably better off not knowing.

"Frank is gone," she told Debbie. "He went early this morning." It was the first time she had put into words what had been on her mind all day. Linda, who had tried several times to start a conversation with her, had finally gone off in disgust with Marilyn Edwards.

"Gone where? I haven't been talking to you for a dog's age, remember. I don't know nothing about what's goin' on."

"He's gone to Alberta. To Fort McMurray. I must've told you that before. I've known ever since the night of the party that he was going."

"My God, Fort McMurray is goin' to be a second Newfoundland soon. Harry been talking about goin' out there, too."

"How *is* Harry?" Heather couldn't have cared less how Harry was but it was only polite to ask.

"Oh, he's all right," said Debbie, not sounding very sure. "He's doin' a bit of taxiing now. He gave up that security job. Couldn't stand the boss. He's one of them get-rich-quick types, you know, like Dave Antle used to live over on the corner of the street, remember him? He had to move in there on the back because he thought it was beneath him to live on *Gaspar* Street." Dave had been in school with Lorraine, and afterwards had gone to work at Woolco as a management trainee. Lorraine had laughed at him because he wore three-piece suits to work. He had switched to real estate now but he still wore three-piece suits.

"Mike says he's a queer," Lorraine had told her. "He won't even talk to him. Of course Mike thinks everyone is a queer if they're dressed up either bit at all."

"Let's go over as far as Rice's for some chips," said Debbie when they reached the corner. Heather's heart lurched at the sight of a car that looked just like Frank's. It was driven by a young man wearing a cowboy hat on his long, stringy hair.

Rice's was crowded, as usual, but they managed to get a table in the corner. Heather recognized several girls from school, including Darlene Snelgrove, looking paler and quieter than usual. Shirley was there too, sitting at the counter with Randy. She couldn't understand why Shirl wore all that mascara, and that dark eye shadow. She was much prettier without it. Shirley called out to them as they went by but Randy ignored them completely. He looked sullen today, sitting on the stool, opening and shutting his pocketknife, snapping it open and shut, open and shut.

They ordered chips, dressing and gravy. "Did you go to see him off?" asked Debbie.

"Are you kiddin'? He left six o'clock. I'm too fond of the bed to go anywhere that hour of the morning." Heather knew she wasn't fooling Debbie any more than she was fooling herself. She would have given anything in the world to have gone to the airport that morning, but there was no way she could have got out there. Frank had sold his car to one of his friends who was going to drive him out. "What about your mother?" she had asked him the night before,

82

remembering that pale, patient face and wondering how Mrs. Marshall felt about Frank leaving.

"No, I'm not lettin' her near the airport. She wouldn't be able to keep from bawlin', and that's all I'd need. I don't like goodbyes." He hadn't asked her if she'd like to come out. They hadn't talked much last night, anyway. Could Debbie tell just by looking at her what had happened the night before?

A couple of nights earlier Frank had asked her if she was on the Pill, saying immediately afterwards that he'd known she wouldn't be, as if he would have been disappointed in her if she had been. She had seen him every night that week; her mother was so preoccupied with Nan, who was due to have exploratory surgery on Monday, that she hadn't known or cared what Heather and Shirley were doing. Anyway, she'd been home before eleven every night.

"Mom thinks nothing can happen to a girl before twelve o'clock," Shirley said once, after Eileen had screamed at her for coming in at three-thirty in the morning. "God, last night I was oney over minding the house with Joyce. I never even seen Randy, he was gone off somewhere with the boys."

Frank hadn't really pushed her to do what she had done last night; she'd wanted to as much as he had. They'd been lying together in the back seat, their hands moving feverishly over each other's bodies, saying very little, kissing with a kind of desperation.

"You know what I wants to do, don't you, Heather?" he said quietly, his mouth against her neck.

"Yes," she whispered.

"I won't really do it," he said. "I'll just, you know, lay it there on yours." They talked in circles, or in riddles, never naming the parts of their bodies they were discussing.

"Will it be...all right?" she asked, a wealth of detail behind those short words.

"Yes, you know it will. You won't get pregnant or anything. I won't put it inside."

It had felt so good, so warm and hard and alive. Once he'd put his penis against her, she wouldn't have been able to bear it if he'd taken it away too quickly.

"I didn't mean for that to happen," he said afterwards, leaning over the seatback to get some tissues from the glove compartment. She felt all sticky and messy but it didn't matter. So this was what all the talk was about, all the books, the movies, the songs, the innuendos. Nothing had prepared her for how it would really be. "I meant to take it away, just in time, but I couldn't. I just couldn't."

"I didn't want you to. Don't worry." She had heard so much for so long about men and boys coaxing women and girls, wheedling them, even taking them by force, that she was led to believe that females were passive observers, or at best, receptacles for the lusts of men. What about the lusts of women? She didn't like the word lust, though; it didn't seem appropriate for the way she'd been feeling. And she couldn't imagine feeling that way with anyone else but Frank.

"I hope I didn't hurt you," he said as they drove home. "I know you never did nothing like this before." His words reminded her of what she and Shirley used to call the "bump, bump, bump song," a hit for Carroll Baker a few years earlier, *I Know You've Never Been This Far Before*. They had laughed at it, and made fun of it. It didn't seem funny at all now.

"No, you didn't hurt me," she assured him. "You didn't even try to get inside." Would it have hurt very much if he had? Would she have bled?

"I had sense enough for that," he said, grinning at her with that grin she was sure was stamped forever on her brain. "I don't want anything to happen to you."

When she got home she crept into the house and up the stairs, wanting to take a bath before she had to face her mother or Shirley. In the bathtub she looked down at her body, surprised that it didn't look any different. She knew there was no chance of pregnancy without penetration; she'd gathered from the hints of Debbie and some of the other girls that what she'd done with Frank was what many girls did with their boy friends when they weren't on the Pill or "using something." I wouldn't have stopped him, though, no matter what he wanted to do, she said to herself. I couldn't have. And she let the hot water lap over her, touching the places that Frank had touched and would not be touching again for a long time, or perhaps ever.

The waitress brought their order. "Mmmm, those chips sure hit the spot, don't they?" said Debbie. "Or are you too lovesick to care about food?"

Heather wished Debbie would lower her voice. The tables were close together; she didn't want the whole world to know about her and Frank.

"I must say, I never thought you had it in you." Debbie looked at Heather with admiration. Heather almost said "I didn't," stopping herself just in time. "Now you know all that stuff I was tellin' you is true. There's nothing like havin' a boy friend is there, especially one like Frank?" Was that just a faint note of envy in Debbie's voice?

"See that girl over there at the table by the door, the one with the blue top on?" Debbie continued. Heather was relieved that she'd got off the subject of Frank. "She goes to your school, don't she?"

"Yeah, that's Darlene Snelgrove. I don't really know her, just by name. She's not in my class."

Debbie leaned across the table toward Heather and lowered her voice. "I heard she had an abortion," she said, her lips just barely moving. "Shockin' white-looking, ent she?"

Heather looked at Darlene as well as she could without making it too obvious. She was pushing her chips around on the plate with her fork, as if she didn't want to eat them.

"Did she really, Deb? My God, no wonder she looks sick."

"I don't see how anyone can do that, do you?" Debbie's voice was rising again; Heather put her fingers to her lips. "I mean, you might think it's just cos I'm a Catholic but that's not it at all. I don't care what anyone says, it's murder."

Heather pictured Darlene in the hospital, in the operating room, waking up afterwards. She wasn't sure how abortions were done but she knew you had to be put to sleep for them.

"Mom is the same as you are about abortions, and she's not even a Catholic. But really, Deb, what would you do if you got pregnant?" As soon as she stopped speaking she realized the implications of what she had said. "I mean, you know, you know what I mean."

Debbie laughed. "My God, girl, you're gone some red in the face. You're shockin' for blushin', ent you? I'm frightened to death I'll get pregnant, when I lets myself think about it. But Harry says I won't, he knows all about what to do." She paused to drain the rest of her Pepsi, the almost empty tin making a hollow sound. "If ever I did, I don't know what I'd do. Ma'd die altogether if that happened to me, it'd be just like Mom all over again. I think I'd go away somewhere and have the baby, not let Ma and Pop know anything about it. Maybe I'd keep it, get my own little place. I'd rather give it up for adoption than do what Mom did with me, though. One thing for sure, I wouldn't be able to dump it on her, when she didn't even want *me*." Debbie looked tired, and more thoughtful than Heather had ever seen her look before. "God, what're we talkin' about that for? Worry about something when it happens, that's the proper thing to do."

Heather wasn't ready to let the matter drop. "You wouldn't get married, then?" She pushed the rest of the dressing to the middle of her plate. It was getting cold, the gravy congealing around it.

"Married? My God, no. And even if I wanted to, I can't see Harry gettin' hisself tied down. There's lotsa time for that." A boy had joined the three girls at the table, a fair-haired, blocky boy wearing a Booth Braves jacket. Darlene brightened up when he sat down; there was more colour in her cheeks now, and her eyes looked livelier.

"Who was the fella, you know, that Darlene...?" She let her voice trail off.

"Who did she get pregnant for, you mean. I don't know, girl, it's hard to say. They says she been with everything." It was hard to figure Debbie out sometimes. She talked a lot about all the boys she'd been out with, and the ones she'd like to go out with, but apparently she had her own code of what was acceptable and what was not. Heather remembered Darlene at the party, and the boy who was with her. Had he just drifted out of her life, not knowing anything about her pregnancy? Maybe he hadn't been responsible, or hadn't been sure that he was. She shivered as she realized that Darlene probably wasn't even fifteen yet.

"Are you cold, Heather? It *is* a bit chilly here today, with the door open so much. Put on your jacket, girl."

"No, that's all right, I'm warm enough." She pulled her chair closer to the table, vowing not to look Darlene's way any more.

The restaurant was full now, with not a seat to be had either at the counter or at the tables. Heather listened to the hum of voices. Most of the others there were students like herself, getting together to laugh and talk and joke before they had to separate and go home to homework and parents' complaints. She wondered about Darlene's parents. Surely they must know what had happened to her. How did they feel about it? Had they been angry with her, hurt, disappointed? She thought about her own mother's reaction if anything like that happened to her, and held herself tight to keep from shivering again as she imagined how Eileen would shout and rave and swear if she were faced with such news about her or Shirley.

Shirley was still sitting on a stool at the counter, but Randy wasn't beside her any more. Shirley was moving her shoulders and arms in time with the music from the jukebox, speaking now and then to her friend Joyce who worked part-time as a waitress at Rice's. She and Shirley didn't know much about each other, really, not like the sisters she read about in books, who told each other everything, went around together as if they were friends, shared a kind of empathy that could not be shared with anyone else. Were there any sisters like that, really, or were they just a figment of some writer's vivid imagination? Eileen wasn't at all close to her two sisters, either, not nearly as close as she was to Mollie. Muriel, who was two years older than Eileen, and Patsy, two years younger, both lived far away, Muriel in Minnesota and Patsy in Brampton, Ontario. Muriel had married an American serviceman; the marriage had evidently worked out better than Eileen's. "But how do we know that, Mom?" Eileen asked once when Nan was talking about how happy Muriel and Bob were together. "Sure they were okay when you were there, but that was only for two weeks. Anyone can put on an act for that long. Muriel always made out everything was all sunshine with her, anyway. It's just showing off."

Patsy had married Leo Connors, a boy she'd gone to school with. "Just imagine, two of my children married to Catholics," Heather had heard her grandmother say. "It's funny how they overlooks their own kind and makes for the wrong colour. Of course Leo is a good young fellow (Leo must have been at least thirty-five when she said that), I must say that for him. She could've done worse. And none of the young people goes to church any more, so what difference do it make?"

"I wouldn't waste my time goin' to church lookin' at hypocrites," Eileen had sniffed. "Whatever I am, the whole world knows it. When I sees that George Walker — you know, he's in the choir down to St. Stephen's — and that fella Kennedy up in the band where you goes, Mom, I could vomit, that's the truth. George Walker have had a girlfriend this years, and him so lovey-dovey with his wife. And that Kennedy, sure I saw him myself into the Strand with that one Mason lives up by Mollie, you knows who I mean, Mom. It just turns my stomach."

"Now, Eileen, they're not all like that. And you're not supposed to look at other people. Our Lord told us not to judge, that's for him to do. You're just supposed to worry about what you're like yourself."

"How is your grandmother now?" Debbie asked, as if she'd been reading Heather's mind. The crowd was thinning out; Darlene and her friends had gone. Bertie Lane was sitting at the counter next to Shirley; she was teasing him, as she often did. He was eating a hamburger, and drinking a bottle of Pepsi with loud, slurpy noises.

"Just about the same, girl. They're operatin' on her Monday, looking for more cancer, I think. She looks some sick, and her stomach is all swollen up." Heather tried not to think about the colour of Nan's skin; it was beginning to look really sallow, almost yellow.

"Ma was wondering about her. She don't know her very well, just from seein' her over to yere place, you know. Ma is frightened to death of cancer herself, but who's not? Why in the name of God can't they find out what causes it? Pop says it's the tin food, he says he never heard talk of anyone havin' cancer when he was young." Debbie paused for a moment, as if to stop herself from being too serious. "That Terry Fox, he was some sweet, wasn't he? I cried my eyes out when he died. 'Member we went down to see him when he started his run down there by City Hall?"

Heather remembered. She'd expected to feel really sorry for this doomed young man setting out on the impossible task of running across Canada on one good leg and a stick one. "He'll never make it," a man in the crowd had muttered. "Poor youngster, I gives him about as far as the overpass. He haven't even got a decent artificial leg." But when she saw that flushed, confident face topped by the childish curly hair, the firm set of the young mouth, she had actually found herself envying him. It must be wonderful to believe in something that much, to be so certain that what you did would make a difference. Some people said he was running away from his fear but, whatever the reason, he'd had the nerve and the strength not to sit at home waiting for the cancer to finish him off. There'd been a play in the high school drama festival the year before called *The Valiant.* "The valiant only die but once" was the line that stuck in her mind.

"Yes," she said now. "The Cancer Society got an awful lot of money out of that, but what are they doin' with it? They don't seem to be any farther ahead."

"My God, we're some gloomy today." Debbie gave her shoulders a shake. "Your grandmother'll probably be okay. Marie O'Toole's aunt was nearly gone with it and they gave her some new kind of treatment. Marie says it's almost like she's after comin' back from the dead. They'll probably give your grandmother that. And p'raps it's not cancer at all she got. Anyway, it's not like she was a young person."

Heather looked at her watch. "I think I better go. I promised Mom I'd go up to the hospital with her tonight. She hates goin' up by herself."

"I don't blame her. I hates hospitals, don't you?" Now it was Debbie's turn to shiver. "And everywhere you looks up to St. Clare's there's a crucifix on the wall."

"I didn't think you'd mind things like that, Deb. After all, you *are* a Catholic."

"It puts me too much in mind of dyin', girl. God, we can't get off that subject today, can we? How come your grandmother didn't go to the Grace, anyway?"

"Her doctor put her in St. Clare's because that's the hospital he works at. You know Nan, now, she's not gonna argue with a doctor." They put on their jackets and gathered up their bags of books.

On the way out they stopped to talk to Shirley who was still sitting at the counter, with Bertie Lane beside her. He was eating a plate of chips; there was a smear of ketchup on each side of his face. Without even stopping to swallow the food in his mouth he turned to Heather and said: "Hedder, will you marry me?"

"Oh, Bertie, I'm some jealous," said Shirley, her face mock- sad. "I been sittin' here with you this ages and you never asked me to marry you. Anyway, it's no good asking Heather. She already got a boyfriend." Shirley had raised her voice a little; two or three people at a nearby table glanced over at them.

Heather found herself turning crimson again. "Oh, Shirl, why can't you shut up?"

"That's a lie for her, ent it, Hedder?" said Bertie. "I'm your b'y friend, ent I?"

"Yes, Bertie, you knows you are." Heather forced herself to give him a pat on the shoulder, trying not to look at his mouth. "You don't have to worry about me."

"Are ye goin' home, now, or what?" asked Shirley, reaching down to the floor for her purse. "I think I been here long enough." She opened the purse, took out a little round mirror and looked at her reflection. "God, I looks like something shot at and missed."

Heather hoped Bertie wouldn't leave with them, but of course he did. As they walked along, he kept falling behind and asking them petulantly to wait for him. After a while Heather slowed her steps to match his; Shirley and Debbie walked in front of them.

"What was wrong with Randy today, Shirl?" Debbie asked. "He looked like a thunder cloud."

"Oh, someone told him I was down to Smitty's with another fella and he got right sulky." Shirley didn't sound too concerned.

"And were you?"

"No, girl, not really. Myself and Joyce went down the other night when Randy and them were playing darts up to the Sports and these two fellas we knew just sat at our table for awhile. God, fellas are some hard to get along with, aren't they? Sometimes I thinks we're better off without 'em."

Heather was relieved not to have to join in the conversation. She was tired of talking; she wanted to think about Frank. She pictured him as she'd last seen him, in the car just before she got out. He'd been wearing an orange and brown striped shirt and a leather jacket; his hair was still rumpled from their time in the back seat. "Are you going to write to me?" she asked. He hadn't said anything about writing. "I'm not much of a hand for writin' letters but I'll see what I can do," he'd promised then. "I don't know what my address is gonna be yet but as soon as I gets one I'll let you know." Heather was already composing a letter in her mind.

He'd be there by now, in Alberta. Of course it would be much earlier there. Was he feeling alone, lonely, was he missing her at all? He'd planned to stay for a day or two with a friend in Edmonton before going on to Fort McMurray. He'd said he was going to phone his mother as soon as he got there because "you knows what she's like, she'll worry herself sick if I don't." If only she knew Mrs. Marshall well enough to phone her, to talk to her about Frank. The poor woman probably didn't know she existed. As she walked towards home, Bertie shuffling along beside her, she answered his few questions mechanically, as if she were a computer, and thought all the while of Frank.

"Are you going up to the hospital tonight?" Shirley asked when Heather caught up with her after leaving Bertie behind at Murray's Store.

"I told Mom I would, what about you? You hardly been up at all."

"I can't stand hospitals." Shirley shivered as Heather had done earlier. "And besides, Nan don't care if I goes up or not. You were always her favourite."

Heather knew that was true. Nan had said it herself, the day she told Heather she was leaving her the little pink teapot in her will. "I was goin' to leave you that nice blue glass vase I had, too," she'd continued. "You know, the one you used to like when you were small and I had it in the middle of the dining room table. But the cat knocked it down and smashed it in a thousand pieces. I sat down and cried to break my heart when that happened. You know how much I thought about that vase."

All through supper Heather continued to think about Frank. She was so quiet Eileen asked her if she was getting the flu— "It's all over town." When the time came to leave for the hospital she was almost glad. She knew she wouldn't be able to keep her mind on homework tonight.

# *Eight*

"It was the way he told us," Eileen said for the twentieth time that night. "I mean, my God, cancer might be an everyday thing to him but it's certainly not to us. My own mother, too. 'Your mother has about three months to live, Mrs. Novak,' he said, as cool as any cucumber. 'There's nothing we can do for her. The cancer is too far advanced.' And then he start tellin' us about what organs it's in, the pancreas, the gall bladder, fringing the intestines. Just like we wanted to know any of that stuff." She paused to wipe her eyes again, taking another tissue from Mollie's outstretched hand.

"Was that when Herb...?" Shirley began. Her mother interrupted immediately.

"No, no, not right away. Herb was like he was in a daze first. He hardly said a word, just kept starin' down at the floor. And then, after a while he looked up at the doctor and said 'Are you sure, doctor? Are you *sure*?' Poor Herb, he do think the world of Mom, even if he would drive ya up the wall sometimes. And the doctor just looked at him and said 'Of course I'm sure, Mr. Abbott. And I think Mrs. Abbot should be told about her condition. She's entitled to know. We could move her into the Palliative Care Unit if you like. She'd be very comfortable there.' That was when Herb tried to hit him. 'An' that's what you wun't shift her into no Pall'ative Care,' he said, movin' right close to the doctor. He had his fist up, too. 'An' that's what

93

you're *not* goin' to shift her into that place where they're all give up to die. I'm taking her home with me and I'm looking after her myself, till she gets better. You're not gonna tell her none of that nonsense, either, cos it's a pack of lies.' He looked so funny, Herb did, as small as he is up against that big tall doctor." Eileen seemed about to smile but remembered just in time that she couldn't allow herself to smile now. She sniffed and dabbed at her eyes with the tissue; Mollie handed her another one. "I'm tired talkin' about it," Eileen said, as she had at least six times already. "Don't any of ye ever go to that Dr. Armstrong, will ye? I wouldn't have him for...for a sick cat."

Heather sat in the corner of the living room, in an old wooden rocking chair Nan had given them after Herb had bought her a fancy new upholstered one on their first Christmas together. For the past two hours they'd all been sitting in the room together, her mother on the chesterfield with Mollie close beside her. Shirley was slumped down in the other corner of the chesterfield, and Lorraine sat in the armchair in front of the television set which flickered from *Happy Days* to *Three's Company* to *Too Close for Comfort* and then to *Happy Days Again* without anybody paying attention. Eileen's eyes and nose were red, her face puffy and swollen.

Heather stroked the cat in her arms, wishing she were a cat herself. It must be nice to live from day to day the way cats did, being fed, stroked, sheltered, without ever having to think about anything or anyone. Without ever realizing that some day you were going to die.

"Myrtle Griffin had Dr. Armstrong when she had her gall bladder out," said Lorraine. It was the first time for months that Heather had seen Lorraine without Jason. When Eileen had phoned, telling her hysterically about Nan, Lorraine grabbed her coat and rushed right out of the house, leaving Jason and Mike at the supper table. "He'll have to stay in tonight," she told them when she arrived, breathless from her run uphill to her mother's house. "He won't go off and leave Jason, he's not that far gone yet."

"Myrtle says she wouldn't have nobody else," Lorraine continued now. "She thinks the world over him."

"Yes, but she got better," said Eileen. "It's all right for her. But Mom — my *mother* — is goin' to die." She started to cry again, loudly this time.

Heather looked up at the ceiling; she didn't want to look at anyone else in the room. Lloyd, her mother's old boy friend, had stuccoed the ceiling several years before, right after Eileen had finally managed to stop the leak in the roof. Everyone had been putting stucco on their ceilings then. Lloyd had really let himself go; the long squiggles and swirls of stucco hung down like icicles frosted over with thick vanilla icing, the curly bits on the ceiling itself like rosebuds on a wedding cake. The ceiling had a grimy look to it now; there didn't seem to be any way to wash stucco.

Lloyd had papered the walls at the same time; he was more of a handyman than any of Eileen's other boy friends. The paper was cream with a dark-red pattern on it; it looked much too ornate for the poky little room. Just above the skirting boards the paper had been scratched and torn in several places — "Jesus, you got my nice wallpaper ruined," Eileen had scolded the cat when she first noticed it. Shirley claimed Puss thought his name was Jesus, that he pricked up his ears when the television evangelists were holding forth. Eileen no longer paid any attention to the scratch marks; like the faded green chesterfield, the photographs crowding the cream-painted mantel above the blocked-up fireplace and the soiled brown and beige carpet on the floor they had become part of the living room now.

"I should go up to the hospital," said Eileen, wiping her eyes once more. "I told Mom when I left this afternoon I'd be up again tonight. I don't think she hardly understood what I was sayin' to her. She was awful groggy. And so white-lookin', like she didn't have a drop of blood left in her body."

"Left in her body," echoed Mollie and then, getting to her feet, "I don't think you're in any shape to go up there tonight, Eileen. You just sit right there now and I'll get you a nice drop of tea. Did you take that Valium I brought down to you?"

"Yes, I took that right away. It don't seem to be doin' me much good, though. Have you got another one there? I got to take something goin' to bed or I'll be awake all night long goin' over and over what happened up to the hospital." Eileen stood up and looked in the long, wooden-framed mirror over the mantel. "God, what am I like? I looks almost as bad as poor Mom." She wet one of her fingers and drew it along the arch of her eyebrows.

Mollie put a cup of tea and two jam-jams on the TV tray she had placed in front of Eileen. "Come on now, girl, you got to keep your strength up. I got a nice bit of sugar in the tea, that'll do you good. I often heard Mercedes Walsh say you should eat lots of sugar after gettin' a shock, and she's a nurse. You're not goin' to do your mother one bit of good if you gives out. Come on, now, drink it while it's nice and hot."

She sat down beside Eileen again, and handed her the tea. In her pale turquoise uniform pantsuit, her short, dark hair neatly brushed back from her face, she reminded Heather of a Sunday School teacher she'd once had who had a talent for organizing the concerts and pageants that marked the special days of the church year. Heather liked Mollie but she got nervous when she was in the same room with her for too long. Mollie had a disconcerting habit of repeating the last few words of other people's sentences. She and Shirley and Lorraine had laughed at this so often in private that she was always afraid they were going to forget themselves and do it some time when Mollie was there.

Heather took her eyes off the ceiling and looked around the room. Apart from her mother, everybody else looked much as usual. Lorraine had no makeup on at all tonight; the bright spots of colour in her cheeks were natural. Shirley hadn't been home for supper; the jacket she had flung off when she came in from Joyce's was still lying behind her on the back of the chesterfield. As for Heather herself, a lump had come up in her throat when her mother, just back from the hospital, had told her the news about Nan. She hadn't been able to eat any supper, not even a cup of tea or a glass of milk. Her stomach felt as full and uncomfortable as if she had just eaten a heavy, starchy meal.

Shirley went to the television set and began to switch from one channel to another so fast that the fleeting images on the screen looked as surrealistic and unreal as figures in a dream.

Heather had dreamed about Frank the night before, dreamed that they were sitting on the edge of a swimming pool, very much like the

96

one at the Aquarena, except that the bluish-green water had come lapping in over the sides like gentle waves on a beach on a perfect July day. In the dream she had been conscious of feeling rather than of talking or listening, feeling peaceful and content just as she'd felt when she and Frank were together in the car. She hadn't wanted to awaken from the dream, had wanted to crawl back into it after Eileen shouted to tell her she was going to be late for school if she didn't get up right away.

"Turn off that television, Shirl," Eileen said sharply. "We got more on our mind than TV tonight. Oh, my, I s'pose I better get ready to go up to the hospital."

"I told you you're not fit to go up there tonight and I'm not lettin' you go," said Mollie, as if she were Eileen's mother now. "You're going to have a nice hot bath and go to bed. The girls can go up in your place."

Shirley looked at Mollie, seemed about to say something, then shrugged and looked across at Heather and Lorraine.

"Yes, Mom, the three of us'll go up," said Lorraine, pulling herself to her feet. "God only knows when I'll get out of the house again."

"...out of the house again," Mollie repeated softly. "Now, isn't that grand, Eileen?" she continued, as if she were talking to a very small child. "I just got to run across the street to Lanes' with some Avon stuff. Would you believe six bottles of Lover Bay aftershave?"

In spite of herself Eileen laughed. "Who ordered them, Bertie or Jack or the old man? I'm surprised at you, Mollie, sellin' the likes of them something like that."

"I'm not supposed to know what they does with it," Mollie said, pulling on her coat. "If they drinks it instead of using it like it's supposed to be used that's their business, not mine. Poor old Mr. Lane, he's in such misery with his legs I'd hardly blame him."

"It's cheaper than liquor, anyhow," said Shirley, shaking the wrinkles out of her jacket. "C'mon then, girls, if we're goin' to the hospital let's get on the road. It's almost time for visiting hours to be over."

"Oh, that's all right," said Eileen, beginning to look and sound a little more like herself. "When anyone is as sick as Mom is the hospital don't worry about visiting hours. My, that drop of tea did me good, Mollie, I must say. Ye go on now, Mollie'll keep me company. It's just the shock of it all, you know. And that doctor, the way he got on." She drained her cup and replaced it on the TV tray. Her hands were steadier now.

Outside a light flurry of snow was falling.

"We shoulda put boots on," said Lorraine as they hurried up over the hill, slipping a little. "I needs a new pair, by rights, but I don't know where the money is gonna come from."

"God, how long is it since the three of us went anywhere together?" said Shirley, pulling the collar of her jacket up around her neck. "Brrr, it's some cold out tonight. We're gettin' winter early this year."

"It'll be Christmas before we knows it," said Lorraine. "Poor Jason, he wants everything he sees but I'm certainly not gonna be able to get him much this year. He don't know the difference between cheap and expensive yet, anyway, thank God. I can probably pawn him off with anything."

" 'Member how whenever Nan'd come to the house near Christmas, when we were small, how she'd always sing 'He see you when you're sleeping/He know when you're awake?' " said Shirley.

"Yes, and Heather'd correct her every time —'It's not he _see you,_ Nanny, it's he _sees_ you,' " said Lorraine in a mock little-girl voice. "And then, the next time Nan'd come down, we'd go through the same thing over again."

As they spoke, Heather could picture the scene clearly, Nan, plump and pink-faced then, dressed in that wine-coloured coat with the grey fur collar, pointing her finger from one to another of them as she sang.

"Do you think we should write and tell Dad about Nan being sick?" Heather hadn't even known she was thinking of her father until the words were out. "Nan always thought a lot about him, from what she told me."

"Aw, he forgets all about her now, girl," said Lorraine, giving Heather a little spank. "Sure he hardly knows we're in the world, let alone Nan. But write to him if you wants to."

"Mom didn't even want to let Muriel and Pats know," said Shirley. "She said they never bothered about Nan when she was well so why should they be told she's sick. But Mollie said she should phone them."

When her father stopped writing to her, a few months after his second marriage, Heather vowed that she'd never write to him again. Surely to tell him something like this, though? But she didn't want to go through all that again, waiting for letters that never came.

When they got to the hospital Nan was dozing, opening her eyes, half-smiling, then closing them again. The room had a sickly smell, a mixture of urine, disinfectant, dusting powder and cologne. Herb was walking back and forth from the bed to the window, from the window to the bed. He nodded at the girls when they arrived, and then seemed to forget they were there. A nurse came in and, without a word to anyone, pulled the curtains around Nan's bed.

"How is she?" Lorraine whispered to Herb. Like Heather, she had never been able to make up her mind what to call him.

"She's going to be all right." Herb sounded almost as if he was talking to himself. "Don't you fret, your grandmother is goin' to be all right. Doctors don't know everything. I'm getting the Major to pray for her Sunday. Prayer can work miracles, you know, if you got the faith."

"A fat lot of good that'll do," muttered Shirley.

"Shhh," said Heather, but Herb didn't look as if he'd heard Shirley anyway. Heather hoped Nan hadn't heard Herb; he'd been so opposed to telling Nan she had cancer and here he was now talking about miracles. Like Shirley, Heather didn't believe prayer would do much good but surely if Herb wanted to believe it could it was just as well to leave him alone. Anyway, you couldn't be too sure.

"Fred was up," Herb said, still pacing around the room. "He didn't stay very long. His wife was with him. Daisy never even knew they were there."

The bed that had been occupied by the old, old woman was empty now, stripped of its sheets and blankets. Heather wondered if she had died. The girl's bed was empty, too, but the blankets were rumpled, as if someone had been under them a few minutes before. Heather thought she had seen the girl in the corridor, leaning heavily on her boy friend's arm as they walked slowly along. Mrs. Mercer was still in her bed; she was drinking Diet Pepsi tonight, and reading the Herald TV Guide. "Your grandmother is miser'ble, my dear," she said, looking at Heather over the top of the magazine. "And they're forever pokin' and firkin' at her. I don't know why they can't leave the poor creature alone."

The nurse emerged from the screened-off section and pulled back the curtains to reveal Nan in the bed once more. "Where's your mother to?" Nan's voice was weak, the words slurred. "I wanted to see your mother." The intravenous equipment stood beside the bed; Nan picked at the tube that was attached to a vein on the back of her hand. "They never found nothing, did they?" she asked Herb, who had finally come to rest near the head of the bed. "You know, when they opened me up?"

"Don't you worry about that now, Daisy," Herb said, patting her arm. "Everything is going to be all right." Heather realized as she listened that Herb probably considered it a sin to tell a lie, even to reassure his wife.

"Where's Eileen to?" Nan asked again. There were tears in her eyes. "I wanted to ask her something."

"She'll be up again tomorrow, Nan," said Lorraine, smoothing the blanket over the thin body. Nan's stomach wasn't swollen any more; the doctor must have drained off the fluid in the operating room. "The nurse'll give you something to go to sleep and you'll see Mom tomorrow."

"It's just as well for us to go on again," said Shirley. She was standing at the window, looking across at the headlights of the cars on the south side arterial road. "We can't do nothing here."

Nan didn't notice when they left. Herb was sitting down by the bed now, his hand on Nan's wrist just above the intravenous attachment. In the corridor outside they met the girl and her boy friend. She smiled at them, seemed about to say something and then changed her mind.

"Whew, am I ever glad to get out of there!" said Shirley when the elevator stopped at the main floor. They had ridden down in silence; none of the other occupants of the elevator had spoken either. They had all kept their eyes fixed on the floor numbers lighting up above the door. "I hope when I gets old I dies right quick of a heart attack. It must be shockin' to be just fadin' away like Nan is."

"She's not like herself at all," said Lorraine. "It's funny to see her actin' so peevish and everything."

"Herb'd drive anyone up the wall," said Shirley, sounding exactly like Eileen. "God, it's good to be out in the fresh air. I hates the smell of hospitals, don't you?" The snow was still falling, in big flakes that made patterns on their coats.

Heather said nothing. She tried to picture Nan as she used to be but all she could see was the frail figure they had just left in the hospital bed, an old and shrunken and useless figure. Why did such horrible things have to happen to people?

Back at the house they found Mollie sitting at the kitchen table, a cup of coffee in front of her. The kitchen was tidier than it had been for a long time. There was a sweetish smell in the air from the Avon talcum powder and cream sachet Mollie had left on the counter for Eileen.

"I got your mother put to bed," she said when the girls came in. "She took a sleeping pill. I always carries a few in my purse. You never knows when you're goin' to need one. She'll be good till the morning now."

Mollie was enjoying her new role. She was in no hurry to go home. Lorraine sat down and chatted with her for a few moments, telling her about Nan, sounding as if she were talking about a half-senile old stranger. Shirley had gone straight to the living room and turned on the television. Heather began to feel unutterably weary. Her shoulders ached; she wondered if her legs were strong enough to carry her up to bed.

"Have a cup of tea and a bit of jam toast now, Heather," urged Mollie after Lorraine had gone. "Your mother told me you never et a bite since you found out about your grandmother. That won't do her any good, for you to starve yourself."

"I'm not hungry," said Heather, even her voice sounding tired. "I'm going to bed."

"...going to bed," murmured Mollie, still sitting at the table. "Don't wake up your mother now, will you? She needs her sleep."

Heather had just crawled into bed, her socks still on to warm her icy feet, when Shirley came into the room. "God, do Mollie get on your nerves as much as she do on mine?" she asked, sitting down on the bed.

Heather nodded. "She's good to Mom, though. I s'pose we're lucky to have her around."

"I dreads to get up tomorrow morning and face it all again, don't you?" said Shirley, pulling her feet up under her. "I'd like to be able to run away somewhere." Heather thought of the many times, after she'd been reading about sisters who were close friends, or watching Pat and Alice on *Another World*, that she'd wished she could have the same kind of relationship with Lorraine and Shirley. Especially Shirley.

"Where's Randy all the time?" She hadn't heard Shirley speak of him all week.

"Who knows? We're broke up, I guess. I don't really want to talk about it." Shirley was silent for a moment; in the near darkness her face looked thoughtful. "What about that fella you met at the party, Frank, was it? Have you heard talk of him since he went away?"

"He's only gone a week." She didn't tell Shirley how she'd scrabbled through the mailbox every day as soon as she got home from school, how she hated to go out in case Frank should call long distance. Long distance! How important did she think she was to him, anyway? Even if he'd wanted to call her he didn't have that kind of money to throw around, after spending almost every cent on his fare to Alberta.

The day before she had gone down to Woolworth's, telling herself she had to buy a new exercise book which she could just as easily have picked up at Murray's over on the corner. She'd taken it to Frank's mother's checkout, trying not to stare at the thin woman whose red lips and rouged cheeks only emphasized the lines around her mouth and eyes. All the while Mrs. Marshall was ringing in the sale, passing her back the change, putting the exercise book into the brown Woolworth bag and stapling the saleslip carefully on it, Heather tried not to think about how much she was hoping the woman would mention Frank's name to one of her co-workers, say she'd had a letter from him, talk about how he was doing. Heather's hand had actually trembled as she took the parcel, but all she said was "Thank you very much."

"Is it all right if I gets in bed with you tonight, Heather?" Shirley asked. "Mollie is still downstairs and I can't very well pull out the chesterfield and get in bed while she's there. Besides, I just don't feel like listening to her any more tonight."

"Sure." Heather moved over to the wall side of the bed. She hoped she wouldn't dream about Frank and throw her arms around Shirley in her sleep.

"What about the birth control pills now, Shirl?" she murmured as they settled down together. "You gonna throw them away, or what?"

"Like ducks I am," said Shirley sleepily. "I got 'em now, I'm gonna keep on takin' 'em. It's just as well to be on the safe side."

Her words reminded Heather of the Ramses poster she'd seen that night when she was in the car with Frank. What was he doing tonight? Had he already found another girl, a good-looking, know-it-all mainlander, to talk to, and do other things with, the same as he'd done with her? She was probably just a distant memory to him already, that strange, quiet girl who went along with everything. She thought of him as he'd looked when she said goodbye to him that last night. "Not goodbye, so long," was what he'd really said. She could see his face as plainly as if she had a sharply-focused photograph in front of her eyes.

"Goodnight," Shirley murmured, drawing up her knees. It was nice to have a warm body lying beside her, even if it did remind her of Frank. But then, everything reminded her of Frank. Everything but Nan. The way Nan was now made her think of nothing except sickness and death and being cold and being alone. She wondered if Herb was still at the hospital, pacing back and forth, back and forth. It seemed so funny, so out of place, for an odd little man like Herb, with his wide, flowery ties and brightly-coloured shirts that Eileen laughed at, his thinning grey hair and his old-fashioned way of talking, to be in love. But what else could anyone call the way he felt about Nan? Surely Nan could never have felt about him anything close to the way she herself felt about Frank. It must be all very different when you were older.

# Nine

Heather had often heard Nan say "You can get used to anything." She had never believed it before but now she was discovering that it was true. Eileen went back to work, and even started going out to clubs on weekends again. One night Heather heard her telling Mollie on the phone about a man she'd met at the LeMarchant Club. "He's a nice fella, a real gentleman, like. He works on one of the oil rigs, you know? The only thing the matter with him is the way he talks. He puts me right in mind of 'erb." Eileen often deliberately dropped the aitch in Herb's name, trying to say it just as he himself pronounced it. "He's from around the bay, see, and you knows what they talks like. It's hard to get romantic with a guy who says h'Eileen and 'eart. That was one thing about Gary , he really talked nice." The only times Eileen ever spoke wistfully about her ex-husband was when she remembered his accent or the way he danced. And his teeth. "Funny about the Yanks, almost all of 'em got their own teeth. Gary's teeth were lovely." Eileen had had all her top teeth out when she was nineteen, and had been wearing dentures ever since. Herb and Nan had no teeth left at all; both wore upper plates but not lowers. Herb's false teeth were small and even and very white; they reminded Heather of the pretend teeth children used when they dressed up for Hallowe'en. Heather's own teeth needed attention; she hardly ever went to a dentist now that she was too old to come under the government's free dental care plan for children. Linda Stone went every six months. She had been wearing braces for almost a year and often talked of root canals and capping and other things that Heather knew nothing about. "What odds if you do have to get them all out?" Eileen would say when Heather said anything about going to the dentist. "Them dentists charges shockin' prices for fillings. At least when you gets 'em all out you got no more worry with toothache. I used to suffer like a dog. It's all right for the Stones and people like that to be forever gettin' their teeth looked at. They got so much money they don't know what to do with it anyway."

True to his promise, Herb took Nan home eight days after the operation. She didn't look much like Nan any more, but Heather found that she was even getting used to that. The new Nan was a frail woman who whimpered a lot, something the old Nan had never done. She got up late in the mornings and rarely dressed; just wandered around the house all day in the new blue quilted housecoat Herb had bought her. Herb took over the running of the house, cooked the food, washed the clothes, scrubbed the floors. Nan, who had been so proud of her housekeeping, sat back or lay back and watched Herb doing what she had done for many years. Sometimes, now, Heather found it hard to recall the old Nan with her hearty laugh, her quick movements, her enjoyment of a good joke, her warmth and compassion toward her family. She had become a quiet old woman, preoccupied with the changes in her body. Most days now she didn't even wear her false teeth; her hollow cheeks and skinny body made her look like a refugee from Bangladesh or Somaliland.

"You should thank God for Herb," Mollie said to Eileen one night after they'd come back from visiting Nan. "Looka the worry you'd have if it wasn't for him. Sure he's as good as a woman."

"He always seemed more like a woman than a man, anyway. He was cook in the lumberwoods for years, and after that he cooked on one of the coastal boats. You got to give the devil hes due, I s'pose. I don't know what I'd do without him. I wouldn't be able to give up my job to look after Mom and someone'd have to do it. Unless we put her into that pall'ative place, whatever they calls it. I never been inside that, and I don't want to be. Lilly Sharpe tells me it's marvellous up there but I hates the thoughts of goin' to a place where everyone knows they're gonna die. It'd be right morbid like, wouldn't it?

"...wouldn't it?" murmured Mollie, and then, briskly. "We all got to die, girl. 'It's only a postponement for all of us,' tha's what I heard a minister say once. But I know what you mean. Still, some people are glad enough to have that Palliative Care Unit. It takes a lot of worry off the family."

During the eight days after Nan's surgery, when, as Eileen put it, "they opened her up and sewed her up again," Herb had never left the hospital. He'd wanted to sit in the chair beside Nan's bed all night long but the head nurse had had to get firm with him about that. She couldn't stop him from spending his nights on the leather sofa out in the waiting room, the "No Smoking" waiting room, of course. He slept in his clothes and washed himself hastily each morning in the washroom across the hall. Every couple of days he'd hand Eileen a neat little parcel containing his dirty underwear and shirts and she'd bring him clean clothing. They never talked about what they were doing.

"I know Herb is right embarrassed because I'm doing hes washing," Eileen told Heather one night as they walked down from the hospital. "But someone got to do it. It's all bad enough him bein' up there all the time without having him stinkin' the place up along with it. I must say, though, he's really clean over himself, for a man. I wish I could get ahold of that old checked jacket he wears. And them funny ties. He musta had them since the Year One."

Frank had been gone almost a month now and Heather still hadn't heard from him. She had made several trips to Woolworth's but hadn't yet managed to hear his mother so much as say his name. "She's going to catch on to what you're doin' if you goes down too much," said Debbie, having caught on herself. "Why don't you write Frank if you're so anxious to hear from him? You knows what fellas are like." Debbie didn't see Harry any more now. She was going out with an American sailor from the Argentia Naval Base; he came into town whenever he could.

Heather said nothing. She couldn't write to Frank, even if she'd let herself; she didn't have his address. She tried hard not to think about him so much, but it wasn't easy. A face on television, dark eyes, the sound of a voice, someone whistling, everything reminded her of him. "Did he mention my name, just in passing?" crooned Anne Murray's creamy voice from the radio one morning when Heather was eating her breakfast. "And, by the way, did he men...tion my name?" She was ashamed to admit to herself that she thought of Frank much more often than she thought about her grandmother.

One night at the drugstore she noticed the Christmas cards on display near the prescription counter. "To Someone Nice Across the Miles" said one in red letters. The card was white, with a picture of a long, winding, train track on it. She picked it up but put it back on the rack when she read the sentimental verse inside. Her eyes moved to the humorous card section; that was the kind she always bought for Debbie and Lorraine and Shirley and Linda. (Not Nan, though; Nan had always liked what she called "mushy cards.") There was one with a dog and a cat looking slyly at each other, and a funny, four-line verse. After all, what was wrong with sending a Christmas card to a casual acquaintance? She took it to the counter and paid for it without fully realizing what she was doing.

When she got home she remembered, if she had ever really forgotten, that she didn't have Frank's address. She had no reminders of Frank, not even a photograph. Their courtship, if it could be called that, hadn't gone on long enough for them to take any pictures. She did have that newspaper picture of him with his hockey team, that she had cut out of the paper but his face on that was all blurry and dark. She didn't need a picture to remember what he looked like. His brown eyes, his mouth, amazingly soft for a boy's, the few freckles on his nose and forehead, the tiny triangular scar on his cheek that he'd got from falling out of his highchair when he was two, the way his hair curled, especially when the weather was damp, the way he grinned all over his face, not just with his mouth. And his voice, especially the way he said her name. Most of the boys on Gaspar Street called her Hedder, just as Bertie Lane did. Frank had always been careful to pronounce the th. She remembered particularly the way he said it when they were parked in the car at night. It had been "Heather?" then, with a question at the end of it. He was probably saying another girl's name in exactly the same way now.

"I wonder who's kissing her now/I wonder who's showing her how." Nan used to sing that song, over and over again, half to herself, when Heather had spent so much time with her after Pop Morgan's death. She'd sung it as she peeled vegetables, set the table for supper, washed the dishes afterwards. She would get a song in her mind early in the morning and sing bits of it at intervals throughout the day, hardly knowing that she was doing it. Heather couldn't remember the last time she'd heard Nan sing.

When Eileen and Heather were visiting Nan one night, three women from the Salvation Army Home League came to see her. Two of them were about Nan's age; a much younger woman, Mrs. Allan, had driven them to Nan's in her little brown Chevette. Mrs. Allan said very little, just sat in the rocking chair moving gently back and forth, back and forth, as the other two talked to Nan about the Home League, her soul and how it would be Christmas before they knew it. They had brought an enormous basket of fruit, bananas, rosy apples, pears, green grapes, plums and several other kinds that Heather didn't even know the names of. Nan probably wouldn't be able to eat any of it; she had all she could do these days to keep down a cup of tea and a milk-lunch biscuit. The tall, heavy woman — Mrs. Baker her name was — read from the Bible, a long, dreary chapter from Revelations about a pale horse and a pale rider. She was very pale herself; her frizzed grey hair framed a long, shiny face that looked as if it had been waxed.

After the reading Herb played his accordion and the women sang:

*There's a land that is fairer than day*
*And by faith we can see it afar*
*For the Father waits over the way*
*To prepare us a dwelling place there*

and then the chorus :

*In the sweet bye-and-bye*
*We shall meet on that beautiful shore.*

Mrs. Baker couldn't carry a tune; perhaps to compensate she sang so loudly that Eileen said afterwards that she must have been heard by the people in the houses five or six doors away. Mrs. Allan's voice was sweet and true but it was hard to hear her through Mrs. Baker's monotonous shout. The third woman, Mrs. Ellis, who was so short her feet didn't quite touch the floor from the straight-back chair she was sitting on, joined in the singing only occasionally. The rest of the time she kept her eyes closed and murmured to herself words too low for anyone else to understand. Nan didn't sing at all, just sat still in the armchair, dabbing at her eyes with a tissue, and blowing her nose. Eileen and Heather left shortly afterwards, while Herb was serving the three women tea and his own homemade raisin buns, along with the pineapple squares that Nan's next-door neighbour, Mrs. Lodge, had brought in earlier. Eileen, saying tersely that Heather had to do her homework, had declined Herb's invitation to "stay for a lunch."

"What a hymn to pick at a time like this," Eileen said as soon as they left the house, her anger making her move more quickly than usual. "And that Scripture passage, they musta gone lookin' for the gloomiest one they could find. Think they woulda sang "How Great Thou Art" or something cheerful like that, and read a nice happy chapter from the Bible. Did you see Mom cryin', tryin' to make out she had a cold in the head? I didn't feel like cryin', I can tell you. I was too mad."

Heather knew from past experience that it was useless to argue with her mother. Besides, this was one time she agreed with her. She thought of how much Nan would have laughed at those women a few months earlier, especially Mrs. Baker's powerful, tuneless voice. Nan had always prided herself on her singing; when she was a young woman she'd sung in the church choir. Salvationist though she was, Nan's sense of humour had allowed her to see the funny side of religion as well as of everything else. She had no sense of humour now; her smiles were wan little shadows of what they had been. What was there to smile about when you knew you were going to die soon? Nobody had told Nan she had cancer; Herb had forbidden it, Eileen going along with him for once. But Heather was sure she knew. With her loss of weight and strength, her lack of interest in food, her eternally queasy stomach, how could she not know? She never talked about it, though. Instead she wondered aloud how long it would be before she was better, when she'd be able to go to church again, why she couldn't work up an interest in Christmas this year. No, there wasn't much to smile about when you were dying, no matter how much you and everybody around you pretended that you weren't. Heather thought of all the lovely deaths in the L.M. Montgomery books, the smiling demise of beautiful, consumption-ridden Ruby Gillis to whom "death, after all, had come as a friend and not as the grisly spectre she had anticipated," the hopeful death of the schoolteacher, Mr. Carpenter, who was convinced that soon he'd know "everything there is to know," the laughing death of the old Irish servant, Judy Plum, who quoted a comic rhyme seconds before the end. Perhaps her mother had been right all along. Perhaps most books of that kind *were* a pack of lies. Eileen was still talking, still mad, but Heather was no longer following what she said. She was glad when they got home so that she could escape upstairs while her mother repeated her angry outpourings to Shirley.

In her room she found a parcel lying on the bed. A blue corner of what looked like a Kotex box protruded through the open end of a brown paper bag. Shirley must have thrown it there. When she saw it, Heather realized that it was a long time since she'd had her period. She was menstruating the night she met Frank at Donna's party; she remembered wondering if he knew, thinking of the old stories she'd heard about how boys always knew when a girl was "like that." It was nothing strange for her period to be late. She hadn't even begun to menstruate until a couple of years before when she was nearly fourteen; ever since then her periods had been irregular, sometimes two in a month, sometimes nothing for two months or more. "If I was like you I'd be scared to death I was knocked up," Debbie had said. "Of course, you don't have to worry about nothing like that."

It was a good thing she hadn't gone all the way with Frank. "All the way." What a strange expression. She'd got it out of a book, or books. Nobody talked like that any more, if they ever had. Debbie and Donna and the others talked about "doin' it" or "havin' a bit" or "gettin' a bit" or "givin' in." They always made it sound very general.

It would have been so easy for Frank and her to have gone "all the way" that night, the night before he left for Alberta. She remembered the feeling of his hard, warm penis lying against her...her...she still didn't know what to call it. Vagina sounded so technical, so much like a word in a textbook. She knew all the vulgar words too, of course, but she didn't like them either, perhaps because almost every time boys or men used them, usually when they were running each other down, they sounded so vile, so contemptuous, so brutally cruel, as if there was nothing worse a person could be called, unless it was fag or queer. The boys who'd had the fight at Donna's party had used them in that way. The warm sensation that had washed over her when she and Frank lay touching, the feeling of utter peace mixed with strong desire, the nothing-else-matters urgency, that indescribable sense of release, had nothing to do with such words, or at least the common use of them. Even the hot, thick flood of semen that escaped him as he held her so tightly she thought her bones would break had not repelled her as she might have expected it to do. Frank had wiped it away himself, wiped her as tenderly as if he were dressing a wound. But he hadn't even tried to get inside her.

As she climbed into the bath now, looking at her flat white belly and the curly dark hairs further down, she recalled how long she lay in the bath when she came home the night before Frank went away. She'd known she should wash herself thoroughly; the stuff smelled unpleasant and must be gotten rid of as soon as possible. Her mother had laughed derisively at a scene on *Another World* where fastidious Rachel had jumped out of bed and immediately pulled her clothes on after a very physical episode with Mitch. That night as she lay there she had relived every moment, every second of that evening with Frank, hardly believing that what had happened had actually happened. She'd smiled at the memory of letters to Ann Landers and Dear Abby on the question of "giving in" to boys. She hadn't felt that she was "giving in" at all, unless it was to her own powerful urges. Frank hadn't seemed surprised at her reaction. Was that because it was so much like that of other girls he'd gone out with? She didn't want to think about that now any more than she had at the time. She just wanted to think about Frank.

When she got up the next morning she almost tripped over a bucket of water that Eileen had left at the foot of the stairs. The last sound she'd heard as she dropped off to sleep the night before was Eileen's angry voice, criticizing Herb, Nan's Home League visitors, the Salvation Army as a whole, the doctors, the hospital and, finally, the world itself. She realized now that her mother must have finally dealt with her anger by scrubbing the kitchen floor. Puss was moving around the bucket inquiringly, dipping his head and nose over the top of it and then hastily drawing back again.

"There's nothing in that for you, Puss." Heather looked into the bucket to see if her mother had left the scrub cloth in the water; she had a habit of doing that. More than once she had flushed the cloth down the toilet with the dirty water. Years ago, when Eileen had used Sunlight soap for cleaning, she had lost many bars and half-bars of it that way. Heather put her hand into the cold, greasy water; sure enough, a slimy piece of old towel lay at the bottom of the bucket. Why couldn't her mother ever remove it right away, and flush the water down while it was still warm and soapy? It felt so much worse when it was left around like this. When she squeezed the water out of the slippery cloth she felt her stomach turn over; a sweeping sense of weakness forced her to sit down on the stairs. After a few moments she picked up the bucket and made her way to the bathroom, the squeezed-out floor cloth in her other hand. As she threw the water into the toilet the stench of stale urine became almost overpowering. She reached for the deodorizer on the flush box and sprayed it into the air. The sweet, cloying smell filled her nostrils; her knees began to weaken again. She pulled down the toilet seat cover and sat on it. Beads of cold sweat stood out on her forehead. She wanted to vomit but there was nothing to come up; she'd hardly eaten anything at all yesterday and of course she hadn't had breakfast yet this morning. She tore off a piece of toilet paper and wiped the sweat off her forehead, thinking as she did so of the death dew lying cold on the brow that the Salvation Army people sang about in the hymn ending "If ever I loved Thee, my Jesus, 'tis now." It was one of the many that Nan used to sing cheerfully as she did her housework.

She'd better eat some breakfast right away; this nausea must be caused by her empty stomach. She had always been afraid of throwing up; when she was a small child she prayed every night that she wouldn't vomit. That prayer had been succeeded by an even more fervent one that asked God to make sure she wouldn't die in the night. It had probably come about because of a prayer she seemed to have always known but that she realized now had originally been taught to her by her Grandmother Novak and later repeated after Lorraine and Shirley. For a moment she could almost feel a tall, gaunt presence standing over her, urging her to repeat the words:

*Now I lay me down to sleep*
*I pray Thee, Lord, my soul to keep*
*If I should die before I wake*
*I pray Thee, Lord, my soul to take.*

She couldn't remember what Grandmother Novak looked like except from a few of the old snapshots her mother had kept. Nevertheless this...this apparition was present now, as it had been a few times before. Once, when she was sleeping at Nan's, years before, Heather had said she was afraid to say her prayers, afraid that the Lord would steal her soul, and herself, while she slept. Nan had put her arms around her and taught her a new prayer:

*Heavenly Father, hear my prayer*
*Keep me in Thy tender care*
*Guard and guide me through the night*
*Bring me safe to morning light.*

Heather liked that one much better; after a while she had stopped praying that she wouldn't die in the night. I'll have to die some night, or some day, the practical side of her had argued, so it's silly to keep on praying that way forever. She had always loved sleeping at Nan's, for Nan was never too busy to lie down with her. Sometimes she sang, or chanted, as Heather drifted off to sleep:

*Wynken, Blynken and Nod one night*
*Sailed off in a wooden shoe*
*Sailed on a river of crystal light*
*Into a sea of dew.*

The words had sounded so beautiful. They looked beautiful, too, in the book Nan had given her one Christmas. It was still in the old wooden bookcase at the top of the stairs.

The smell of the kitchen — greasy cup towels, decaying orange peels, congealed fat in the frying pan — almost sent Heather running to the bathroom again. With shaking hands she poured cornflakes into a bowl and ate them quickly, without adding milk or sugar. Then she made herself a cup of tea. By the time she sat down to the table with the tea and a slice of dry toast she was beginning to feel a little better. It must have been the empty stomach.

It was still dark in the kitchen; she'd had to switch on the light. No wonder, it was only six-thirty. What in the world had made her wake so early? She usually slept until at least eight o'clock, unless her mother hauled her out of bed before then. She'd have plenty of time to get ready for school this morning. Eileen and Shirley wouldn't be thinking about getting up yet.

When she opened the fridge door to look for something for lunch, the intermingled smells of the leftovers made her stomach turn over again. She sat down at the table and ate a couple of dry crackers. Her mother had told her that when she was pregnant she'd had to keep a box of crackers on the night table so that she could swallow a few before she got out of bed in the morning. Well, I'm not pregnant, anyhow, she thought. It's got to be something I ate.

She felt gradually better as the day went on. Only once, when she went into Murray's on her way home from school did the queasiness return. The smell of the new box of apples, just opened on the floor, was overpowering.

"What's the matter?" Debbie asked as Heather gripped the counter for support. "You're some white-lookin' all of a sudden."

"It's nothing," said Heather, making a tremendous mental effort to stop her knees from wobbling. "I'm okay now."

"P'raps you're gettin' the flu," said Debbie. "There's a bad kind goin' around."

"Yes, I had it the other day," said Mr. Murray, placing four of the rosiest apples on the counter. "It was only a twenty-four thing but it was awful while it lasted."

"Got anything to take for it?" Mrs. Murray called from the back of the store. "Contac C is good. Or even a drop of hot lemon, to sweat it out of you." Heather couldn't wait to get outside.

"Do you want me to come in with you?" Debbie asked when they finally reached the house. "You still don't look the best."

"No, I'll be okay." More than anything else in the world, Heather wanted to be left alone. She hoped Shirley wasn't home.

There was nobody in the kitchen. The queasiness was gone now, but she was still shaky and weak. Suddenly feeling ravenously hungry, she took a loaf of bread out of the bread tin and made herself a plate of peanut butter sandwiches. Then she ate an apple flip that someone had left on the counter. None of this spoiled her appetite for supper.

"They had a special on," Eileen told Heather and Shirley as they sat down to eat the Kentucky Fried chicken she'd brought home. "And I just felt like splurgin'. 'What odds?' I said to myself. 'When you're careful you're no better off.' "

The three of them ate without speaking, pausing occasionally to feed a little chicken to Puss who was waiting patiently near the table.

"Mom used to love this," Eileen said, her eyes glazing over as she looked at the remains of the chicken in the cardboard bucket. "She could never get enough of it, and now...." She shook herself, straightened her shoulders and went to the stove to turn on the burner under the kettle.

Heather didn't go to see Nan that night. She tried to concentrate on her homework but before she knew it she was nodding over her books. It was only a few minutes after nine when she gave in and went to bed, not even taking a book with her. By the time her mother and Shirley got home she was deeply, soundly asleep.

# *Ten*

For a week Heather continued to feel sick every day. For a week she kept telling herself that it was the flu, or mononucleosis, or even her nerves. She'd heard her mother and Mollie and Nan, when she was well, talk about the strange and bizarre things nerves could do to a person. Sometimes, after visiting Nan, she almost convinced herself that she had cancer too. Hadn't Nan's illness started with nausea and vomiting? Heather had actually vomited only twice, a mouthful each time, but she knew this was because she still had such a fear of throwing up. If she could have loosened up and allowed herself to, she knew she would have been vomiting three or four times every day. She had known, or known of, several young people who'd had cancer. Vera Dalton, a girl who'd been in her class from kindergarten to grade seven, died of a brain tumour when she was fourteen. And Debbie's cousin, Pam, was a patient at the Janeway now with leukemia.

So far Eileen and Shirley had noticed nothing. Heather kept out of their way as much as possible during the day. Her mother already had enough on her mind with Nan but that wasn't the only reason she didn't tell her how she was feeling. She wasn't sure what the other reasons were. The nausea hardly ever bothered her at night; in fact she almost always felt voraciously hungry in the evenings. She welcomed the bananas and oranges and cookies and chocolates that

Eileen brought home from Nan's, those awkwardly-presented contributions from neighbours and friends. "I can't eat any of that, Eileen child," Nan would say. "Take it home for the girls."

"My God, Heather, I believe you're after losin' your appetite and pickin' up a horse's," Eileen said one night after watching Heather devour a plateful of potted meat sandwiches. "You used to be so picky over your food. Be careful you don't get fat, now."

The next morning Heather was sicker than she'd ever been before in her life. After actually throwing up on the street on her way to school she decided she'd better go home and lie down. All morning she lay on the chesterfield in the living room, watching Donahue on television as he talked with a group of men about why they preferred to wear women's clothes. Her bones and her head ached; her whole body was painfully weary. She felt too sick to question what was wrong with her.

She fell asleep, and awoke to a feeling of complete disorientation. *The Young and the Restless* was on television now; she must have slept for over an hour. Still dazed, she pulled herself up slowly, testing to see if her head and her stomach felt any steadier than they had earlier. Slowly, cautiously, she moved toward the kitchen. I'm like an old woman, she thought. I'm like Nan.

She warmed up a can of tomato soup and managed to drink half a bowlful, with a few dry crackers. After rinsing her bowl and spoon and leaving the saucepan to soak in the sink she sat down again, pinching her nose to block out the sour smell of the cup towel on the counter and the balled-up J-cloth in the sink. I'm sick, she said to herself over and over. I'm really sick. She wanted to go upstairs and lie down on her bed, to pull the blankets right up over her head and cry herself to sleep.

Instead, she picked up the telephone directory and opened it up to the yellow pages. Doctors, where was the listing for doctors? She couldn't find one. She flipped over the pages until she finally came to the heading Physicians and Surgeons: Adams, Dr.G.B., Haemotology; Bessell, Dr. J.A., General Practitioner; Blackwood, Dr. H.J., Surgeon; Cant, Dr. J., Urologist. She spread the book open in front of her on the table. When was the last time she'd been to a doctor? It must have been years ago, when she needed a health certificate to go to Guide camp. Eileen didn't think much of doctors. "A couple of 222s or a good shot of whisky is as good as anything they can give you," she often said. She had, however, gone to the Outpatients' Clinic at the hospital to get a prescription for the Valium she'd begun taking soon after she found out about Nan's cancer.

Dixon, Dr. Elaine M., General Practitioner. She had never been to a woman doctor. Still holding the telephone book, Heather went to the phone and dialed the number. "Dr. Dixon's office," said a confident young voice. For a moment Heather forgot why she was calling.

"Hallo, this is Dr. Elaine Dixon's office. Can I help you?" The voice sounded a little impatient now.

"Hallo, could I make an appointment, please?" The bulky directory slipped off her knees to the floor.

"Could you speak up, please? I can't hear you very well."

Heather cleared her throat. "I'd like an appointment with Dr...." God, now she couldn't remember the doctor's name. "With the doctor, please," she finished. "As soon as possible."

"All right, let me see now. I can give you one Monday morning at ten-fifteen. Will that be all right?"

"Well, yes, I guess so, but I'd like to get something sooner if I could, please. Isn't there anything available this afternoon?" Her hand trembled on the receiver.

"No, I'm sorry, we're booked solid this afternoon." The voice didn't sound apologetic at all, just crisp and businesslike.

Heather's throat felt the way it had once when she was little and had to eat a small dish of dry cornmeal at someone's birthday party. It had been part of a game. "It's a kind of...emergency," she said, feeling cold beads of perspiration on her forehead again

After a pause, the voice, sounding a little more human, said, "Well, if you'd like to come at about five o'clock I'll try to squeeze you in before Dr. Dixon goes home. She might have a cancellation."

"Oh, thank you so much." She was about to hang up when the voice, slightly impatient again, cut in with "Could I have your name, please?"

"Heather Novak."

"Have you been to see Dr. Dixon before, Heather?" Heather? The receptionist must have guessed that she was very young.

"No."

"Okay, then, Heather, don't forget your MCP card. You know where we're located, do you? We're up here in the Taylor Building." And with a sharp click she was gone.

Heather got to the doctor's office at about quarter to five. The afternoon had been interminably long. Shirley, who'd gone out early in the morning, still wasn't home when Heather left the house. Every time the phone rang she just let it ring. After all, she was supposed to be in school, wasn't she? Sometimes the school secretary phoned the homes of absent students to check up on them. Heather had a good record that way. She had always liked school; being home in the daytime depressed her. The nausea wasn't nearly as bad in the afternoon as it had been in the morning. When she got her bath she scrubbed herself vigorously all over; her skin was red and almost sore by the time she was finished. Her mother had always washed herself very carefully, and talked about it afterwards, on the few occasions that she had gone to a doctor. Eileen liked to retell an old story about a woman who'd scrubbed her swollen left foot before she went to the doctor's surgery, but had neglected to wash the right one. "Poor thing, she was some embarrassed when he asked to see her other foot, to compare it with the bad one," Eileen would conclude each time, as if she'd never told the story before. Heather had always considered it a stupid story, and wondered now why such silly things stayed in the mind.

The waiting room was crowded. Most of the patients were women, two or three of them obviously pregnant, others with small babies in their arms. One woman's husband was with her; the only other male in the room was a young fellow a few years older than herself, probably a university student, judging by the pile of books on the floor beside him. One baby kept spitting up milk on his mother's shoulder; she patted him rhythmically on the back. The mother's eyes were bloodshot, as if she hadn't slept the night before. When the smell of the sour milk reached Heather's nostrils she was afraid she was going to be sick again. She picked up a magazine and turned her head in the opposite direction.

It was after five-thirty when she finally got in to see the doctor, a dark-haired, slight young woman who looked a little like Janet on *Three's Company*. She listened carefully to Heather's halting story, interrupting now and then with a brief question.

When Heather had finished speaking, Dr. Dixon leaned back in her chair and stared at the wall behind Heather's head. Unlike the waiting room walls, which were covered with posters warning the patients against smoking and telling them that "Breast fed is best fed," the walls in here were bare except for the doctor's qualification certificate with its odd, Latinized words, a couple of reproductions of oil paintings and an enlarged, framed photograph of the river in Bowring Park. When Heather had noticed that one on her way in it reminded her of Frank; she realized with a shock that she'd hardly thought of Frank at all in the last few days. She knew this was only because she'd been feeling so sick, yet she wondered at herself. Only a week ago she would have believed that nothing in the world, no calamity, no miracle, could drive Frank from her mind for more than a few minutes at a time.

Dr. Dixon removed her gaze from the far wall and looked into Heather's face. "Do you have a boyfriend, Heather?" she asked.

"Yes...no, I mean, I don't really know." The skin on Heather's face was tight and hot; the realization that she was blushing made her angry with herself.

"What I'm trying to ask you, Heather, is...are you sexually active?" She looked as if the words were almost as hard for her to say as they were for Heather to hear. She probably hadn't been in practice for very long.

Sexually active. That was what the doctor at Planned Parenthood had asked Shirley and her friend when they went there for birth control information. It must be one of those new phrases, like "down the road" and "at this point in time."

Heather kept her eyes on the desk blotter as she replied. "No, not really, I don't think so, anyway." This doctor was going to think she was retarded. "I mean, I've never had...intercourse...or anything like that."

Dr. Dixon looked tired; there were greyish-blue smudges under her dark eyes. "Heather, could you explain to me exactly what you and your boyfriend did? I'm sorry to have to tell you this, but your symptoms are very much like the symptoms of early pregnancy."

"Oh, I can't be pregnant. I just know I can't be. It must be something else. I was afraid I might have cancer, like my grandmother." Heather knew that later, when she went home, she wouldn't be able to believe that this conversation had actually taken place.

There was the beginning of a smile on Dr. Dixon's face but when she spoke her voice was serious.

"Just tell me, Heather. I'm not going to laugh at you, or bawl you out. I talk to girls like you almost every day." She sighed, and then picked up a pen and pointed it at the pad of paper on her desk.

Girls like you. What kind of a girl did she think Heather was, anyway? Someone like Darlene Snelgrove? Or even, perhaps, like Loretta and Elsie Sheppard? Still, she'd better say something. The doctor was waiting.

Slowly, with many pauses, she told Dr. Dixon what had happened between her and Frank. It all sounded so ugly, so common, when she tried to put it into words. She used the scientific names for the sex organs; now the whole experience was moving from ugly and common to clinical and cold. If only she could explain to this doctor the way it had really been between Frank and herself.

When she had finished, Dr. Dixon looked briefly at the wall again and then said, "Do you remember the date of your last period? I should have asked you that before. My mind is all topsy-turvy today. I've been so busy." A strand of dark hair had fallen forward across her face; she tucked it back behind her ear.

"Let me see, it was just before Donna Power's party, that was the first part of October. Or was it September? Donna's parents were gone off in the country somewhere." This was all nonsense.

Dr. Dixon frowned, and picked up the calendar on her desk. "Hmm, tomorrow is the first of December. You've certainly missed one period, then, and it's just about time for another.

"But I'm like that, Dr. Dixon. I really am. I've been like that ever since I started to menstruate."

Dr. Dixon was writing on the pad in front of her. She looked up. "I'm not doubting your word at all, Heather. I'm sure you're a very honest girl, and a good girl, too. But, like so many other girls your age, you don't know as much as you think you do about all this business." She scribbled on the pad again. Her writing was all squiggles; it was impossible for Heather to figure out what she was writing down.

"I'd like for you to go to Planned Parenthood tomorrow, Heather, and take a pregnancy test. I don't think I'll even examine you now. There's not much I can find out at this stage."

"You can find out that I'm still a virgin." Heather was surprised to hear her own voice saying those words, surprised, too, that it sounded so strong, not trembly at all any more.

"I have no doubt that you are, Heather. Unfortunately, I've seen this kind of thing happen to virgins before." She folded her arms in front of her on the desk, leaned forward and smiled. For a moment she looked more like the girl she really was than a doctor delivering a serious message to a nervous patient. Then she stood up, and Heather realized this was a signal for the visit to end. "You go up to Planned Parenthood tomorrow — you know where it is, do you? — and they'll do the test while you're there. It's quicker that way than if I send you to the hospital. Let's hope it's negative, but if it's positive come back to me as soon as you can and we'll have a talk. Come back anyway, if you're still feeling sick, even if it's negative. Meanwhile, try not to worry too much. It's not the end of the world." She touched Heather's arm, then let her hand drop.

"Thank you," said Heather, at the same time wondering what she was thanking her for. "Goodbye." Her legs carried her out of the office, across the waiting room, where there remained only one mother and baby, and out into the street. It was only when she reached the sidewalk that her knees began to buckle. She stood by the bus stop, leaning against the pole for support.

Somehow she got home.

"Where in the name of the Lord were you?" Eileen asked. She was sitting at the kitchen table, finishing up her supper. "I bought a couple of cold plates into Dominion, they were sellin' 'em off half-price. I knew Shirl wouldn't be here because she's relievin' one of the girls up to Mary Brown's. But then, when you weren't here, I didn't know what to make of it, so used to you bein' around the house when I comes home." She got up and went to the stove to turn on the kettle, looking sideways at Heather. "My God, girl, you're some white-lookin'. Are you sick, or what?"

"I think I'm gettin the flu," said Heather, shrugging off her coat. "There's a lot of it on the go up to school." Her knees were still wobbly although not as bad as they'd been when she came out of the doctor's office.

"You're gettin' something, girl, and that's for sure." Eileen was sitting down again, her shoes on the floor, her stockinged feet up on the chair next to her. "My feet are some tired today. Just look at 'em, how swollen up they are. And I s'pose I got to go in and see Mom tonight, although all I wants to do is lie down on the chesterfield and watch TV. Pour a drop of water on that teabag for me, will ya, Heather? That's the girl. I'm perishin' for a cup of tea."

Heather hoped Eileen wouldn't notice how her hand shook as she passed her the cup. Then she sat down herself and gripped the table in front of her, hardly aware of what she was doing.

"Don't you want your cold plate? I put it in the fridge for you. I know you're dyin' about salad and that and when I saw 'em marked down in the supermarket I thought I'd get one for ya. Carol came to pick her mother up from work so she gave me a run, too, and we went into Dominion on the way home. She's a lovely girl, Carol is. Mollie is some lucky with her family."

Eileen sighed and drank some tea. "I don't like them teabags I bought the last time," she said, wrinkling up her nose. "They were on special, so I thought I'd buy 'em. But they're not like the Tetley. Anything cheap is no good, they tastes like that old senna tea Mom used to make for us years ago, for a tonic."

Heather tried not to think about the taste of tea. There was something about the taste, and the smell, that made her feel sick just to think about it. Funny, usually by this time of day she was hungry, with no sign of the nausea.

Over the rim of her teacup Eileen looked long and hard at Heather. "If you could only see yourself," she said, pulling a face. "You're like death warmed over. Have your supper, now, you're probably hungry, that's all is wrong with ya. There's a lovely bit of macaroni salad there, and that beet salad you likes."

Heather swallowed hard. Her mother looked different, like someone far away and strange, almost like someone seen in a movie when the picture is fuzzy and out of focus.

"I'll have my supper later," she said, standing up quickly and pushing back her chair. It fell over behind her, the four legs upended to show the dust and wool that had collected around the little metal discs on the bottom. She righted it and pushed it into the table again.

"I think I better go up and lie down, Mom," she said, wondering if she'd make it up the stairs to the bedroom without falling. "I'll have the cold plate byme by. It'll keep. Thanks for getting it for me." She was out of the kitchen before her mother could reply.

When she reached the bedroom, her legs like wooden stilts that had been lent to her for the day, she flung herself down on the bed and pulled the blankets up over her head. She was glad it was dark in the room; there was nothing she wanted to see. Sometimes, when she went to her bedroom late at night, she would get out Frank's hockey picture, creased and recreased so many times that tiny holes were appearing in the folds. Tonight she knew she wouldn't have wanted to look at a big glossy photograph of Frank, even if she had one. When she closed her eyes she wanted to see only blackness. What she saw was her father's face as it had been in the wedding picture when he and Eileen looked like teenagers themselves. She wouldn't have been surprised if she'd seen a whole jumble of faces in her mind, Dr. Dixon's, the faces of the people in the waiting room, even her mother's face, startled and puzzled when Heather had left the table so suddenly. But her father's face, why?

She closed her eyes as tightly as she could but the image was still there, a tall, skinny young man with the shy, forced smile that people used to have when they were getting their pictures taken, when there was nobody around to tell them to say "cheese" or "sex" or "whisky." She had often wished she could remember what her father looked like in the flesh, and not have to depend on old photographs. But try as she might the only memory she could conjure up was a face from a picture. She had learned that face by heart, that longish, thin face with the closely-cropped light hair and the thoughtful-looking eyes. Just as a few short weeks ago she had memorized Frank's face. But it was only her father's face she saw tonight.

As she lay there in the darkness, her head burrowed inside the heavy, slightly musty blankets, she remembered the night she and Frank had dropped into a new restaurant on their way in Topsail Road. He was hungry that night, had missed his supper because he'd been relieving at the garage. As he ate his hamburger and she her chocolate sundae, they listened, or half-listened to the songs coming from the big juke box in the corner. Sandwiched in between Rod Stewart's raucous *Do Ya Think I'm Sexy?* and Olivia Newton-John's *Physical* was a much older, softer kind of song that Heather had heard years before on Nan's record player. The song hadn't affected her much one way or the other at the restaurant, but now she could recall the mellow crooning as if the record were being played right here in the room:

> *You're the end of the rainbow, my pot of gold,*
> *You're my little angel, to have and to hold,*
> *You're sugar...you're spice, you're everything nice*
> *And you're Daddy's...little...girl.*

Her eyes started to sting; soon her cheeks were wet with tears. She sniffed as her nose began to run. She was too tired to get out of bed and look for a tissue. As the song played itself over and over again in her head, with her father's face still before her, the hot tears came faster and faster, and then she started to sob. She tried to smother the sound, afraid her mother would hear, but it was no use. Her shoulders moved of their own accord; noises that she didn't know she could make were coming from her throat. Now she didn't care who heard her. All she wanted to do was cry and cry and cry.

# *Eleven*

Heather sat in one of the orange and brown chairs in Clinic 3, waiting. She'd been there for over two hours. So far she'd only been examined by the gynecologist. She still had to see a psychiatrist, a social worker and a nurse. Dr. Potter, the gynecologist, was a tall, bored-looking man who talked very little. She'd felt sure she was going to faint when she lay on the examining table waiting for him, her feet in stirrups. "Try to relax," he'd told her two or three times. "When you stiffen up like that it's bound to hurt."

When he had finished with her she felt bruised and sore. She had expected Dr. Potter to ask her how she'd managed to get pregnant when she was still a virgin. He hadn't said a word about that, just hummed absentmindedly as he felt around inside her with his slippery gloved hand. She still felt the soreness now as she sat waiting, and her pants were wet. She wanted to go to the washroom to check; perhaps it was her period starting at last. But she was afraid to leave the waiting area, afraid the receptionist would call her name while she was gone, conclude she had left and go on to the next person.

Clinic 3 was crowded, full of women and girls. Dr. Dixon had told her that on Wednesday mornings this clinic was used only for people who wanted abortions. Heather wondered what it was used for on other days of the week, people with broken bones, perhaps, or

126

heart trouble. Were people in the other clinics staring over at the ones in Clinic 3, or was she imagining that?

Over the top of her magazine, a torn *Newsweek* dated two years earlier, Heather looked at the women and girls around her. A few of them were about her own age, but there were also women in their twenties and thirties. One girl sitting next to a thin, anxious-looking woman who was probably her mother, looked about twelve. She was reading an Archie comic book, her eyes darting quickly over each page before she turned to the next one. Her dark brown hair hung in two plaits to her shoulder blades; her mother kept flicking them back when they fell forward as the little girl bent her head over her book. An older woman about Eileen's age sat staring at the wall, not reading, not doing anything. She wore no makeup; there were dark circles under her eyes. As she continued to stare she started to tap the arm of her chair with her fingers, gently tapping in a kind of rhythmical way, almost as if she were patting a dog, or a small child. She looked familiar; Heather tried to remember where she had seen her before.

Only two of the women had men with them. One man looked uncomfortable in his neat blue suit, as if he were more accustomed to looser, freer clothing. The other, a much younger man wearing faded jeans and a roll-neck sweater, was showing the girl with him a picture in the magazine he was reading, and explaining what was going on in it. She didn't look at all interested. Apart from that there was no conversation.

The receptionist was leaning over her desk, looking for something in the drawer. Under her tight-fitting white pantsuit Heather could see the outline of her underpants. She turned around and looked at Heather.

"What was your name again?" she asked, frowning over the loose-leaf binder on the desk.

"Heather Novak."

"Oh, yes, that's right. You've already seen Dr. Potter, haven't you?"

"Yes."

"Dr. Buchner will see you next. He's running behind today, had an emergency first thing this morning." She lowered her voice as she said the last few words. An emergency. That probably meant someone had tried to kill herself. Or himself. More men than women committed suicide, Heather had read somewhere, but more women than men attempted it. Her mother had told her a story about a girl she'd gone to school with who had killed herself because she was pregnant.

"Her mother and them pretended she went over that cliff by accident, but what was she doing away out there by herself in the middle of the night, anyhow?" Eileen had said. "We all knew she was into it; it always shows up fast on the skinny ones. Some said she was pregnant for her father; he was a real odd type."

Since her own pregnancy had been confirmed at the Planned Parenthood clinic, Heather had hardly dared let herself think about what her mother's reaction would be if she knew. She'd be angry, of course, and cruelly disappointed. Surprised, too; so many times she'd looked hard at Shirley and then said to Heather: "At least I got no worries about *you*." She would probably feel that Heather had done it just to aggravate her. Whenever anyone told Eileen about some young girl who was deeply into drugs, or mixed up with the wrong crowd, or pregnant, or even the victim of an accident, the first thing she'd say was "I pities her poor mother."

But the real reason Heather couldn't face Eileen was that she knew her mother would make her have the baby and then give it up for adoption. And muddled and confused though she was, sick, terrified and abandoned as she might feel, she knew she would never be able to do that.

Unlike many of the girls she knew, and the older people as well, Heather had never been especially fond of babies. When Jason was born she hadn't been able to utter all the oohs and aahs that Eileen, Nan, and even Shirley and Lorraine considered the only proper way to greet an infant. Heather found Jason easier to deal with now that he was older, now that he could talk a little and understand what was said to him. In all the dreams she'd wallowed in, about the house she'd live in, the career she'd have, the places she'd visit, it had never occurred to her that a baby might be a part of her life. She had occasionally imagined herself the mother of two children, a boy and a girl, but it always seemed as though they had miraculously come to her, handsome, clever, loving children aged about five and seven.

She turned a page of the magazine and came upon some bloody-looking pictures of injured children in Lebanon, their sombre dark eyes huge and questioning in their thin faces. A soldier in one of the pictures looked a lot like Frank. He had joked once or twice that there must have been an Arab amongst his forefathers; people often said he looked foreign. Frank. She hadn't thought about him much since her first visit to Dr. Dixon. She'd been living in a dream, or a nightmare. No, not really a nightmare, not now, anyway. She felt much too numb for that. She walked through the days the way patients from the Waterford Hospital walked through Bowring Park. Most of them moved stiffly and slowly, like sleepwalkers with their eyes open. Why didn't she cry, or shout, or scream? Since that first night, the night of the day that Dr. Dixon had told her she was probably pregnant, when she'd cried so much her pillow was still damp the next morning, she hadn't shed a tear.

She had a strange sensation of being watched. She looked up from the magazine to find all eyes in the waiting area on her, all eyes but those of the woman who was tapping the arm of her chair. The receptionist must already have called her name. "Heather Novak," she said again, and then, impatiently, "Are you all *right*, Heather? Dr. Buchner will see you now."

All right. What a crazy question to ask at a time like this. For a moment she felt like replying, "No, I'm not all right. I'm all wrong."

Dr. Buchner, a sad-eyed man of about sixty, his dark, grey-streaked hair still thick on his rather broad head, was sitting at his desk reading a letter.

"Good morning, Heather," he said with a smile and a faint trace of an accent. "Sit down, my dear." He waited a moment and then continued: "I have here a letter from Dr. Dixon. She tells me that you are pregnant."

It was the first time since Dr. Dixon's early speculation that Heather had heard her condition put into words. The nurse at Planned

Parenthood had said her test was positive, and had advised her to come back later if she wanted to talk to someone about birth control. Then she referred her back to Dr. Dixon. The gynecologist had simply told her he'd be doing her procedure if she was approved. And Dr. Dixon had smiled that sympathetic, wistful smile of hers and asked her if she'd considered termination.

Termination. Procedure. She hadn't heard the word abortion at all. Dr. Dixon and the others had probably been trying to spare her feelings. What did it matter? For days now her only feeling had been that she had no feeling. Even the nausea had vanished, as if now that her pregnancy was confirmed nature could, for a little while at least, remove its signals.

"You poor little thing," said Dr. Buchner, lifting his eyes from Dr. Dixon's letter and looking straight at Heather. His eyes dropped to the letter again, then moved back to Heather's face. "You poor, poor little thing."

As he continued trying to make eye contact with her, Heather kept on looking down. Then, certainly as much to her own surprise as Dr. Buchner's, she burst into tears.

For a long time she just sat there crying, with Dr. Buchner sitting patiently on the other side of the desk, his mild grey eyes moving back and forth from the letter in front of him as she continued to cry. At one point he pushed a box of tissues toward her from the corner of the desk. She was sobbing loudly now, so unlike her usual self that it didn't even bother her to wonder if her noisy weeping could be heard in the waiting room outside. She was no longer a thinking, rational person but a creature responding to intense pain. The numbness was gone, at least for the moment. It was only later she realized that this was the only time since she'd been a tiny child she'd really let herself go in the company of a stranger. She hardly ever broke down even in front of her mother or her sisters.

Her crying was quieter now. The whole thing was like something that was happening to her over which she had no control. Control. The little two-syllable word, flickering through her consciousness, reminded her of the movie *Ordinary People* that she and Debbie had seen the year before. "I'm not big on control," the psychiatrist — he was the actor who played Alex on *Taxi* — had said to the hero of the story, a boy who'd become severely depressed after the drowning death of his only brother. Even while she was watching the film Heather had wondered at a psychiatrist getting out of his bed in the middle of the night to counsel a patient. Now here she was herself, completely out of control in front of a man she'd never seen before, and would probably never see again. She wiped her eyes with a tissue, and blew her nose hard.

"How do you feel about all this?" The doctor's accent was a little more pronounced than it had been before. He sounded so much like a psychiatrist in a book that, in other circumstances, Heather probably would have laughed.

When she didn't answer, Dr. Buchner repeated his question in a slightly different form. "Are you sure you really want this termination?"

After another long pause Heather said, "Yes, I'm sure. I don't like the idea but I just can't face having a baby and giving it up for adoption." Her eyes were stinging now that the tears were all gone. She took another tissue and blew her nose again.

Now it was the doctor's turn to pause. For a few moments he played with the little glass paperweight on his desk, moving it from one hand to the other, back and forth, back and forth. It was the kind of thing that you shook to make a snowstorm. Finally he looked straight at her and asked "Have you considered keeping the child yourself? Is there any possibility that your mother could take it? It's only right that you should consider all the possibilities."

Heather felt dangerously close to tears again. "I haven't told my mother," she mumbled into the tissue in her hand. "I'd rather die than tell her. She doesn't believe in abortion but she wouldn't be able to look after a baby herself even if she wanted to. She works."

"Umm," said Dr. Buchner, drawing a wavy line on the prescription pad in front of him. "You haven't told your mother. What about your father? A girl of your age — how old are you, anyway?" He opened Dr. Dixon's letter again, and spread it out on the desk in front of him.

"Nearly sixteen," said Heather, feeling younger and smaller than Jason. "I'll be sixteen in January."

"Sixteen," repeated the doctor, and looked at her again for a long moment. She hoped he wouldn't call her a poor little thing again; she didn't want to cry any more. She would have thought Dr. Buchner talked to so many girls like herself that it would be all routine to him by now. Perhaps he was just filling in for someone else, another psychiatrist who usually dealt with the abortion cases.

"My father doesn't live here," Heather said, looking down at the green desk blotter. "My mother...they're divorced. He lives in the States. I haven't seen him since I was small." As she spoke she could see her father's picture again, only this time it was the one of him in the blue Sunday suit that she thought she could remember being smudged with Shu-Milk from her white summer shoes. She bent her head lower, so that any tears wouldn't be visible.

Dr. Buchner reached across the desk and patted her arm. "Don't be afraid to cry, my dear," he said. "Tears are nothing to be ashamed of." He sat back in his chair and became businesslike again.

"Have you seen the social worker yet?"

"No, I think I have to see her next."

Dr. Buchner took off his glasses, polished them with his handkerchief and put them on again. "Did Dr. Dixon tell you that technically you can't have a termination without your father's permission?"

Termination. There was that word again. A rose by any other name would smell as sweet. Or as bitter.

"I don't know. She might have. I'm so mixed up these days I can hardly remember what anyone said. She did think I should tell Mom, but I don't believe she said anything about Da...my father." She saw her father getting a letter from her, the first one for a long, long time, opening it perhaps a little guiltily because he'd never had her up for a visit, and then dropping it on the floor when he read what it had to say.

"Well, the social worker will advise you about all that. My job is to report to the therapeutic abortion committee about your emotional condition." He paused again, folded Dr. Dixon's letter into tight creases and said, "Heather, do you have trouble sleeping, have you contemplated taking your own life?"

Before she could think about what she was saying she answered the second question: "Oh, no, I'm too afraid of death for that."

"Ah," said Dr. Buchner, looking directly at her again. "That is not what the committee will want to hear. You know, don't you, Heather, that in Canada abortions may only be performed if the woman's physical or mental health is in danger?"

Heather did know that. One of her religion assignments at the beginning of the school year had been to write a paper on abortion, giving the pros and cons. That was one of the many times that Eileen had pronounced on her opposition to abortion for any reason. After studying the magazine articles at the library, Heather had become more confused than before about her own feelings. There'd also been a number of letters to the editor in the *Telegram* around that same time, most of them from pro-lifers, as the anti-abortionists called themselves, with a few from pro-choice people, or pro-abortion as the Right-to-Lifers called them.

Pro-life. Pro-choice. Pro-abortion. Anti-abortion. Words, that's all they were, words. Words like "termination" and "pregnancy" and "sexually active" and "all the way." What did all those words have to do with how a person really felt when something like this happened to her? One thing for sure, it could only happen to a her. The hims didn't have to worry about it.

Some of the letters from the pro-lifers had been nasty, throwing around words like murder and killing and slaughter, talking about the dead "babies" the way the anti-seal hunt protestors talked about "baby seals." "Abortion today, euthanasia tomorrow" was a favourite headline. And the Knights of Columbus had taken to putting red *Abortion is Murder* bumper stickers on their cars. Words again. Nothing but words.

"Yes, I know that," she said finally, wishing she could explain to him or to herself the chaos of thoughts pushing at each other inside her skull. And then, summoning up courage she didn't know she possessed, she continued: "What are you going to say about me?"

"About you? What do you want me to say about you, child?"

133

"Why, that,...that it's okay for me to have an...abortion." Should she have said termination, to keep up this conspiracy the others had started?

"I'll do my best for you, my dear. But don't count on being approved. The committee has been turning down a lot of women lately. They're under pressure from...various groups." He made a few more notes on his pad; Heather didn't want to know what they were.

"The social worker will talk to you about that permission business. I agree with Dr. Dixon that you should tell your mother. You might find her more understanding than you think."

Heather got up to go, sensing that the interview was over. When she was almost at the office door Dr. Buchner spoke again.

"You will get a call from the social worker. But remember, even if you are approved you can always change your mind, right up to the last minute."

What in the name of God did he mean by that? Was he trying to tell her not to have the abortion? What did he mean by saying he'd do his best for her?

The social worker was young, about Dr. Dixon's age. She told Heather her name was Deirdre Attwood. A nurse who came into the office to ask her a question called her D.A. The office was already decorated with Christmas tinsel and red and green streamers.

"I'm not going to ask how you are, Heather," she said. Her eyes were large and very blue; she was pretty enough to be a movie star or a TV hostess.

"Do you see many girls like me?" Heather asked, not knowing until the words were out that she was going to ask the question.

"Yes, unfortunately. Oh, I'm sorry, I didn't mean that the way it might have sounded."

Heather nodded. She was tired, tired of explaining something that she didn't understand herself. She still hadn't quite accepted the fact that *she* was pregnant, she herself, not Debbie, Donna, Shirley, Darlene Snelgrove but her, Heather Novak. For a moment Dr. Buchner's question about killing herself did not seem as absurd as it had earlier.

Deirdre Attwood was reading something on the desk in front of her. "Now, you're under nineteen, so you'll need either your father's or your mother's permission. Technically I think it's the father's, but ever since I've been working here we've accepted the mother's. Most girls seem to be closer to their mothers than they are to their fathers." She went on to tell Heather that the abortion committee was to meet at five p.m. that day. She would sit in on it, and as soon as she knew anything she'd call Heather at home. "If everything is okay you'll have the surgery Friday morning." Surgery. Yet another name for it. What else would they think of to call it?

"Oh, no, don't call me," said Heather when she realized the full impact of Deirdre's words. "I haven't told Mom yet and she'd want to know what you're phoning about and everything." She could picture herself getting the phone call, with Eileen's eyes and ears nearby.

"Okay, then, you call me early tomorrow morning, about nine o'clock or so. I'll know for sure by then." She wrote a number on a slip of paper and passed it across the desk to Heather. "But Heather, you should tell your mother right away. She's got to sign this permission slip, see, right here? There's no way you can be approved without your parents' permission."

"I could phone my father," said Heather. Her voice sounded like someone else's. "He's in Iowa. I'm sure he'd understand more than Mom would."

"But we need written permission, Heather. Perhaps a telegram would be all right, I don't know. I still think you should talk to your mother as soon as you get home today. Lots of other girls have felt like you do but everything worked out fine."

"Were any of their mothers against abortion?"

Deirdre smiled. "We've had girls in here whose mothers were in anti-abortion demonstrations the week before."

"I don't know," said Heather. "I'll have to think about it." Her mother was hardly ever home these days, between work, visiting Nan and going to the LeMarchant Club either with Mollie or with her new boyfriend, the one who worked on the oil rig. Heather tried to imagine having a heart-to-heart talk with Eileen, talking to her even the way she was talking to the social worker now, or had talked to Dr. Buchner earlier. She'd shout and rave and yell. No, surely anything would be better than telling her mother.

Deirdre Attwood asked her a few more questions, about birth control, about Frank ("the father," she called him), about Heather's plans for the future. The future, what was that? Heather could not see past the moment when the abortion would either be approved, or not.

"You can call me any time afterwards, too, Heather," Deirdre was saying. "You know, when it's all over. It's not the end of the world." Dr. Dixon had used those very words. She led Heather to another small office where the nurse was waiting to speak to her. "You've got a long life ahead of you." She laid her hand on Heather's shoulder for a moment, and then was gone. Heather knew the words had been meant to cheer her up but at this moment they sounded like a dreary life sentence.

Like Deirdre, the nurse, whose name was Mrs. Andrews, was pleasant and understanding. Heather didn't know how they could stay that way when they were talking to people like herself all the time. Mrs. Andrews explained the physical procedure, the fasting beforehand, the general anaesthetic, and told her how to get to day surgery. Heather wasn't really taking in what she was saying. She was tired of listening to people, no matter how nice and friendly they might be. Surely they weren't all nice and friendly, though. Some of them must be mean and disapproving. She was relieved, in an abstracted way, that she hadn't had to talk to anyone like that.

"I'll do everything I can to make things easier for you when you come in on Friday," said Mrs. Andrews. She was a short, thick woman of about forty-five; there were a few strands of grey in her smooth brown hair. Heather wondered if she had any children of her own.

"That's if I'm approved." Heather felt like some kind of wind-up toy; words and sentences tumbled out of her mouth at intervals the way they came out of the talking doll Nan had given her once for her birthday.

"Oh, yes, of course, if you're approved. I don't see why you wouldn't be."

As she followed the nurse back to the waiting area, Heather tried to extend her thoughts to all the others in her predicament, to the women and girls she'd seen at the clinic, to Darlene Snelgrove, to the girl Eileen had known who had thrown herself over the cliff, to every female she'd ever heard of who'd been pregnant with a child she couldn't have. Try as she would, at this moment she could summon up no sympathy for anyone except herself. Years before she had startled herself with a strange thought, a thought that had formed itself into a group of words in her mind: we're all me to ourselves. At times those words made perfect sense, made her feel part of something marvellous and awesome. Later she'd realized that this must be what people meant when they talked about oneness with the universe. Right now they made no sense at all.

On the bus home she sat next to a girl of about eighteen with a baby in her arms. It was the only empty seat on the bus. The child wore a pink snowsuit with a hood, the two points of which stood straight up like rabbits' ears. She reached out her tiny fingers to touch the shiny buckle on Heather's purse. Her mother jerked her away and the baby started to cry.

"Oh, my God, Krista, don't start bawlin' now." The girl took a bottle out of her jacket pocket and shoved the nipple into the baby's mouth. She held the bottle with her left hand; there were no rings on any of her fingers.

Watching the baby sucking contentedly, Heather wished for a moment that she could do as this girl had done, have the baby and keep it. Then she knew, with a deep sense of sadness, that such a course was not for her. For the time being she forgot her fears about the permission slip that had to be signed, her fears of the operation itself (would she die?) her fears about the guilt that might torment her for the rest of her days. Whatever happened to her later in life, whatever children she might have in the future, she was not going to have this one. Tears stung her eyes as she turned away from the baby in its mother's gently-swaying arms and looked instead at the brightly-coloured advertising poster for chocolate Turtles ("Get Yours Today") that decorated the upper part of the bus.

# Twelve

That night was the longest one of Heather's life. She had slept very little; when she did drop off she dreamed about her father. He was standing in a sunshiny garden, wearing the blue suit he'd worn in the old snapshots. She'd been trying to talk to him; he kept looking in the opposite direction, as if he hadn't heard a word she'd said. Finally he walked away, still not acknowledging her presence. In the distance she heard a mournful mewing sound and awoke to find Puss snuggling down at her feet. She sat up in bed and stroked his smooth fur; he purred so loudly that she was afraid he'd wake Eileen in the next room.

She didn't sleep any more after that until daylight. Every time she closed her eyes she saw the orange and brown furniture in Clinic 3, the woman who had kept tapping her fingers on the arm of her chair, the steely-cold stirrups in Dr. Potter's examining room, the glass paperweight on Dr. Buchner's desk. Everything was in motion, the chairs moving of their own accord, the paperweight with its own snowstorm inside it sliding across the desk. Dr. Buchner's smile detached itself from his face and floated around the room like the grin of the Cheshire cat in *Alice in Wonderland*. The smile began to talk in a language Heather couldn't understand. Then her mother's voice cut in, calling her name.

Heather woke up, drenched in sweat. The cat jumped, scratched his neck and settled down again. "Heather," Eileen shouted. "Are you gettin' up today or tomorrow? Come on now, it's nearly eight o'clock."

Heather got out of bed and stumbled out to the hall, the dream still heavy in her head. Lately most of her dreams had been scary or tormenting; she couldn't recall the last time she'd dreamed about Frank, or had any kind of pleasant dream at all. Her mother's bedroom door was open, the bed unmade, underwear and pantyhose strewn all over the floor. She leaned over the stair railing. "I'm not going to school today, Mom," she called. "I got a pain in my stomach."

Eileen came out of the kitchen and looked up the stairs to where Heather was standing. She was wearing her aqua uniform pantsuit with a striped terrycloth apron over it. The apron emphasized the thickness of her waist, the waist that she'd proudly told Heather and her sisters had been the tiniest of all of her friends'.

"God, it's not like you to miss school," Eileen said, wiping her hands on the apron. "Would you like a drop of hot ginger wine for your stomach? I bought a bottle of the essence last night; Mom said she thought 'twould do her good. Of course I had to explain to Herb that it's not really wine at all, that there's no alcohol in it. I still don't think he believed me."

Heather sat down on the top step, her bare feet touching the worn rubber stair treads. "How is Nan now?" Her tone was polite, as if she were asking about an acquaintance she hadn't seen for years.

"Fadin' away, girl, fadin' away. She was askin' for you again last night. Try to get in to see her soon, won't you? Fred and Bun were there last night. Fred had a few drinks in; I s'pose that was the only way he could face it. Of course that worried Mom up. She said to me after she hope he don't turn out like Pop."

The words passed over Heather's head. She could almost see them there, different shapes and sizes and colours. Her mother, standing at the foot of the stairs, holding on to the railing, was like a figure in a picture or a television show. Her voice sounded unnatural, unreal. Heather had read stories of people who'd been clinically dead and had come back to life, stories of how they left their bodies and hovered over them, watching the frenzied doctors and nurses at work. She felt now as if she were, like them, on another plane, looking down at herself sitting on the stairs with her mother's words flying around her.

How could Eileen fail to notice her strangeness, her apartness from the whole scene? She was still talking; Heather tried to make sense of her words.

"Anyway, are you sure you don't want a drop of ginger wine? You needs something to pick you up, girl. You're as white as a ghost here lately."

Heather stood up. "I'm going back to bed," she said, turning. "Don't bother with the ginger wine. I'll take an Enos when I comes down."

"All right, then. You knows where the Enos is to, do you? It's in the cupboard over the stove, right next to the molasses. If that pain don't get better you'll have to go to the doctor."

Heather climbed back into bed, still feeling as if she were watching herself doing it. The cat was scratching himself again. Heather wondered abstractedly if he had fleas. She'd had little red itchy spots on her legs last spring that Eileen had said looked like flea bites. For a few days she was ashamed when she had to strip down to her shorts for gym, afraid the other girls would recognize the little lumps for what they were, knowing that girls like Linda would never have flea bites.

All at once Heather felt sorry for her mother, perhaps for the first time in her life. Up to now she'd mostly thought of her as a happy-go-lucky, good-time person who didn't concern herself with anything but the surfaces of life. She'd believed her main reason for not telling Eileen about her pregnancy was Eileen's opposition to abortion. It had occured to her briefly that her mother would be disappointed in her but that hadn't seemed to matter. She'd always considered her mother someone who could put troubles behind her and go on to the next thing. Now she saw her as an oddly tragic figure, a person who hadn't asked much from life and certainly hadn't received much. Here she was now preoccupied with Nan's illness and the problems of daily living, knowing nothing about what was happening to her youngest daughter, the quiet one, the studious one, the one who was going to make something of herself.

All the while she was thinking those thoughts Heather still had the feeling that she was observing herself. She'd had it a few times before in her life; it was an uncomfortable sensation that was hard to describe. Right now she was almost glad she felt this way, detached from herself and what was happening to her. Perhaps it would make what she had to do a little easier. Yesterday she had cried and cried, first in Dr. Buchner's office and then again later. Today she did not feel like crying at all. She had often wondered, especially during history lessons, what condemned people thought about in their last days, what Anne Boleyn had been thinking when they led her to the executioner's block, what was on Joan of Arc's mind when the fire was lit under her. Perhaps they'd been observing themselves too, had been detached from what was going on. "Or at least her head was," she could imagine Linda laughing if she had ever spoken those thoughts about Anne Boleyn. But they weren't at all funny to Heather today.

After her mother had left for work Heather crept down the stairs. She didn't know why she was creeping; a thunderstorm wouldn't wake Shirley in the mornings until she was ready to wake up. When she saw the tiny bottle of ginger wine essence on the counter she remembered how Nan used to make up a huge glass jar of it every Christmas; she could almost smell the warm gingeriness of it when Nan brought the mixture to a boil and offered her a hot cup of it, stingy and sharp. Nan had always made fudge on Christmas Eve; Heather would help her colour it pink and green and yellow with drops from the little bottles of food colour that Nan called cochineal. Nan had sung while she was making fudge, or homemade candy as she called it, just as she had sung when she was doing other jobs around the house. Because it was Christmas time she would usually sing carols; her favourite was *Once in Royal David's City*, especially the verse

*He came down to earth from heaven*
*Who is God, and Lord of all,*
*And his shelter was a stable*

*And His cradle was a stall.*
*With the poor and mean and lowly*
*Lived on earth our Saviour holy.*

Nan had always wiped her eyes after she sang that. Sometimes it made Heather cry too. Later, when she was old enough to understand, she wondered how the Virgin Mary had really felt when she found out that she was pregnant. Surely the Bible didn't tell the whole story.

She wished she could cry now. What had been detachment from herself earlier was now turning into a cold numbness. She turned up the heat but that didn't help. Her feet especially were icy. She pulled on a pair of white socks that were balled up on the washer, and threw her mother's old red sweater over her shoulders.

She picked up her purse and began to look through it for Deirdre Attwood's phone number. Ah, here it was. Perhaps she should have a cup of tea first; Deirdre wouldn't be at work yet. It was only a quarter to nine.

She still hadn't told anyone about her pregnancy. Several times she'd almost told Debbie, especially on one beautifully fine day when they'd gone for a walk together up over Signal Hill. She suggested the walk because she thought it would give her a chance to talk without being overheard. Debbie had grumbled that she wasn't much for walking but had gone along cheerfully enough.

"You're awful quiet lately," Debbie said as they made their way slowly up the hill. "You never did talk anyone's ear off but you're even quieter lately. Is anything the matter?"

Now, she told herself. Say it now. Go on, say it now.

Just at that moment a car passed them, a car full of boys who stuck their heads out through the window and yelled out what they'd like to do to the two girls. Debbie shouted back, then turned to Heather and asked:

"Well? What were you gonna say?"

The moment had passed. "Nothing. Nothing, really. If it was anything I forget it now."

A couple of days after she first went to see Dr. Dixon she was at Linda Stone's for supper. The nausea had been really bad then but she'd promised Linda the week before and she didn't know how to back out. As earnestly as ever the child Heather had prayed not to vomit she prayed it then. Please don't let me throw up, at least until I get outside, she pleaded silently over and over again. As she tried to show some enthusiasm for the beef stroganoff, the crisp green salad, the hot French bread and the partridgeberry pudding she'd glanced at Linda's father, comfortable looking in the brown corduroy pants and green sweater he'd changed into when he got home from work, at her mother, smiling and at ease in her checked pants and yellow blouse, at Linda herself, looking, in her brown wool knickers and Indian top, and with her shining reddish-brown hair, as if she'd just stepped out of the pages of *Flare* magazine. Mrs. Stone's freshly-made Christmas fruit cake was cooling on the kitchen table when they arrived, the smell of the mixed peel and the cherries, the spices and the flavourings reaching them as soon as they opened the front door. The nausea had vanished for the moment; Heather found herself really enjoying the smell.

"I'm late with my Christmas cakes this year. Has your mother got hers made yet, Heather?" Mrs. Stone had never met Eileen but she always asked after her.

Heather had a vision of her mother on Christmas Eve, hastily mixing up a cherry cake and slapping it into the oven, having bought her dark cake at Sears. Up to that moment she'd been thinking that perhaps she'd get up the nerve to tell Mrs. Stone about her pregnancy, or at least ask Linda to tell her, but after the question about the cake she became defensive about her own mother and hadn't felt at all like confiding in this...this stranger. Mrs. Stone was involved in all sorts of good causes like Planned Parenthood and the Status of Women Council and Amnesty International and Unicef; that was why Heather had considered telling her. But she had known then that she couldn't. She was pretty sure that if Nan had been well she would have been able to talk to her. Nan would have been disappointed but would have tried not to show it. Telling her was out of the question now.

Funny, this impulse to tell someone. What could anyone else do or say, after all, that would help? Perhaps, when this was all over, if it ever was, she'd be glad she hadn't told anyone except the professionals who had to know, glad that her shameful little secret would be hers alone. She certainly didn't want Frank ever to know. She didn't really blame him for the freak thing that had happened, felt that it had been as much her fault as his, but, when she thought about him at all, she couldn't bury the bitterness as she compared his situation with her own. What was really strange was how rarely she thought about Frank at all those days. Ever since she found out she was pregnant, her thoughts, previously so full of him that there was no room for anything else, had turned sharply in another direction.

She'd told Deirdre Attwood that perhaps she'd try to get her father's permission. Maybe she should phone him right now. No, not now, it would be very early in the morning in Iowa, and a telephone call would frighten him. Besides she didn't even know his number. Maybe she should try to get it from Information.

She looked at the cup in front of her, still full of tea. When she tasted it, it was already cold. She emptied the cup into the sink, and looked at the clock. Two minutes after nine. She picked up the piece of paper with Deirdre Attwood's number on it and went to the telephone.

As she dialed the number the sensation she'd had earlier of watching herself returned more powerfully than ever. Who was this person sitting calmly on the chair, waiting for someone she hadn't known existed until yesterday morning to answer the phone? Who owned the lifeless voice that said politely, "May I speak with Deirdre Attwood, please?" as if she were about to make an appointment with the eye doctor or the dentist?

"Hallo." Deirdre's voice sounded as far away as if she were talking to Heather from the other side of the Atlantic Ocean. "Oh, it's you, is it, Heather? I'm glad you called me nice and early." She hesitated, as if waiting for Heather to say something. Heather heard this strange, new voice of hers ask, as though she were checking on a library book, or a parcel at Sears, "Have you got any news for me?"

"Yes, Heather, I have." Why didn't she get to the point? And then, "I'm pleased to tell you the committee has approved your request. Be in here tomorrow morning by 7:30 and go straight to day surgery. Remember I showed you where it was?"

Deirdre continued to talk but Heather neither reacted to nor ever remembered afterwards what she said. She wasn't observing herself anymore now, but was again one with the girl in the chair holding the receiver in her damp hand. She was frightened, more frightened than she had ever been when as a small child she'd been afraid she was going to die in the night, more frightened than she had been that day she got lost at the Avalon Mall. For the first time in her life she wanted to close her eyes and die right where she was. She'd read in books and heard in movies and songs that there were worse things than dying but she had never believed it before. Almost every centimetre of her skin became coarse with gooseflesh. Not only was her heart pounding against her ribs, it seemed to be banging against the walls of her stomach as well.

Deirdre was still talking. "Mrs. Andrews gave you a permission slip, didn't she? Have you told your mother yet, Heather?"

"No." Heather had begun to tremble. She couldn't say anything else because her teeth were chattering.

"Well, remember what I told you. I still feel you should. I'm sure she'll take it much better than you think she will. You know you have to fast tonight, don't you? Don't eat anything after supper."

Don't eat anything after supper. Didn't this person on the telephone know that she was never going to eat again?

"Heather? Heather, are you still there?"

"Yes. Yes, I'm still here. Thanks for all your help."

"Are you okay, Heather?" The voice was anxious, concerned.

"Yes, I'm okay. I'll get the permission."

"All right, then, that's fine. And don't forget what I said to you yesterday about calling me afterwards if you need any help."

Afterwards. What was afterwards? And what help would she possibly ever need from this sympathetic social worker who talked to girls like her every day in the week? Deirdre had mentioned birth control. Birth control. That was a laugh. If this nightmare was ever over she was never going to look at a boy or a man again. Never ever, if she lived to be a hundred.

"Thanks again," said Heather, and replaced the receiver.

When she finally looked up she saw Eileen's bottle of Valium on the counter, next to a glass that looked yellow from the Tang in the bottom of it. She went over and picked up the bottle, turned it around and around in her hand. It was almost full, must be a new bottle. Perhaps the answer was here. Perhaps if she swallowed all those pills and went back to bed she'd just go to sleep and never wake up. She was tired, weary right to the bone. She didn't want to think about permission, or termination, or procedures, or anything at all. She took the cover off the bottle and turned on the tap.

As she was running the cold water into a glass she heard a noise behind her and turned to see Shirley, tousled and sleepy-looking, coming into the room.

"Oh, hi, Heather? Why aren't you in school? I know I'm up early but surely God it's not that early, is it?" She smoothed her hair back from her face, and brushed a crust of sleep from her eyes. "What're you doin', takin' one of Mom's Valiums, are you? I'm after takin' a few myself. They makes you feel like you haven't got a care in the world." She went to the stove and turned on the kettle, then sat down at the head of the table. "I don't know why I got up so early. I had a funny dream, it was really scary, and I just couldn't get back to sleep, half afraid to, to tell you the truth. Now what am I gonna do with myself all day?" She stood up again and took a mug from one of the hooks on the wall near the stove. "I better get myself a cup of coffee, I s'pose."

Heather emptied the glass into the sink, replaced the top on the Valium bottle and put it on the counter. The words on the prescription label had burned themselves into her brain. "Dr. Evans," it said at the top and then, underneath, "Valium 5 mg. Take as required. Mrs. E. Novak."

She sat down at the table across from Shirley. Her hands weren't trembling any more, but goose pimples were still standing out all over her body.

"Shirl," she said, and Shirley looked up from her coffee, her sleepy eyes a question. "Shirl, what would you say if I told you I was pregnant?" There, she'd said it. She looked down at the table, wondering what had made her blurt out those crazy words.

Shirley smiled. "You're jokin', of course. Just tryin' to wake me up, are ya? You, pregnant. That's a laugh." She took a sip of coffee.

"Shirley, I'm not joking." As if to prove it, Heather began to cry, not the loud, sobbing kind of crying like yesterday in Dr. Buchner's office but a quieter, hopeless kind of weeping that gave little relief.

"No, you're not jokin', are you? It's really true, isn't it?" Shirley was fully awake now, her blue eyes wide open, an embarrassed look in them. She made a move as if to get up from the table and then sank back in her chair again. "Tell me about it, Heather," she said, her eyes on the coffee mug in her hand. It was a white mug, with the words "Toronto the Good" stamped on it in red. One of Eileen's friends had brought it back to her as a souvenir. "It was Frank, I suppose, was it? Tell me all about it."

Later, Heather couldn't remember a single word she'd said. She knew she talked for a long time, and that the more she talked the less she cried. Shirley didn't leave her chair, didn't get up to come to where Heather was sitting and put her arms around her or pat her. She just stayed where she was, and listened. When Heather had finished she didn't speak for a long time. Then she said, "Heather, you're gonna have to tell Mom. You just got to. You're not goin' to be able to get that thing done tomorrow without her permission, you knows that yourself. She'll be all right, don't worry. You knows her bark is always worse than her bite."

"I just can't tell her, Shirl, I just can't. No matter what happens I can't tell her. You know how she feels about abortion, and besides she got enough on her mind now with Nan and everything. I was thinkin' about phonin' Dad. The social worker said a telegram from him would be okay."

"Don't you do no such thing!" Shirley looked her straight in the face for the first time that morning. "Don't go draggin' him into this. He don't give a damn about us now, anyway, and besides he might be even worse than Mom about givin' permission. He's kind of religious, isn't he? No, if you got your mind made up you're not goin' to tell Mom I'll write out a note for you and sign Mom's name. They'll never know the difference into the hospital. Tell them your mother is too sick to come in with ya." She got up, came around to Heather's end of the table and stood behind her. "I still can't believe it, girl. That's the kind of thing should've happened to me."

Heather felt calmer now than she'd been for a long time, but the earlier detachment from herself did not come back. "Would you really do that, Shirl? You wouldn't mind?" She picked up her purse from the floor and found the sample permission slip the nurse had given her. She handed it to Shirley.

"I_____ hereby consent for my daughter_____to have a termination of pregnancy under general anaesthetic,"

"No problem," said Shirley after she read it. "No problem at all." She made her right hand into a fist and lightly punched Heather between the shoulder blades. "Now don't go worryin' yourself sick. It'll be all over by tomorrow night. You should go back to bed, girl, and get a bit of rest. You looks like something the cat dragged in." She paused and then, not looking at Heather, said, "I'll go into the hospital with you tomorrow if you wants me to."

As Heather climbed the stairs to her bedroom, she wondered what would be happening to her now if Shirley had not come into the kitchen.

# Thirteen

"Every time I been in here yet I got lost," Shirley grumbled as they walked down one hospital corridor and up another looking for Day Surgery. "Up to the Grace and St. Clare's now, it's easy to find your way around. They got this place laid out some queer."

Heather's head was whirling from walking around in circles. From that and from thinking, and from not having had any breakfast. Deirdre had taken her to Day Surgery on Wednesday, but now she had no idea where it was. She was afraid she was going to faint before they got there.

"Aw, shit, this is not it either," Shirley said as they came face to face with a door marked Nuclear Medicine. "What time are you supposed to be there, Heather?"

"They told me seven-thirty." She looked at her watch. "It's almost that now."

"I don't care, I'm gonna ask someone. Hey, nurse," Shirley called to a young woman in white who'd just passed them. "Can you tell us where Day Surgery is at?"

The nurse or whatever she was (she wasn't wearing a cap) looked bored as she pointed in the opposite direction. "Straight down that way, and then turn right," she said, with a glance at Heather that took in every part of her, from her feet to the top of her head.

"It wouldn't have hurt her to crack a smile," mumbled Shirley as they walked along in the direction indicated.

When they finally found Day Surgery Heather recognized some of the people she had seen in the clinic on Wednesday. The little girl with the plaits was there, her mother beside here. So was the woman who'd kept tapping her fingers on the arm of her chair, and several of the others. Most of them had someone with them, a mother, a husband, a boyfriend or a girlfriend. Heather was glad, after all, that Shirley had insisted on coming with her.

She hadn't wanted her to, at first, but Shirley was determined to come. Heather had told her mother that she was going to the Aquarena for an early morning swim. Luckily she had done that several times before, usually with Debbie.

"Don't you go gettin' a cold out of it now," Eileen warned. "It's freezin' out, so don't go comin' out of there with your hair wet."

"They got hair dryers there, Mom," Heather explained patiently. Eileen shrugged, looking unconvinced.

"I think I'll go swimmin' with you," Shirley said then, as if she'd just thought of the idea. "I can sure use the exercise." She winked at Heather behind Eileen's back. For a moment Heather felt intensely annoyed with Shirley. It was all right for her to joke and carry on. Nothing was going to happen to *her*. Instantly she was ashamed of herself. Perhaps this was the only way Shirley could handle what was happening.

"Well, if the two of ye catches yere death, don't blame me," Eileen had warned. "I got enough to worry about now with Mom without ye gettin' brownkitis or pneumonia. Still, I s'pose anything that gets Shirl up early in the morning can't be all bad."

They had got up at six-thirty, creeping around the house so as not to wake Eileen. Heather had been awake since five o'clock, looking at her watch every five minutes. She had probably slept for no more than an hour during the whole night. Every time she closed her eyes she saw a hospital stretcher, a masked face, a gleaming scalpel. She knew the doctor wouldn't be using a scalpel on her but she couldn't get the image out of her mind. She could almost sense the sweet, cloying smell of ether in her nostrils. Two or three times she jumped up in bed, struggling for breath.

Shirley had insisted on calling a taxi. "I got a loan off Joyce last night," she said, showing Heather a crisp new twenty dollar bill. "Just don't ask me where she got it. It's none of our business, anyway."

Now in the Day Surgery waiting room, Mrs. Andrews came toward them. "Good morning, Heather," she said, taking her hand. "Is this your sister? She looks a lot like you."

It was the first time anyone had ever told Heather that. She thought she and Shirley were as unlike as it was possible for two sisters to be.

"Shirley, this is Mrs. Andrews, the nurse I told you about."

"Pleased to meet you," said Shirley.

Mrs. Andrews smiled and nodded. "Okay now, Heather, you just take a seat there until someone is ready to prep you. We're extra busy this morning. You haven't eaten anything, have you? Good. Is your mother coming in?"

"No." Heather's voice was so low that she shook her head in case Mrs. Andrews hadn't heard her.

"No," Shirley repeated loudly. "Mom is sick. Her nerves are awful bad lately. Her mother is dying with cancer, see."

"Oh," clicked Mrs. Andrews. "Oh, I'm so sorry. Cancer is a terrible thing, isn't it? My mother died of it, too." And then, after a pause, "Did she sign the permission slip?"

"Yes, she signed it," Shirley said quickly. "You got it there in your purse, haven't you, Heather?"

Heather opened her purse and, hands trembling, began to feel around for the piece of paper. Panic shot through her when her fingers didn't locate it. Then she remembered she'd put it in her jacket pocket. She handed it to Mrs. Andrews who read it quickly.

"That seems to be all right," she said finally, folding the note. "I'll just keep it for the files."

She knows, Heather thought. She knows my mother never saw that piece of paper. She glanced at Shirley who was sitting down reading a *People* magazine, and looking entirely unperturbed.

Heather had a quick vision of the files Mrs. Andrews had mentioned. In her mind's eye she saw a pale beige folder with her name on the side tab. "Heather Novak," it would say. "Age 16. Abortion." Oh no, of course the word abortion would not be there. "Termination," the file would say.

Perhaps it should say murder. The words rang as clear in Heather's ears as if someone close to her had spoken them aloud. She looked around the room as if to discover who had said them. Her face was burning hot and then stiffly cold. She picked up a magazine from the long rectangular table in the centre of the room. As she absently turned the pages her eyes fell on a picture spread of a glamorous-looking young woman in a number of different brightly-coloured outfits. Her eyes were made up in a spectacular fashion, her lips glossily red, and there was a rosy splash of colour under each high cheekbone. "You don't need to take on the expense of buying special maternity outfits," the blurb at the top of the page read. "Do as our gorgeous model Agatha Nichol is doing. Wear stylishly long loose sweaters, or blouses that fit in around the breasts and then flare out. Agatha is seven and a half months pregnant; she still looks and feels fantastic."

She let the magazine slip to the floor and looked at Shirley who was avidly reading the cover story on Dolly Parton. She sat back in the chair and let her eyes move around the large room. Almost all of the chairs were filled now. It was obvious that not all of the patients were there for the same reason she was. One woman must have been at least sixty, and there were a couple of older men in the room now who appeared to be there for purposes of their own rather than with a girl friend or wife.

The chairs in this room were upholstered in the same orange material as the ones in Clinic 3. Heather tried to count them, to keep her mind off what was coming next. It was useless. Every time she got to seven or eight she had to stop and start again because she could never remember where she had left off. The carpet was also orange. Along one wall stood a row of tall, narrow, cream-coloured lockers. Every now and then a nurse would appear through one of the several doors in the room carrying a plastic garment bag which she hung in one of the lockers. Heather recognized a student nurse as a girl who'd graduated from her school a couple of years before.

The older woman Heather had seen in Clinic 3 on Wednesday was staring blankly in front of her. Unlike most of the other patients, she was alone. She was tapping the arm of her chair just as she'd been doing at the clinic. Heather thought she could detect a rhythm to the tapping:

*Shine on, shine on harvest moon up in the sky,*
*I ain't had no lovin' since January, February, June or July.*

Heather shook her head hard, as if to shake the words away. She didn't want to remember those words here in this place on this grey December morning. Against her will she thought of how full and brilliant the moon had been that night, the night she'd stepped outdoors at Donna's party, the night she'd met Frank coming into the house with his cases of beer just as she'd been about to leave. If only she hadn't gone to that party. If only she'd left two minutes before Frank arrived. If only she had never met him. Two weeks before she wouldn't have believed it possible that she'd ever wish she'd never met Frank. The thought would have been ludicrous.

Shirley nudged her, an open package of Juicy Fruit gum in her hand. "Have a stick. Chewin' is not the same as eatin', is it?"

Heather put the gum into her mouth and started to chew. Almost immediately it began to break into tiny pieces, the way Juicy Fruit always did. Perhaps it would help the dryness. The inside of her mouth felt as if somebody had lined it with thick blotting paper. The sweet taste of the gum reminded her of the days when she used to look through Nan's handbag (pocketbook, Nan always called it) for gum and candy. Once, when she was very young and Nan had been babysitting, she'd taken an Ex-Lax, deceived by its chocolately appearance, and had spent the night running to the bathroom.

The little girl with the long plaits was reading a Judy Blume book. Heather had read a few of those herself; they often dealt with sexual and other taboo subjects that most teenage books left strictly alone. Her mother looked through one of them once, and then threw it down on the kitchen table in disgust.

153

"Is that what they got on the go for girls today? I never seen the likes of it. Do your teacher know you're readin' that kind of trash?"

"The teacher thinks they're okay," Heather had mumbled, not knowing why she was defending the books. She didn't like them nearly as much as she liked L.M. Montgomery.

"No wonder young people are as bad as they are today," Eileen had continued. "If that's the kind of stuff they're readin', on top of what they sees on TV, I wouldn't make any wonder they're as bad as what they are."

Eileen enjoyed the sexual intrigue on the soap operas; her employer had installed a television set at the beauty parlour so that the customers and staff could keep up with the adultery, rape and murder that was commonplace on shows like *Another World, All My Children* and *General Hospital*. She loved the *Three's Company* reruns featuring Mrs. Roper with her eternal innuendos. She could also listen to, and tell, an off-colour joke without batting an eyelash. But let her catch a glimpse of a naked woman on television, or hear profanity or a four-letter word in any context, and she became as virtuous as a cloistered nun. "See, that's where our tax money is going," she'd say to Mollie or whoever else happened to be around. "That CBC, that's all they minds. I'spose it's because their programs are so slow and boring and that's the only way they can get people to watch them."

Heather heard herself sigh. She looked around to see if anyone else had heard her. The little girl in plaits was still reading, turning the pages quickly. She reminded Heather of herself a few years before. How in the world had this...this...child ever become pregnant? Linda Stone's mother had been very angry a couple of years before when a local psychiatrist who was a staunch opponent of abortion said on television, in answer to a question about a pregnant twelve-year-old, that perhaps it would do the girl good to have the responsibility of parenthood. Mrs. Stone had written a biting letter to the editor. "Haven't that woman got anything better to do?" Eileen had asked when she saw it in the paper.

By the look of her, the child's mother was in far worse shape than her daughter. There were purple blotches under her tired eyes, as if she hadn't slept for a good many nights. She kept flicking her daughter's plaits back over her shoulders. They were dark brown and glossy, tied with two stiff green ribbons.

Shirley nudged Heather. "Looka this bit here about Robert Wagner and all his new girlfriends. Wouldn't that poison you? Didn't take him long to get over poor Natalie, did it? There was something really screwy about the way she died, anyway."

Heather glanced at the magazine pictures without seeing them. Did Shirl really think she could possibly be interested in something like that now, or was she just trying to help her get her mind off herself? She picked up another magazine and pretended to read it.

When she looked up again the student nurse she'd recognized earlier was standing in front of her.

"Heather is your name, right?" the girl said, looking up from the chart in her hand. "I've seen you somewhere before. Do you go to Bishops?"

Heather nodded.

"So did I. My name is Sandra Locke. I think my brother Tim is in your class, isn't he?"

Heather nodded again, wondering if Sandra talked about her work when she went home. Nurses weren't supposed to, but who knew for sure?

"Come with me now, Heather," Sandra went on. "I'm going to prep you."

Heather wanted to run away, to throw herself under a bus, to jump into the harbour, to go to sleep forever, anything but face what she had to face.

"How long will she be?" asked Shirley, closing the magazine.

"Oh, she'll be a while. The O.R. is really busy this morning, so she'll be waiting in the prep room until they're ready for her."

"I'll probably go to the cafeteria to have a cup of coffee and a smoke then, Heather. I'll be back here for you later on, okay?"

"Okay," said Heather. Shirley gave her shoulder a squeeze; Heather's eyes filled with tears as she watched her sister walk away.

In the prep room Heather took off all her clothes and put on a yellow johnny coat that tied at the back.

"Don't worry, no one's gonna see your backside," said Sandra as she helped her into the gown. "No one except me, and I don't count, do I?"

"What about the nurses and doctors in the operating room?" said Heather, pretending to catch the other girl's mood.

"Oh, you'll be asleep then, so that don't count either." Heather watched her, young and sturdy in the neat white polyester uniform. Did she have a boyfriend? If so, did she go "all the way" with him?

As Heather lay down and pulled the white sheet over herself she noticed that there was a figure in the other bed, a body so thin that it was barely discernible under the sheet. Heather recognized the older woman who'd been tapping on the chair arm in the clinic and then, this morning, outside in the waiting room. She was lying on her back, staring at the ceiling.

"Hallo," said Heather, surprised to hear her own voice.

The woman turned her head.

"Hallo," she said, in a voice as expressionless as a robot's. And then, lifting herself on her elbow she asked, with a little more expression in her voice this time, "Aren't you Eileen Morgan's daughter?"

Heather's heart began to race. Did everyone in this place know her? No wonder so many women and girls went to Montreal for abortions.

"Yes," she said. What use to deny it? Then, on an impulse, she blurted out: "But Mom don't know about this, so don't tell her, will you?"

She felt a sudden bond with this woman, as if they were fellow conspirators in a secret plot, or prisoners of war planning an escape. She looked at the woman again, and realized who she was. "You used to live next door to my grandmother, didn't you?"

"Yes, that's right," said the woman, lying back on the pillow again as if she was too exhausted to keep her head up. "We rented there for years but we left it and moved into St. John's Housing three years ago. Sorriest thing ever I did. I wish we had stayed where we were to. Your grandmother and them were wonderful neighbours. The crowd I got 'longside of me now, they wouldn't help you out if you were dyin'. All they does is watch people and report 'em when they makes a little bit of money on the sly from the Welfare." After saying this she closed her eyes, as if the effort of speaking, after so much silence, had been too much for her. From a neighbouring room came the sound of loud, spontaneous laughter. The woman opened her eyes again and said, "Well, I'm glad someone got something to laugh about."

Sandra came back, a razor in one hand and a pan of soapy water in the other. "Okay, Heather," she said briskly. "Draw up your knees and open your legs for me now, that's right. Don't tense up now, it's not going to hurt a bit."

While Sandra was shaving Heather, another, much older, nurse came in to shave the woman in the next bed whose name, Heather remembered, was Sullivan. Sandra talked to Heather as she worked, about the weather and the decorations in the stores and the terrible prices everyone was going to have to pay for Christmas presents this year. The older nurse shaved Mrs. Sullivan without saying a word except what she absolutely had to say. Her lips were tightly closed; there was a grim expression on her face as if she were doing an exceptionally unpleasant chore and the less said about it the better.

"I don't believe she likes me," Mrs. Sullivan said after the two nurses had left the room. "Perhaps she don't agree with what I'm gettin' done. Of course as far as that goes I don't think I agrees with what I'm doing myself." For the first time since Heather had seen her in the clinic Mrs. Sullivan smiled, a small smile that didn't quite spread to her eyes. "I'm a Catholic, see, and I've always tried to be a good one. But I got seven youngsters now and my youngest little girl is retarded. I'll be forty-four my birthday and my blood is down all the time." Her voice sounded tired, as if she'd rehearsed what she was saying many times before. "But I still don't think what I'm doin' is right." She reached for a tissue and blew her nose. "When I was pregnant the last time I used to get up on one of the kitchen chairs and jump off it, tryin' to bring on a mis, and that didn't bother me a bit. After though, when Sheila was born, I wondered if that was what made her retarded but I was afraid to ask the doctor." The words came out of her in quick little bursts.

For the first time that day, no, for the first time in weeks, Heather stopped thinking about herself and what was going to happen to her. She wanted to reach over and touch Mrs. Sullivan's hand.

"I'm sure no one in the world could blame you for what you're doing," she said.

Again, Mrs. Sullivan tried to smile. "Oh, I wouldn't be too sure about that," she said. "I never told a soul I was gettin' it done, not even my husband. He just gave up drinkin' about three weeks ago — he joined AA — and even if I had to tell him I was expecting that would've been enough to set him off again. It's some relief to talk about it, though." She paused and then said, "I seen you at the clinic Wednesday and thought you looked familiar. Don't worry, I won't tell no one about you if you don't tell no one about me." The smile was a little wider now; Heather smiled back.

Mrs. Andrews came in, looking as at ease and unworried as if she were a receptionist in a business office.

"We'll soon be ready for you two ladies," she said. "I just got to give the two of you a needle in the bum and then we'll be wheeling you down to the O.R. Don't try to get out of bed after I give you the needle, okay? It'll make you nice and groggy."

As the needle began to take effect Heather felt drowsier and drowsier. Nothing mattered any more. Then suddenly it was terribly urgent that she remember the words of a song that had been going through her head when she was trying to get to sleep the night before.

"Mrs. Sullivan," she said slowly, the words sounding strange in her own ears. "Do you know a song about a lonesome valley? I think Tennessee Ernie Ford used to sing it."

"Oh, I loves Tennessee Ernie," said Mrs. Sullivan, her voice sounding sleepy too. "Something about a lonesome valley, you say?"

"Oh, I remember it now," said Heather, as if it were the most important thing in the world. She began to sing to herself:

*You gotta walk that lonesome valley*
*You gotta walk it by yourself*
*Nobody else gonna walk it with you*
*You gotta walk it by yourself.*

"What's all this about a lonesome valley?" That was Mrs. Andrews' voice. "It's not very lonesome around here this morning, let me tell you. We're going to take the two of you out to the O.R. now. Have you ever had an anaesthetic before, Heather? No? Well, there's nothing to it. Dr. MacLean will just give you a needle in the back of your hand and then you'll know nothing until you wake up and it's all over. I'm sure you know all about it, Mrs. Sullivan."

Mrs. Sullivan nodded. "When I was havin' the youngsters I used to really look forward to bein' put to sleep," she said, her words slurred. "I always had a hard time, even on the seventh one."

Mrs. Andrews helped Heather roll onto a stretcher and Sandra helped Mrs. Sullivan. Heather was glad it wasn't the older, tight-lipped nurse. As they were being wheeled away Sandra started to sing softly:

*Rudolph, the red-nosed reindeer*
*Had a very shiny nose;*
*And if you ever saw it*
*You might even say it glows.*

Heather had sung that with her class on the Christmas concert in Grade Four. She had peered down into the darkened auditorium, trying to pick out her mother and Nan. Sure enough, Nan, who had helped Heather to learn the song, was singing along with the group.

In the operating room Heather found herself surrounded by masked figures in green gowns. She couldn't tell which were men and which women. She heard a female voice say, "She makes a marvellous beef stroganoff. I must try her recipe," and then, "Okay, my love, just you move right in there. It'll be all over before you know it." Then a male voice said, "I'm just going to prick your hand with this needle, okay?" After she closed her eyes she saw the bright green, jewel-like islands she used to see almost every night just before she went to sleep when she was a little girl. Then everything went soft and black.

# Fourteen

Heather opened her eyes to see the masked people still standing over her. They looked like green-clad giants.

"Jolly Green Giants," she heard a thick voice say, and then realized it was her own. "Are you going to give me another needle, or what?" Her throat felt very sore.

"No," a female voice said. "No, my love, it's all over. You were very good. You're going to the recovery room now."

"Guess what?" said another female voice coming from farther away. "Guess what. I'm a grandmother. My daughter-in-law just had a baby girl. Isn't that great?"

"Hi, there, Granny," a male voice said, and then somebody else said "Shhh!"

Heather kept trying to hold on to the thoughts that were tearing furiously through her head. Was it really true that she wasn't pregnant any more? What had she been very good at? She felt something warm running down her legs.

"Oops, she's bleeding," a male voice said matter-of-factly. Was it Dr. Potter's?

"Okay, doctor, I'll put another pad on her." It was the same female voice that had said she'd been very good. Heather felt the sanitary napkin being slipped into place.

The blood was rushing out of her body. "Am I going to bleed to death?" she asked hoarsely, as if she were asking the time, as if it didn't matter much one way or the other.

"No, my love, you're going to be fine," said the female voice. Heather could see lips moving behind the mask.

"Whash...whash your name?" Heather asked. It was somehow very important that she find out.

"Mrs. Keats," said the voice. " 'ilda Keats, I should say. We're not formal 'ere."

"You sounds just like 'erb," said Heather. "Oh, sorry, I mean Herb." The words were tumbling out of her mouth, like the blood from the other end of her body.

"Well, 'e must be from Bonavista Bay like myself. I'm a bayman, and proud of it."

"Take the baymen out of St. John's and you wouldn't have much left," said the male voice.

*I do' want your maggoty fish*
*Thash no good for winter,*
*I can buy it better'n that*
*Down in Bonavista.*

Heather heard her cracked voice singing. Why couldn't she just shut up?

*Sods and rinds to cover your flake*
*Cake and tea for supper,*
*Codfish in the spring of the year*
*Fried in maggoty butter.*

sang a male voice with a pronounced Scottish accent.

"You don't pronounce the words right, Dr. Maclean," said Mrs. Keats, laughing. She sang the verse again, in a bay accent so exaggerated that it would have made Herb sound like an elocution teacher. After she had finished someone laughed loudly.

"Whash so funny?" said Heather, feeling aggrieved. Maybe this is how it feels to be drunk, she thought drowsily.

When she opened her eyes again she was in another room, surrounded by people lying on stretchers like herself. She wondered if she had died and was now in some weird sort of antechamber to another world. Then she realized she must be in the recovery room.

In the distance she could hear bells ringing, softly, sweetly. In the same *Reader's Digest* article where she'd read about people rising out of their bodies when they were at the point of death, the one she'd been thinking so much about the day before, she'd also read that sometimes those same people saw a celestial light and heard bells ringing.

A young man in white approached, carrying something. She touched his arm. "Am I dying?" she asked. Again, it didn't seem to matter one way or the other. She just felt she had to know. She thought about Vera Dalton who was in her class right up through school and had died of leukemia when they were in grade seven. She had lost all her hair. Once, when Heather and some of the other girls went to the Janeway to see her, she was wearing a little white cotton cap.

The young man smiled, showing metallic braces over very white teeth. "No, indeed you're not dying," he said. "I'm going to take your blood pressure now."

As he tightened the band around her arm he asked, "Why did you think you were dying?"

"Well, people often do die in hospitals, don't they?" Why was she saying all those nutty things? She just couldn't control herself. "And anyway, I'm sure I heard bells ringing and I bet you didn't."

"Yes, I did. That was the chapel bells. There's a service in the chapel this morning and they were trying out a new set of chimes someone donated to the hospital."

"It was a lovely sound," said Heather. Now she could feel big tears rolling down her cheeks. Was she going crazy, or what?

"Why am I acting so foolish?" she asked.

"Oh, it's just the anaesthetic," the young man said. "There you go, now. Your blood pressure is just fine."

"Oh, thank you. Are you a male nurse?"

"Well, I'm a male, and I'm a nurse, so I guess that makes me a male nurse." He smiled and then went on. "How do you feel now" — he looked at the plastic bracelet on her arm — "how do you feel now, Heather?"

162

"Okay, except my throat is sore and it hurts a bit to talk but I keep on talking anyhow."

"Your throat is sore from having a tube down it. That'll go away soon." He faded from her vision as she drifted off to sleep again.

When she next awoke she recognized the little girl with the plaits in the next bed. She was crying.

"What's the matter?"

"My throat hurts," said the little girl. "I want to go home." She began to sob loudly.

"Don't do that," said Heather. "You'll make your throat worse. You'll be okay soon. Thash what that nurse who's a boy told me." Her own voice still sounded thick and strained, as if she'd been strangled.

The little girl continued to cry. One of the nurses came to her and wiped her face with a towel, talking to her in a voice so low that Heather couldn't catch the words.

"Heather," said a voice from the stretcher on the other side of her. "Heather, is that you?" Like her own and the little girl's, the voice was hoarse, croaky, but Heather recognized it as Mrs. Sullivan's. She tried to turn toward her but it hurt to move.

"Yes, it's me. Are you okay?"

"I guess so, but I've been saying all kinds of crazy things. The nurses must be havin' a great laugh at me."

"Me, too."

"Well anyhow, girl, we're over it. That's the main thing, isn't it?"

"Yes, I couldn't believe it was over, could you? When I woke up I was sure I still had to go through it."

"So was I."

Mrs. Sullivan was resting her chin on her elbow. Her face was as white as a dead person's. Heather could see the perspiration glistening on her forehead.

"Oh, I'm going to be sick," said Mrs. Sullivan, turning even paler. "Nurse," she croaked and then, with all her might, "Nurse!" The young man who'd taken Heather's blood pressure moved quickly toward Mrs. Sullivan, a kidney-shaped basin in his hand. Mrs. Sullivan urged and vomited.

Heather wondered that she didn't throw up herself. When she was small the sound or sight of someone else vomiting had sometimes proved too much for her. The euphoria produced by the anaesthetic was beginning to fade. She was starting to realize where she was, and why.

There were a lot of people in the recovery room now, not all of them women. On the other side of Mrs. Sullivan lay an old man with a bristly grey moustache. He was snoring; a nurse was calling his name.

"Mr. Sparkes. Wake up, Mr. Sparkes. I want to take your blood pressure."

"Them guns," muttered the old man. "Them guns are too loud. Why don't they stop shooting? The war is over, ain't it?"

"Yes, Mr. Sparkes." The nurse's voice was soothing. "Yes, the war is over, but I still got to take your blood pressure. Be a good boy, now. I'm not going to hurt you."

Mr. Sparkes, who was at least fifty years older than the little nurse, stretched out his arm obediently.

Heather could still hear the odd muffled sob from the little girl but she wasn't crying as hard as she had been. She glanced back at Mrs. Sullivan whose face was beginning to look a little more lifelike.

"That poor old man, he's certainly not here for the same reason we are, Heather," Mrs. Sullivan said, trying to smile. "All the same, men do get the best of it in this world, don't they?"

"I guess they do." Heather tried to place Frank in this worldwide communion of men. (Frank? Who was Frank? He seemed more distant than Barney Snaith, Valancy's lover in *The Blue Castle,* or her own father, far away and innocent in Iowa.) "But I wouldn't like to have to go to war, would you?"

"No. No, I don't s'pose I would, although sometimes anything looks easier than a houseful of youngsters all screamin' for money you haven't got and a husband comin' home drunk every night and smashin' up the few dishes you got left. But no, I don't s'pose I would want to go to war, really."

The young male nurse was advancing toward them again, blood pressure equipment in his hand. "Blood pressure time again, ladies," he said briskly. "I'll do you first, Mrs. Sullivan."

"Age before beauty," said Mrs. Sullivan, rolling her eyes toward Heather. Even lying white and weak on the stretcher she was obviously feeling a great deal more cheerful than she'd been earlier that morning out in the waiting-room, or at Clinic 3 on Wednesday.

The young man and the little doll-like nurse who'd taken Mr. Sparkes' pressure wheeled the two of them back to the prep room they'd been in earlier. Mrs. Andrews came in and beamed at them, congratulating them on their rapid recovery.

But we didn't do anything, thought Heather. Something was done to us.

Now that the anaesthetic was wearing off she was conscious of a burning pain in her abdomen, her hollow abdomen. Where was the...baby...now? She would like to have asked Mrs. Andrews but she didn't dare. It wouldn't have been a baby yet, of course. What had it looked like when the doctor removed it from its dark sanctuary? I've been vacuumed, she thought. Just the way I vacuum the living room carpet for Mom, that doctor vacuumed me out inside. Had the...the pregnancy...come all apart or had it remained in one piece? She sighed heavily and buried her face in the pillow.

"What do they do with the...the...you know, what they took out of us?" When Heather heard the words she thought at first she'd said them to herself. When she looked at Mrs. Sullivan she realized the words had come from her.

"I was just wondering the same thing. It's hard to think about, isn't it?"

"Do they baptize...it, do you think?" Mrs. Sullivan's voice was uneasy. "When I had a miscarriage the priest came and baptized it."

Heather wanted to get them on to another subject. This one was too dreadful to talk about, or think about. "Did you see the priest this morning, before you went in?" she asked. "Mrs. Andrews thought I might want to see a minister but I said no. I don't go to church much, and anyhow I would have been too embarrassed."

"No, girl, I wouldn't dare ask for a priest. He probably would have tried to stop me from going through with it." She turned on her side, wincing as she did so. "Oh, my God, I feels some sore, do you? No, I'm not the same for the church as I used to be. Oh, I tries to make the youngsters go, and young Gerard is an altar boy, but I don't go

165

that often myself. It was different when I was young, I'd never miss Confession and I'd take Holy Communion every Sunday. And when they used to have the Missions I'd go every night. But lately, I don't know, I'm not even as afraid of Hell as I used to be. I guess I've seen too much Hell on earth."

Heather shifted her position, feeling the warm blood coursing out of her again. What if it never stopped? She lay there for a few moments, afraid to move. Then she drew up her knees cautiously, and squeezed her legs together as if to force the blood back into her body.

She looked across at Mrs. Sullivan, her damp, dark hair streaked with grey, the tired brown eyes, the thin, pale lips. When they were in the recovery room Mrs. Sullivan's teeth had been missing, causing her cheeks to sink in, giving her the look of a refugee from the Third World. Giving her the look of Nan. Now, although she had her dental plate in place again, her face still looked very thin. Heather wondered how her mother would look if she was here for the same reason. Mrs. Sullivan was probably even older than Eileen.

"Are you going to tell your mother about this, Heather?" Mrs. Sullivan must have been reading her mind again.

"No." A dark curtain of panic descended on Heather, as it had been doing regularly for the past two weeks. "No, she'd never forgive me. And I don't want to worry her, anyway."

"I think you should tell her. She's your mother, after all. If it was one of mine I'd want to know."

"But you didn't tell your husband, did you?" Heather was amazed at herself, having such a personal conversation with an older woman she hardly knew, asking her the kind of questions she'd never have dared to ask her own mother.

Mrs. Sullivan's eyes filled with tears. She blinked a couple of times and then said, "No, that's true, I didn't. But husbands are different than mothers. If my mother was alive I'm sure I would've told her. She died three years ago. Or I s'pose I would've told her. She was a real strict Catholic, though, went to Mass almost every morning. But I still think she would've understood. You know, she mightn't've thought abortion was right for anybody else but it'd be different if it was her daughter. Of course Mom didn't know what it

166

was like to have a big family, anyway. There was only the two of us cos Dad died when I was three. She had it hard but not the same way I did."

"But you do think your husband really would've minded? Surely he wouldn't want you to have another baby now?" Something inside Heather was driving her to keep on talking. She was afraid of the doubts that would confront her if she remained silent, the doubts about what she'd done, the speculations on what had happened to the living organism inside her that would have been a baby if she hadn't interfered with nature.

"Well, Pat is kind of shy, see. He never was one to talk much. I think that's why he had such a bad drinking problem. And now that he's after givin' it up and everything is goin' pretty good for a change I didn't want to bring another worry on him, so I decided to keep this to myself." She blew her nose. "It's some relief to talk about it, though. I been so uptight this last few weeks I never knew if I was comin' or goin'."

"I think we're the only two here that came by ourselves. I mean, I know my sister Shirley was with me but she only found out yesterday. All the other women and girls got their mother or their husband or their boyfriend with them. I didn't talk to anyone about it either, at least not until I told Shirley yesterday. And I don't say I'll ever mention it to anyone again after this."

"No more will I," said Mrs. Sullivan. She closed her eyes. "Did you see that poor little youngster out there, the one with the long plaits? Isn't that a sin? I s'pose that was some young fella or man that should have had better sense. I hope they locks him up for life."

Mrs. Andrews came into the room, holding two charts.

"Now, Mrs. Sullivan, you didn't have the tubal ligation, after all, did you? That's a pity, really. Then you wouldn't have any more worry."

"No, girl, I didn't," said Mrs. Sullivan. "You got to have your husband's permission for that and I never did get around to tellin' Pat, although I know he don't want no more youngsters any more than I do." After staying silent for so long, Mrs. Sullivan, like Heather, had to keep talking.

167

"Well, you can always come in later and have it done," said Mrs. Andrews. "Try to talk him into it, girl, or persuade him to have a vasectomy."

Mrs. Sullivan laughed what was probably her first laugh in a long time. "Don't hold your breath! I was just tellin' Heather, Pat is so shy. He can't even hardly go to a doctor."

"He wasn't too shy for one thing or you wouldn't have had so many youngsters," said Mrs. Andrews.

Heather felt she was somewhere she didn't belong, overhearing a private conversation between two women with whom she had nothing in common, women like her mother and Mollie.

"Well, according to your charts you're both doing fine," said Mrs. Andrews. "Although we're goin' to have to put you on iron pills, Mrs. Sullivan. The two of you'll soon be ready to go home. I'm going to bring you a bit of lunch and then, after you've had a little rest, we'll let you go. Your sister went out for a little while, Heather, but she'll be back for you soon."

"Lunch," groaned Mrs. Sullivan after the nurse had left the room. "Even the thoughts of it makes my stomach urge."

Heather was still trying to make some sense out of what Mrs. Andrews had said about Shirley. Gone out somewhere, was she? Where? Gone to the Mall, now, probably, to spend the rest of the twenty dollars. Heather's eyes were hot with tears. She reached for a tissue from the box on the bedside table.

"What's the matter?" asked Mrs. Sullivan. "Sure you're all right now, aren't you? I must say I feels an awful lot better now than I have for weeks. I thought my nerves were goin' on me, girl. That Dr. Buchner didn't have to tell any lies to get me approved."

"Nothing, really. Some kind of reaction, I suppose. In one way I think I'm surprised I'm still alive." It was only as she said the words that Heather realized they were true. In the back of her mind, ever since she'd decided to have the abortion, had been the scarcely-acknowledged dread that when the anaesthetic put her to sleep she'd never wake up again. All her old fears of dying in the night, her terror at the implications of the prayer, "Now I lay me down to sleep," had been rekindled at the prospect of the anaesthetic-induced nothingness, the oblivion that she had always feared so deeply.

168

"So am I," said Mrs. Sullivan. "I was afraid of my life I was going to die with a mortal sin on my soul. And I was worried to death about what would happen to poor little Sheila if I was gone. Her father and them loves her but they don't understand how to manage her like I do. She can be really hard to handle sometimes."

"Where is she today?"

"Oh, she goes to school. They got special classes for youngsters like her. That's a godsend. When Pat's aunt had a retarded child, years ago, she had to keep him home all the time and he didn't learn nothing. I told the crowd home I was goin' out to do a day's work today — I does that once in a while to help out — so they won't be surprised if I'm tired tonight. The two oldest girls are pretty good at pitchin' in now. My oldest boy is married and the next fella is out in Alberta."

Alberta. The word had a strange effect on Heather. It was like a reminder to an old woman of a long-forgotten part of her childhood. Alberta. For the past few weeks Alberta had meant Frank. Now it was just a place, like any other.

Heather managed to eat some of her lunch but she couldn't face the sausages with the thin film of grease under them on the plate. She enjoyed the turkey soup, remembering, as she drank it, Herb bragging at the hospital about Nan's delicious soup. That was all Nan lived on these days, soup. She didn't make it herself any more, of course; Herb had taken over that chore with all the others. Sometimes her neighbour, Mrs. Lodge, sent in a pot of soup or a baked custard, and the women from the Home League kept bringing banana breads and apple pies and chocolate cakes that Nan had no appetite for.

"My, them sausages are some greasy, aren't they?" said Mrs. Sullivan, pushing them to the side of her plate. "Ouch, that rubber sheet burns something awful, don't it? I'll be glad to lie down on my own bed."

As Heather continued to drink her soup she recalled the night she'd first gone to the hospital to see Nan, before she had the operation. Nan had complained about the rubber sheet too. That was the first night Heather had gone out with Frank, except for the night of Donna's party. She'd been in such a hurry to meet him that night. She'd had butterflies in her stomach but they were friendly butterflies, not at all like the kind she had later, after Dr. Dixon had told her she

169

was probably pregnant. They'd stopped fluttering after a while, had settled into a heavy, immovable lump in the pit of her stomach. It wasn't there any more now. She felt hollowed-out, light, as if there were no organs inside the skin, just a burning, tearing kind of pain that came and went, and the warm, warm sensation of blood leaving her body.

*First Love, Last Love.* That was the name of one of the books Eileen had brought home from work, a Harlequin romance. Heather had tried to read it; it was the usual Harlequin story of a dark, passionate young man who'd finally preferred a pretty but poor secretary over a rich, glamorous, spiteful model. That was probably the way it was going to be with her, though varying slightly from the situation the book dealt with. In her case first love and last love had happened at the same time.

Sandra, the student nurse who had prepped Heather, poked her head in around the door. "Someone to see you, Heather," she said.

It must be Shirley. About time for her to come back. Heather couldn't understand why she was so annoyed by Shirley's absence, especially when she hadn't even wanted her to come in the first place. Or thought she hadn't.

The door opened and a tall, strongly-built man in a Salvation Army uniform came in. It was hard to tell his age. His hair was dark and thick, his face disfigured by large patches of skin that had been grafted on it from other parts of his body. His eyes, smiling over what appeared to be a completely rebuilt nose, were large and dark. As he walked he leaned heavily to one side. Heather recognized him as Major Forsey, a Salvation Army officer she'd seen several times before when she'd gone to church with Nan. Nan told her he'd been in the Royal Navy during the Second World War and that his ship was torpedoed, leaving him with part of his face and other parts of his body blown away. She had talked to him briefly once when he visited Nan. Herb told her he was a chaplain to the hospitals.

"Hallo, Heather," he said, stopping at the foot of her bed. "I was going through the list of patients and your name struck me as being familiar. You're Mrs. Abbott's granddaughter, aren't you?"

Heather nodded. Was there no escape from people who knew her? She had bound Mrs. Sullivan to secrecy but she could hardly do the same thing with a clergyman. Maybe he would consider it his place to tell her mother; he'd met Eileen at the same time he met Heather.

"I'd like to share a scripture passage with you, and say a little prayer, if you don't mind."

Heather nodded again. After all the talking she'd done this morning, her throat felt closed over. It was still raw and sore.

Major Forsey sat down on the chair beside Heather's bed, after glancing in Mrs. Sullivan's direction as if in question. "Oh, I loves the Salvation Army," Mrs. Sullivan said. "Always did. Many's the time they helped me out Christmas when I never had no money to buy toys for the children. The Army don't care what religion you are."

Major Forsey opened the large Bible he was carrying and began to read:

Wait on the Lord, be of good courage, and He shall strengthen thy heart. Wait, I say, on the Lord.

As he read, Heather was transported back to the Citadel where she had gone with Nan on so many Sunday mornings. She could see the cadets with their tambourines, the young mothers with their babies in fancy knitted suits and dresses, the little girls in the Singing Company with their shining hair all brushed and curled for Sunday.

As Major Forsey continued to read, Heather's mind fixed on a chorus that reminded her more than anything else of those Sunday mornings with Nan:

*And I thank God for the lighthouse, I owe my life to Him,*
*Jesus is the lighthouse and from the rock of sin*
*He has taken me completely so that I may truly see*
*If it wasn't for the lighthouse where would this ship be?*

Tears rolled down Heather's cheeks. She turned her head away from Mrs. Sullivan and Major Forsey, and looked at the opposite wall. When she closed her eyes she could picture Nan and Herb in church, singing that chorus, Herb's right hand raised high, Nan more timid, her hesitant hand just about parallel with her right ear.

She was glad when the Major started to pray. That gave her a chance to keep her eyes closed a little longer. Nan's and Herb's faith had always seemed so strong, but it wasn't helping them much at all in the present crisis. Heather had often heard the two of them sing about heaven as a place they longed to reach, but evidently neither of them was ready for Nan to go there yet.

After the prayer Major Forsey patted Heather's arm and handed her a *War Cry*, and another to Mrs. Sullivan. Then, after a quick "God bless you," he left the room.

"My, that was nice of him," said Mrs. Sullivan. "I wonder if he knows what we're here for." Heather had been wondering the same thing herself.

The next time the door opened it really was Shirley. There was a strong smell of fried chicken from the Mary Brown box in her hand.

"Hi," she said. "How are you?" She stood close to Heather, bending over a little. "I brought you some chicken. I knows what hospital food is like." Heather was touched, but she knew she wouldn't be able to eat a morsel of it.

"What about you, ma'am?" Shirley asked Mrs. Sullivan. "Would you like some? There's loads here."

"You know what, I really believe I would," said Mrs. Sullivan. "I pure loves Mary Brown chicken and my stomach seems to be okay now. I been hardly eating at all lately and I'm really hungry."

Shirley wrapped a chicken leg and a piece of breast in a paper napkin and handed it to Mrs. Sullivan.

"Well, how'd it go, Heather?" she then asked. She was sitting on the edge of the bed. "Was it very bad?"

Heather was almost afraid to speak. She still felt weepy.

"It wasn't too bad," she said at last. "At least I lived."

"You've got another visitor outside," said Shirley, looking down intently at the white sheet she was sitting on.

Heather was really annoyed with Shirley now. She had no right to bring anyone else in on this. It was probably Joyce, or maybe even Debbie. Whoever it was, she didn't want to see them.

"Shirley," she began, "I don't think I...."

Before she could finish the sentence Heather heard, or felt, someone else coming into the room. When she looked up she was sure she was dreaming, still under the influence of the anesthetic that had made her so silly earlier.

"Hallo." The voice sounded far away.

"Hallo, Mom," said Heather, half-convinced that she was talking to an apparition.

Eileen, wearing her imitation leather coat and brown fabric gloves, sat down in the chair Major Forsey had been sitting in. She stretched out her gloved hand, looking as if she wasn't sure what to do with it. Then she laid it on Heather's arm, inside the sleeve of the yellow johnny coat.

"Heather," she said, in a tone that was somewhere between anger and sadness, "Oh, Heather, why didn't you *tell* me?"

# *Fifteen*

"You'll be all right now, Heather, will ya, if I runs in to see Mom? I didn't get in last night and you know what she's like." Eileen was sitting in the rocking chair in the living room, pulling on her boots.

"Yes, I'll be okay. Shirl is here, anyway. You go on."

Heather was lying on the chesterfield, an old rose-coloured chenille bedspread pulled over her. The cramp-like pains in her abdomen that Mrs. Andrews had warned her to expect had already begun. She had given Heather a bottle of tiny white pills to take for them, and told her to be sure to go back to Dr. Potter after six weeks for a checkup.

Dr. Potter. Why did it have to be Dr. Potter? Why couldn't it be Dr. Dixon? She never wanted to see Dr. Potter again.

"Don't forget, though, Heather, if you have a lot of bleeding or severe pain come back in here to Emergency right away," Mrs. Andrews had continued. "I'm sure you'll be all right but don't take any chances." She had also told her matter-of-factly to "abstain from intercourse" for six weeks and not to get in the bathtub for a week. "You can get a shower, though, if you want." Heather hadn't told her they didn't have a shower.

When she'd last gone to the bathroom to change her pad she'd wondered how much bleeding was too much. Mrs. Andrews had said something about soaking through a pad very quickly. Well, it wasn't

174

like that, not yet, anyway, but she did have to change pretty often. She'd stared at the pad in her hand before she wrapped it in toilet paper and threw it in the waste-paper basket.

She was watching, or half-watching, a *Barney Miller* rerun, the one in which Wojo falls in love with a hooker who doesn't look like a hooker at all, or at least not like any hooker Heather had ever seen. Most prostitutes that she knew by sight looked as if they'd been through a great deal. Take Loretta and Elsie Sheppard, for instance. They lived around the corner on Barter's Hill. Both in their forties, they dressed garishly in the styles of ten years before, in clothes that they probably bought at the Goodwill.

When she and her mother and Shirley were leaving the hospital that afternoon, when Mrs. Andrews had been giving Heather her last-minute instructions, a dark-haired girl in tight jeans and a furry jacket was sitting nearby, waiting for someone to pick her up. Even under the heavy makeup she wore, her face looked ghastly pale. Heather had noticed her in the morning, before she went into the prep room. There was another girl with her then, a blonde girl, also heavily made up, in the same kind of outfit. They were talking loudly to each other about the runaround they'd been getting from Social Services.

"Jesus, Bev, who do they think they are, anyway? And when you thinks about the money they wastes," the dark-haired girl said.

"Well, when they told me that, I just said 'Shag you'," said the blonde girl. " 'If that's the way you're gonna be, forget it.' And Karen, I know for a fact half the people up there that morning were workin' on the side. That Jimmy Parsons, sure he got a real racket goin'."

"Kim Squires is gonna have her baby and keep it," said Karen, flicking cigarette ash on the carpet. "Then she'll have a good chance to get her own apartment. They won't pay for an apartment any more if it's just yourself. But s'posin' I never gets an apartment I couldn't face havin' another youngster, could you?"

"No way," said Bev, shaking her head. "I got enough trouble with the one I got now. Mom don't want to look after her no more. She got a chance of a job."

"Girls, you're not allowed to smoke here," Mrs. Andrews had said. "And you shouldn't be smoking anyway, Karen. It makes it a lot harder on you when you take the anaesthetic."

The two girls had shrugged and crushed out their cigarettes under their high-heeled cowboy boots.

"The two of them are always down by the harbour after the Portuguese," Shirley told Heather and Eileen on the way home in the taxi. "They're as hard as nails. I pities the poor Portuguese young fellas, I really do, gettin' in tow with them."

Eileen hadn't said anything. She'd been very quiet, not like herself at all. She had cried at the hospital, had sat down on the chair beside Heather's bed, buried her face in the blanket and cried for several minutes. Afterwards, coming home in the cab, she was almost distant, briefly answering the taximan's questions, leaning back on the seat with her eyes closed.

"Heather, why didn't you tell me? I can't understand why you wouldn't tell me." At the hospital, after she stopped crying, she asked that question over and over again. Heather hadn't known what to say.

"I don't know, Mom," she said finally. "I really don't know. I suppose I was afraid you'd be disappointed. And then I thought maybe you wouldn't let me have the abortion. You always said...."

"Who gives a good God damn what I always said?" Eileen had sat up straight then, and pushed back her hair. She still hadn't kissed Heather, or touched her, except for that first brief pressure on her arm.

"I hope you don't mind me telling Mom," Shirley had said. "I just had to, that's all. I knew she'd be all right about it."

"The fella responsible for this, that's who I'd like to lay my hands on," Eileen had said then. "Men. They're all alike, every one of them. If I had ahold of that guy I'd strangle him with my bare hands." She had spread out her hands in front of her then, and looked at them. They were rough and red from the strong hairdressing lotions that seeped in through the cracks in her rubber gloves. Two of her fingernails were broken; the red nail polish chipped in places. As Heather looked at her mother's hands she recalled a Saturday evening when she was about ten. She and Shirley had been sitting in the kitchen watching as Eileen brushed polish remover on her then long nails. Heather could almost smell it now, the strong, sweetish, slightly sickly smell of the nail polish remover. Nothing special had happened that night; later on Eileen had gone out somewhere with Mollie, her nails all freshly painted a dark red shade. Nan was there and when Heather went to bed she came into the room and softly recited,

*Wynken, Blynken and Nod one night*
*Sailed off in a wooden shoe*

to her as she drifted into sleep. She had thought drowsily as Nan covered her up, "I'm too old for this," but she was glad just the same.

Shirley came in from the kitchen and sat down in the rocking chair. "You want something?" she asked. "Want me to go over to the store and pick up up some juice or something?"

"No, that's all right. There's Tang in the fridge and a little drop of apple juice. Aren't you goin' out anywhere tonight?"

"No, girl, I thought I'd stay in for a change. There's nowhere to go, anyhow. Since I broke up with Randy there's nothing to do nighttime."

"Do you miss him?"

"Not really, not as much as I thought I would. I miss goin' places with him, though. Joyce and all them got their boyfriends and I don't want to be forever taggin' along with them."

"You don't need to stay in with me, you know. I'll be okay."

"No, I don't want to go out, really. I'd just as soon stay in and watch TV."

Heather wasn't used to being treated like an invalid. She'd never really been sick in her life, except for chicken pox and German measles years before, so long ago that she couldn't remember how she'd felt. Apart from that there'd only been the odd cold and a few bouts of stomach flu. She hadn't even had her tonsils out.

It was hard for her to realize that the abortion was actually over, that she was still alive, that she wasn't pregnant any more. She felt her stomach cautiously. It didn't look or feel any different on the outside. The burning was still there inside, and the soreness; she could still feel the blood flowing out of her body. Her throat was sore, though not as bad as it had been in the morning.

The phone rang.

"I'll get it," said Shirley, and then, "It's for you, Heather. Can you take it? Sounds like that girl Linda."

Oh, no, not Linda. Not now. She'd have to answer it, though. She got up slowly and went into the kitchen.

"Hallo."

"Hi, Heather, it's Linda. I was wondering if you were sick."

"Yes, girl, I've been sick," she heard herself say. "I should be back Monday, though."

"What is it, the flu or something? You sound like you've got a sore throat."

The sore throat was coming in handy. "A kind of flu, I guess." Suppose she told Linda the real reason she'd been off? Suppose she were to say, "I was in the hospital today, Linda. Oh, no, nothing serious, just an abortion."

"Do you want to know what we've got for homework? All the teachers piled it on, like they do every weekend. We've got history and French and math, and then there's that assignment Mr. Harris gave us in English. That's got to be in by next Wednesday. It's a real toughie, too."

Heather couldn't even remember the assignment topic. "What pages have we got in history?" She couldn't have cared less, but she had to say something.

"Seventy-nine to eighty-seven. It's a really boring part. Hey listen, do you want to come up to school to watch our basketball game tomorrow? We're playing Holy Heart."

Heather had always felt that her world was far from Linda's but now it was as if they were living on different planets.

"Not tomorrow, I don't think, Linda," she said. "I'm going to stay around home for the weekend and make sure this flu is all better by Monday." What a liar she was turning into. "Thanks for the homework."

"All right, then, see you Monday, okay? Oh, yes, a few of us are taking up a collection to give Mr. Harris a Christmas present. Do you want to go in on it? We thought we'd get him that new *Dictionary of Newfoundland English* that just came out, although some of the girls think a bottle of whiskey would be better."

"Yeah, I'll chip in. Get what you like."

"Okay, see you Monday. Take care."

Take care. The words echoed mockingly in Heather's head as she replaced the receiver.

The phone rang again right away. This time it was Debbie.

"What're you doin', girl. I haven't seen you this dog's age. Are you sick or what?" In the background Heather could hear rock music, very loud. Debbie always kept the stereo on full blast; both her grandparents were deaf.

"I got a touch of the flu," she answered, thinking she'd unplug the phone as soon as Debbie hung up. Talking to people was such a strain, especially having to lie all the time.

Back in the living room Shirley was watching *Too Close for Comfort.* "God, wouldn't it get you the way all the old women in the TV shows are havin' babies? First it was Mr. Carlson's wife in *WKRP* and now it's Ted's wife on this. And they're all so damn *happy* about it. You knows darn well in real life they'd be absolutely poisoned."

Heather said nothing. She felt achingly weary.

*I am a-weary, weary,*
*I would that I were dead.*

Mr. Harris had read them those lines when they were studying Tennyson's *Mariana.* They had sounded romantic and remote at that time. Now they just sounded appropriate. She remembered how on Wednesday (was that really only the day before yesterday?) she had wanted to die. Really and truly wanted to die, for the first time in her life. She didn't want to any more now. She wasn't exactly sure why she wanted to live but she knew she didn't want to die.

"You didn't mind me tellin' Mom, did you?" Shirley was crouching on the floor in front of the television, her back to Heather. "I just felt like I had to. She took it pretty good, didn't she? You know what was the very first thing she said when I told her?"

"What?"

"She said 'Oh, the poor youngster. The poor young thing!' Heather, she sounded exactly like Nan, you know how Nan would start to cry if the least little thing happened to one of us?"

The phone rang again. Heather wiped her eyes. She had forgotten to unplug it.

179

"You stay there, I'll get it," said Shirley. "Hallo? Oh, hi, Mom. Yes, she's okay. No, I don't want to go out. Wait a second, I'll ask her. Hey, Heather, Mom wants to know if you wants anything brought home."

Heather shook her head.

"No, Mom, she don't want nothing. Okay, I'll tell her." She hung up the receiver and came back into the room. "Mom's leavin' Nan's now to come home. Nan gave her a whole lot of fruit to bring out. She said someone brought it to her and she can't eat it."

"She didn't tell Nan about me, did she?"

"I don't guess so. Poor Nan is so taken up with herself now that she don't worry about other people like she used to."

Heather went up to the bathroom to change her pad again. If she kept bleeding like this she'd have to buy more Kotex. Did anyone ever bleed to death after an abortion? She knew they used to in the old days, but what about now?

Before she got back downstairs the phone rang again.

"It's for you again, girl," Shirley yelled. "You're some popular tonight."

Who in the world could it be this time?

"Hallo?"

"Hallo, is that you Heather? This is Theresa Sullivan speaking."

Theresa Sullivan. Who was Theresa Sullivan?

"I don't..." she began, and then she remembered. The first name had thrown her. "Oh, it's you, Mrs. Sullivan."

"Yes, girl. I just thought I'd call and ask how you're doin'."

"Okay, I s'pose. I'm bleedin' quite a bit."

"So am I, but I guess that's normal." She paused for a moment. "I was so glad your mother came in to the hospital. I know how I would've felt if it was one of mine."

"How'd you get on when you got home?" Heather leaned back and rested her head against the wall.

"All right, as it happened. Sheila was home before I was, though. Joanie, she's fourteen, was here too, so it was okay. Sheila was right worried up, though. She's so used to me bein' here all the time."

"Did you get a chance to lie down?"

"Yes, when Jeannette came home — that's my oldest daughter, the one works over to Dominion — I went up to bed for a while. I told her after about what I had done. I think she partly guessed, anyway."

"I'm glad you told her."

Heather switched the receiver to her other hand. "What about Mr. Sullivan?"

"Oh, he's gone out to an AA meeting. I wouldn't care if he went to them twenty-four hours a day. He's grand now, girl, knock on wood."

Heather could hear a faint tap-tap, as if Mrs. Sullivan had rapped her knuckles on a chair or a table. "Listen, Heather, Sheila's callin' me. I got to go. Phone me sometime, won't you?"

"Yeah, I will for sure."

Funny, how easy it was to talk to Mrs. Sullivan. Heather lay back on the chesterfield and pulled the bedspread tightly around her. She had never had a real conversation with a woman that age before. If she had met Mrs. Sullivan at Nan's, or anywhere else, the two of them would have smiled and said something about the weather, and that would have been all. As it was she felt as close or closer to her than she'd ever felt to anyone who wasn't a member of the family. Closer than she'd ever felt to Eileen. She'd always been close to Nan, of course, before she got sick, but that was different. She wondered if Mrs. Sullivan's daughters felt the same distance between themselves and their mother as she'd always felt with hers.

The front door opened, letting in a cold blast of air.

"Anybody home? I got something for ya."

Lorraine came in, a large shopping bag in her hand. "I just had to run over to Murray's for a few groceries; I didn't have no money to go to the supermarket Wednesday but I got my cheque today, thank God. I'm glad I don't have to go up to that welfare office for another two weeks. It gets me right down up there." She sat down in the armchair and put the bag on the floor. Her face was flushed from the cold; there were a few large snowflakes on her coat. She looked at Heather, and then away again.

"How're you doin', girl? Ugh, these boots are some hard to get off."

Heather could tell that Lorraine knew. Her mother must have told her, or Shirley.

"I got some ginger ale here for you, Heather, and a carton of ice cream."

"What about me?" said Shirley, pretending to be offended.

"Okay, baby, you can have some." Lorraine went to the kitchen and came back with a glass of ginger ale and a dish of Neapolitan ice cream.

"It must be great to be waited on," she said, as she handed the ice cream to Heather.

"Yes, I think I'll be sick more often." Heather tried to adopt the same light tone as her sister. She didn't want Lorraine to ask her about the abortion, just didn't want to talk about it any more.

"Who's with Jason?" Shirley had given up on the television and put a Rolling Stones record on the stereo. She didn't have it turned up as loud as usual. As she spoke her shoulders moved up and down in time to the music.

"Mike is over there asleep on the couch," said Lorraine, lighting a cigarette. "He was up on the line all day and he's tired, I s'pose."

"Did he get anything?"

"Four rabbits. I'm so sick of rabbit I could scream. I just put two in the fridge freezer for ye." She blew smoke toward the ceiling, squinting at the dirty stucco. "He haven't been too bad here lately though, I must say. If he could only get a job I think he'd be okay. He hates bein' around the house and havin' no money."

Heather leaned back on the pillow Eileen had put behind her head and tried to analyze how she was feeling. She was still a bit lightheaded from the anaesthetic and the bleeding; she found it hard to straighten up when she walked. Apart from the physical problems, her main feeling was one of deep relief. Was it only last night she had sat here, preoccupied with what was ahead of her, frightened by it, wanting to die and yet, at the same time, afraid to die? She still wondered what had happened to the...pregnancy. Was she really a murderer because of what she'd done? Her abdomen felt as if she'd been scooped out inside like a pumpkin on Hallowe'en. But of course she *had* been scooped out inside. Did Mrs. Sullivan feel the same way? Perhaps she felt worse, because of her religion. But then again, her religion would probably be a comfort to her later on. She could go to Confession, do penance and receive absolution. What could Heather do? Perhaps, sometime in the future, she'd be kept awake at night by memories. Maybe her conscience would bother her badly. Right now she felt too sore, too tired, too sleepy to worry about future feelings.

She didn't realize she'd fallen asleep until she opened her eyes and saw her mother standing near the chesterfield, looking down at here.

"God, Heather, you're white as a sheet. Are you sure you're okay?"

"Yeah, I think so." She pulled herself up into a sitting position, feeling another gush of blood as she did so.

Eileen sat down on the chesterfield. "I can't believe this is happening," she said, looking straight ahead. "I just can't believe this is happening to us."

Heather wanted to say she was sorry, to tell her mother she'd make it up to her. She couldn't find the words.

Eileen picked up the bag at her feet and pulled out apples, oranges, bananas and grapefruit. "Mom had all this stuff given her," she said, handing Heather a banana, its yellow skin mottled with brown. "That's a nice ripe one, Heather; some of the others are still a bit green." Heather peeled the banana and forced herself to eat it. She hadn't wanted anything to eat since the surgery.

"How is Nan tonight?"

"The same, girl, the same. Or perhaps a little bit worse. She don't bother to get up at all now."

"Who gave her the fruit?"

"I think it was the Salvation Army League of Mercy. That's a group they got to go around visiting hospitals and that. I must say they're good to Mom. They can't help it if she don't eat the stuff."

"It'd be better if they'd send flowers, though, wouldn't it?" said Lorraine. She was drinking Pepsi now, and smoking another cigarette. For an instant she looked like the old Lorraine, the carefree girl who had loved to sing and dance and rollerskate.

"No, girl, Mom never liked bought flowers. She always said they reminded her of death. I remember one time Muriel sent her mums on her birthday, and after a couple of days she threw them out in the garbage. Couldn't stand the smell of them, she told me."

"I don't like 'em either," said Shirley. "They puts me right in mind of a funeral home."

For a moment the four of them were silent, Eileen sitting beside Heather, staring straight ahead of her, Lorraine in the rocker, sipping her Pepsi, Shirley on the floor beside the record player which she had turned off when Eileen came in, and Heather herself on the chesterfield, feeling chilly even under the warm chenille spread.

Eileen stood up and shook herself. "Did the paper come? I wants to show you something I was reading into Mom's."

"It's in the bathroom," said Shirley. "I'll get it for you."

When Shirley came back with the paper Eileen knelt on the floor and spread it out in front of her. "Here it is, in the In Memoriam section, you know, where they haves the verses in about dead people. There's one in here about Mrs. Holwell used to live over there on the hill, remember them?"

"Yes," said Lorraine. "I went to school with Sharon Holwell."

"Here it is. Listen, I'll read it. It's really long so I'll just read the last verse."

*And when she goes home to receive her reward*
*She will dwell in God's kingdom and keep house for the Lord;*
*Where she'll light up the stars that shine through the night*
*And keep all the moonbeams sparkling and bright.*

"Ever remembered and sadly missed by her loving husband, seven sons, six daughters and thirty-seven grandchildren."

"Whew," said Shirley. "She musta been glad to die and get away from all that crowd."

"But just imagine," said Eileen, "thinkin' that a woman would want heaven to be like that, dwelling in God's kingdom and keepin' house for the Lord. Can you picture anyone wantin' to do that?"

"Mr. Holwell drinks like a fish," said Lorraine. "Or at least he used to when I was goin' around with Sharon."

"He used to beat up his wife, too," said Eileen. "Ada Brazil told me that. She lived right next door to them and poor Mrs. Holwell would run out there nighttime when he'd come home loaded. If there *is* a heaven, that poor creature deserves something better than doin' the housework in it."

If there is a heaven. Heather had worried about that ever since she could remember. She was very young, about seven, when she began to visualize a procession of all the people she knew climbing a steep hill and then, when they reached the top, disappearing one by one into the faceless other side. She hadn't experienced death in the family then, but shortly afterwards Pop Morgan had died, and later Vera Dalton from school, and the two Pittman boys from across the street who'd gone over the Queen's Wharf in their car. Then there had been her Grandmother Novak. Now Nan was dying, and after that, in slow procession, would come Eileen, her father, her sisters and, finally, herself.

"You didn't show that poem to Nan, did you, Mom?" Heather asked, suddenly afraid she had.

"No, girl, you knows I didn't. I got enough sense not to do that."

"I wonder does Nan really think she's goin' to heaven?" Shirley spoke as if talking to herself.

"If she do she certainly don't talk about it," said Eileen. "No, girl, I think she's the same as the rest of us, for all she's saved and converted in the Salvation Army. She just don't want to think about it."

"How was Herb tonight?" Lorraine asked.

"Same as always. He keeps the house beautiful, I must say that for him. But he's always there, hoverin' over Mom. I never gets the chance to talk to her alone." She blinked a couple of times and looked down at the carpet.

"God, this carpet is filthy. I suppose we'll have to hire one of them machines from Dominion and get it cleaned up for Christmas." She leaned back on the chesterfield, stretching her arms over her head. She let one hand drop on Heather's knees, drawn up under the spread.

"I guess I'll go to bed," she said finally. "This has sure been a day. You want anything, Heather?"

"No, Mom, thanks."

"You're feelin' okay, are you?"

"Yeah, I'm okay."

"Get a good rest tomorrow, now, and by Sunday you'll probably be feeling pretty good. Mom was askin' about you, as usual. She was sayin' something about givin' you that little pink teapot she got."

The pink lustre teapot. Nan had always said she was going to leave it to Heather when she died. They joked about it when Nan first told her. "Some day, when I'm pushin' up daisies, you'll have this." Nan had been washing all her good dishes when she said that, getting ready for Christmas. She'd been wearing an old pair of crimpknit slacks and a green pullover sweater. She rarely wore slacks, always said they made her look too fat. She'd had both her breasts then; in the loose brassiere they hung almost to her waist. After she finished the dishes she cooked liver and onions for supper; Pop Morgan had been alive then. She laughed when she talked about pushing up daisies. Death had been the furthest thing from her mind.

Eileen leaned forward and pushed back Heather's hair. Heather remembered one night when she slept at Linda Stone's, how Linda had kissed her mother, her father and her brother before she went to bed. She'd told Debbie about it, laughing a little and feeling like a traitor. "Ugh," Debbie had said, screwing up her face. "They must be some mushy crowd."

"Sure you don't want nothing, Heather?" Eileen asked again.

"No, Mom, I'm okay. Really."

"All right, then, I'll go on up to bed. Don't ye be too late now, will ye?

She left the room and went upstairs, walking very slowly. Shirley turned on the television; this time it was *Taxi*.

"That Louie, I could flatten him, couldn't you?" said Shirley.

"I likes Alex, though, don't you?" Lorraine moved closer to the screen. "Is he married, I wonder?"

Heather turned her head toward the television. She liked *Taxi*, especially Jim, the burnt-out drug addict. When she saw his troubled face, spaced-out as usual, she thought: He looks the way I feel. Even though she still felt sick and sore, even though she had that hollow feeling inside, there was something pleasant about being here in the warm room with her two sisters, her mother in the bedroom upstairs. It reminded her of Eliza Laidlaw in one of the O. Douglas books. Eliza was a Scottish girl, a minister's daughter who lived in Glasgow surrounded by a devoted family. Perhaps, for a little while, she would pretend to be Eliza, just as, when she was younger, she had pretended to be Nancy Drew or Judy Bolton, fantasizing about mysteries she would solve.

Later, when she had settled herself in bed, she felt the corners of her mouth twitch. She wasn't sure if she was going to laugh or cry. Eileen's words about poor dead Mrs. Holwell rang in her ears. As she recalled Eileen's fake-dramatic reading of the memorial poem about shining up the stars in heaven, her shoulders started to shake. Soon she was laughing helplessly, burying her face in the pillow so nobody would hear her. Was she going nuts, or what?

Nan used to have those laughing jags, as she called them. She would laugh until the tears ran down her cheeks about something that wasn't funny at all, a speech impediment or an odd way of talking. Then she would wipe her eyes, her shoulders still shaking, and say, "That's shockin' for me."

Every time Heather tried to stop laughing she'd hear Eileen's words again and another hiccuping giggle would escape her. I must be hysterical, she told herself, but even the word hysterical sounded hilarious. At last, her head still deep in the pillow, she fell asleep.

# Sixteen

*City sidewalks*
*Busy sidewalks*
*Dressed in holiday style;*
*In the air there's a feeling of Christmas.*
*Children laughing, people passing*
*Meeting smile after smile*
*And on every street corner you'll hear...*

As Heather walked through Bowring's, balancing four different parcels, she hummed along with the piped-in music, hardly realizing what she was doing. Just inside one of the street doors an elderly man with glasses was playing *Silent Night* on his concertina. He was in Salvation Army uniform; beside him was a large, transparent globe hanging from a red metal stand. It was half-filled with silver coins and paper money. Heather had seen the man before when she'd gone to church with Nan. He was a retired officer, a lame man who sat in the same seat every Sunday, giving his testimony often. Sometimes, to prefix it, he sang a chorus or a verse of an old song. She wondered how he felt about competing with the Muzak this way. Pasted on to the globe (Nan and Herb would have called it a pot and radio announcers said kettle) was a strip of white paper with the Salvation Army logo on it in red, and the words God Bless You. Another strip bore the words "Keep Christ in Christmas." Heather felt in her jacket pocket for a quarter and slipped it into the slot. "Thank you and God bless you," said the concertina player, continuing to play as he spoke. As she moved back toward the jewellery counter he began to sing softly:

*Round yon virgin, mother and child*
*Holy Infant, so tender and mild*
*Sleep in heavenly pe...ace*
*Sleep in heavenly peace."*

"Would you like me to put all your parcels in one big bag for you?" asked the woman at the cash. Heather had picked up the pierced earrings her mother had asked her to buy for Mollie. "Here you go, that should be easier for you to handle." The saleslady handed Heather the bag. She was a tall, big woman who usually worked in the cosmetic department nearby. She always dressed in stylish outfits and wore lots and lots of makeup, especially around her eyes. Her eyelids were coloured a soft blue today, she was wearing a royal blue, tightly-fitting dress with a large blue and silver Christmas corsage just above her left breast. She smiled now, and said, "Merry Christmas" as if she really meant it.

Christmas Eve was one of the busiest days in the year at Ricardo's. Before she left for work, Eileen had given Heather a hastily-written list and a handful of crumpled bills, instructing her to buy, as well as the earrings, a pair of heavy socks for Herb, gloves for Lorraine and Mike and a Tonka truck for Jason. "I got him a snowsuit but you knows he's gonna want me to give him something to play with," she said as she'd scribbled the list. "Try to do the best you can with the money, girl. That's every cent I got left. The darn old groceries takes so much. I'm hopin' to get a few tips today, so that'll help out. If you do have any money left, get a couple of packs of tinsel for the tree, will ya? We haven't got half enough, as usual."

The Salvation Army man had switched to something more up-tempo: *I Heard The Bells On Christmas Day*. This time his Muzak competition was Elvis singing *Blue Christmas*.

Heather thought of how, a few short weeks before, such a song would have reminded her instantly of Frank. Now she hardly ever thought about him at all. Sometimes she even found it difficult to remember what he looked like.

Earlier this morning, at Woolworth's picking up the socks for Herb, she heard Frank's mother's voice from a neighbouring checkout. She no longer made special attempts to go to Mrs. Marshall with her purchases; now she just took whichever checkout was least busy.

"I'm certainly going to miss Frank this year," Mrs. Marshall had said to another employee. "Of course I knew he wouldn't be home after only just goin' but I never really realized until last night that he wouldn't be there with us for Christmas dinner. He's dyin' about Christmas pudding, too. I always used to have a small one especially for him." As she said the last words she brushed her hands across her eyes.

"Have he got anywhere to go for his dinner?" the other woman asked.

"Oh, yes, he's getting together with three other fellas who got an apartment in Edmonton. They got a turkey and everything. I'd like to see them cookin' it. One of the fellas is Betty Walsh's son, you know her, she works in men's wear."

Heather had glanced quickly at Mrs. Marshall as she passed her checkout on the way to the door. Her eyes looked sad; for a moment Heather felt as if she were looking at Frank. It was uncanny, this sometime resemblance. She had noticed the same kind of thing before, in her mother and Shirley, for instance, or Lorraine and the pictures of their father. Nine times out of ten you could look at a person and see nothing beyond that person; the tenth time you'd get a glimpse of a relative, especially around the eyes.

"Hey, miss, don't forget your parcel," the checkout girl had called. Heather went back to pick it up and, with another quick glance at Frank's mother who was now Mrs. Marshall and nobody else, she left the store.

Now, at Bowring's, as she made her way downstairs to the toy department, she thought again of Frank's mother. If she'd gone ahead and had the baby Mrs. Marshall would have been its grandmother, and Frank's brothers and sisters its aunts and uncles. Only they would never have known, of course.

For a week or so after the abortion, once the lingering effects of the anaesthetic had vanished, she had slept badly. Every time she closed her eyes she could see the operating room with its green-clad, masked apparitions looking down at her, talking to each other in words that sounded foreign and far away. And every night she would think of the baby, or the fetus, or whatever it was, and wonder if it had been thrown into the garbage, or burnt, or kept in a bottle. Had it been a boy or a girl? Would it have been a healthy child, or would it perhaps have been deformed? She had read in the *Reader's Digest* that sixteen was a bad age to have a baby, both for the mother and the child. And she wasn't even sixteen yet, not until the fifteenth of January. Sometimes she hoped it had been deformed; that made its casual destruction a little easier to bear. Perhaps she'd ask the doctor when she went back for her six-week checkup. But no, she'd better not; if Dr. Potter told her the baby/fetus had been perfect she knew she'd find all this even harder to bear.

She was sleeping better now, as the memory of the operating room and the recovery room became less sharp.

Mrs. Sullivan phoned her once more after that first time. "Just wonderin' how you were," she said. "I'm doin' fine now myself, girl. Sometimes I just can't believe I'm not pregnant any more."

"Do you feel guilty?" Heather had hardly known what she wanted Mrs. Sullivan's reply to be.

"Not near as bad as I thought I'd be. I looks at poor young Sheila and I'm glad she's still the youngest. I hope she always will be. She needs an awful lot of care and attention."

"How is Mr. Sullivan now?" Heather felt as if she knew him.

"Still going to AA, girl. I'm keeping my fingers crossed for Christmas. That's always the worse time of the year for alcoholics. Hes buddies are forever askin' him in for a drink and all that kind of stuff. But so far he's still holding on." Heather heard a long sigh. "'Member how the nurses wanted me to have my tubes tied while I was in the hospital? I couldn't do it then because your husband got to sign a paper for that. I believe though, girl, I'm goin' to bring it up to him after Christmas. I think he'd be all right about it now. I still don't have to tell him about the other thing."

Mrs. Sullivan's words reminded Heather of what Mrs. Andrews had told her about abstaining from intercourse for the next six weeks. She wondered how Mrs. Sullivan was managing. Imagine if she got pregnant again before she could get back in hospital.

Eileen had hardly mentioned the abortion since the day it had been done. For a few days afterwards she'd checked on Heather's eating habits, brought home milk and fruit to her instead of Pepsi and chocolate bars, and asked her obliquely a few times if she was "all right." Now things were back pretty much the same as they had been earlier in the fall. Eileen went to work every day and, most evenings, to Nan's. Weekends she still went out with Mollie; her new boyfriend had gone to work on an oil rig in the Gulf of Mexico and wouldn't be back for months. Shirley was working at the Arcade, just for the Christmas rush.

"I hope you'll look after yourself now, Heather," Eileen said one night as they lingered over the supper table. "Don't put yourself in the way of gettin' like that again." Heather wasn't sure if Eileen was advising her to have nothing further to do with boys, or men, or if she was warning her to be careful. When Eileen got up from the table after giving her that piece of advice she straightened the collar of Heather's blouse and smoothed down her hair

Bowring's was getting more and more crowded. When Heather went into the washroom there were several people ahead of her waiting to get into the toilet cubicles. A small woman with short straight dark hair stood near the hand-drying machine, smoking a cigarette. Heather had often seen her before, mostly in public washrooms like this one or scurrying along Water Street. She always walked very fast, in quick, short steps, darting her dark eyes from side to side as if she was afraid of being followed. Today she was wearing a green coat and short black rubber boots with the tops of white socks showing above them. She was always very neat.

"Shockin' cold out today, ain't it?" she said to Heather, flicking the ash from her cigarette into a nearby sink.

"Yes," said Heather.

"It's nice to have a bit of snow for Christmas though, ain't it?" In every encounter she'd had with this woman, all similar to this morning's, Heather had never heard her talk about anything except the weather. For the first time she wondered where the woman lived, if she had a family, if she would spend tomorrow in a happy group of celebrating people or if it would be like any other day.

After she had used the toilet Heather went to wash her hands but she hated using the hand dryer and there were no paper towels. She put down her parcels, reached into her purse for a tissue and hastily ran the hot water over her fingers, drying them as best she could on the tissue. She carefully avoided the mirror above the sink. She disliked being caught unawares by her own reflection staring back at her, always seeming to her to be much less attractive than any other face in the room. At the next wash basin stood a tall young woman whose thick black hair was gathered into a knot at the back of her head. She touched a powder puff to an already perfectly made-up face and ran a lipstick over her lips. There was a little triangle of colour on each of her high cheekbones. Heather had begun to notice those tiny perfect triangles on some women's faces about a year before. How had everyone suddenly known, at the same time, that this was the latest trend in makeup? Two or three times, in the bathroom at home, Heather had borrowed her mother's cream blush and tried to achieve the desired effect. It was useless. Her cheekbones weren't at all prominent, for one thing, and she was never able to get the colour on in exactly the right place. The woman at the mirror was finished now; with a flick of hand to head she turned and left the washroom.

How was it that some women always looked so gorgeous? Heather knew she'd never be able to apply makeup in a public place like this; there was something about it that always made her nervous and embarrassed. Still not looking into the mirror she ran her fingers through her short hair, picked up her parcels and moved toward the door.

"Merry Christmas, now," said the little dark-eyed woman. Her small darting eyes reminded Heather of the eyes of a cornered rat, or a ferret, although she had never seen a ferret. "Hope Sandy Claws bes good to you," she continued, throwing the stub of her cigarette into the sink. Heather nodded and started to say thank you, and then was almost knocked down by two big parcel-laden women coming through the door.

193

She found a truck for Jason, marked down because it was Christmas Eve. She'd look for the tinsel at the Arcade; that would probably be the cheapest place.

As she left the store she passed the concertina player again, hoping he'd remember that she'd already put a quarter in the pot. It was more than half full now; she could see several five dollar bills, a few tens and even one twenty. Now he was playing *O come all ye faithful* while the Muzak selection was *Frosty the Snowman*. Heather remembered a Christmas years before when Nan had invited Eileen and herself, Lorraine and Shirley to a pork chop supper on Christmas Eve. "We always used to have pork chops Christmas Eve on the South Side," Nan said as she put the steaming plates in front of them. She had riced the potatoes, mashed the turnip with butter and pepper and boiled the green peas that had been lying in soak all day in the big buff-coloured earthenware bowl.

Pop Morgan hadn't been home when they sat down to the table. Nan was talking more than usual, and glancing toward the door every few seconds. They were all finished eating when Pop arrived. Nan had put his dinner in the oven with a pie plate over it to keep it from drying up. There were three other men with Pop, men who'd been in the Royal Navy with him during the war. They were singing as they approached the house; Pop had a really good tenor voice:

*O come let us adore Him*
*O come let us adore Him*
*O come let us adore Hi...im*
*Chr...i...st the Lord*

Pop went to the pantry and brought out the large bottle of dark rum he'd bought the day before. He poured a drink for each of his companions and then insisted that Nan, Eileen and the girls have a glass of port wine. Nan's father, who had worked with Baine Johnston's on the South Side, used to supervise the storing of Newman's port in special casks in a concrete building with small barred windows on Water Street. As Heather walked up Water Street now she could almost taste the pungent warmth of the wine as it had rolled down her throat and made her chest burn. Her mother had mixed some water with it but it had still tasted strong. Pop was in a very good mood that night, at least up until the time she and her mother and sisters left to go home. He and his friends sat around the kitchen table drinking the rum, his dinner remaining untasted in the oven. Nan tried to relax in the front room with the rest of them but every few minutes she'd made an excuse to go to the kitchen.

The snow was falling thickly now; it was going to be a white Christmas. Heather slipped and slid along the sidewalk; the soles of her last year's winter boots had worn smooth. The crowds were thicker, too. People kept bumping into each other and saying, "Oh, excuse me." Most of them were smiling; the wear and tear of the last few weeks was over now and they'd soon be able to relax.

On the corner by the Bank of Nova Scotia three men were standing, leaning against the wall of the building. One was rubbing his gloveless hands together; another pulled up the collar of his long, black overcoat. Their faces were red and shiny; a strong smell of alcohol surrounded them. "Got a quarter to spare there, little one?" the tallest man asked. Heather had often seen the three of them before, hanging around outside liquor stores and banks. She always tried not to look at them, to pass by as if they weren't there, but today she felt in her jacket pocket, pulled out a quarter and passed it to the man who had spoken to her. "Thanks and a Merry Christmas to ya," he said, slurring the words a little. Then he turned toward an approaching couple, his bare hand outstretched again. The man in the overcoat was singing, almost to himself,

*I sell the morning paper, sir*
*My name is Jimmy Brown.*

Across the street a boy from Mount Cashel Orphanage, a yellow and green toque pulled down over his ears, was ringing the handbell that he held in his mittened hand. "Come right in, ladies and gentlemen," the male voice on the loudspeaker blared, inviting passersby to test their luck at the Mount Cashel Christmas Raffle. "Come in and try, come in and buy. We've got toys for the kiddies, chocolates, even a few turkeys. Step right up, ladies and gentlemen, only a few more tickets left. All gone, Joe? All gone."

Heather was tempted to go into the raffle and try her luck but persuaded herself it was better to spend the little bit of money she had left on a cup of tea and a scone at the Speakeasy. Her feet were tired and she still had Barter's Hill to climb.

As she sat in the restaurant, a cup of hot tea in front of her, and spooned apricot jam over the warm, buttered scone, she recalled the Saturday morning she had sat there with Debbie and Donna, that Saturday when Donna had invited her to the party. If she hadn't gone to the party, if she had never met Frank, the past few weeks would have been so different. She looked through the window at the harbour, crowded now with boats and ships in port for Christmas. The South Side Hills stretched up on the other side of the water, the rocks and grass and bushes touched now with the white of the snow. She thought of Nan as a girl, climbing those hills, picking the blueberries that had earned her the money to buy the blue glass vase that she had treasured so much, the one she had mourned for after the cat knocked it down and smashed it.

"It was the first money I ever earned," she had told Heather. "Fifty cents, I got for my blueberries, and I went right over to Goobie's and bought that vase. 'Twould cost an awful lot more than fifty cents now."

Heather had admired the vase, its dark-blue grooved glass covered with a bold design in pink and cream. In the early summer, when the lilac tree in her backyard was in bloom, Nan had always kept the vase in the centre of the dining room table, a bunch of purple lilacs in it.

"That's the only kind of flowers I really likes, lilacs," she had said. "Lilacs and wildflowers, like bachelor buttons and buttercups. There's no smell in the world to beat the smell of lilacs." After her marriage, when Nan had moved from the South Side to live with Pop, the two of them went back to her old home, dug up the lilac tree there and planted it in the garden of the little house Pop had built in the northern part of St. John's, on the higher levels. They'd had only two rooms of the house finished at that time, the kitchen and one bedroom. Pop built the rest of it while they were living in it.

"He didn't drink so much then, first when we were married," Nan told Heather. "It was after the war that he started to get really bad."

When she last visited Nan, a few nights before, Nan had given her the little pink lustre teapot she'd been telling her about for years. Nan stayed in bed almost all the time now, getting up occasionally to sit in the upholstered rocking chair Herb had moved into the bedroom.

"You were always my favourite grandchild," she said, giving Heather's hand a little squeeze with her own thin white one. "But don't tell Lorraine and Shirley that, will ya? Or Fred's youngsters."

Heather cried when Nan gave her the teapot; she couldn't help it. It had always stood on its own shelf in Nan's old-fashioned sideboard, never used for anything as mundane as steeping tea. Whenever she cleaned house Nan would take it down and wash it, polishing it off afterwards with a soft cloth. Then she'd put it back where it belonged.

Nan didn't complain much any more. She seemed to grow weaker every day and to withdraw more and more from those around her.

"Herb wants us to go there for Christmas dinner," Eileen had told Heather and Shirley the night before. "All of us, even Lorraine and Jason, and Mike if Lorraine can coax him to come. He asked Fred and them too, but of course Bun wants to go to her own mother's. He got a great big turkey, over twenty pounds, and he says he's gonna make Mom come to the table. It's not for what she'll eat, poor thing. I'd sooner stay home but I s'pose it's the least we can do. And I'll get a rest out of it, anyway." Eileen had stared blankly ahead of her when she said that, then blinked and went to the sink to wash the dishes.

Heather climbed the shallow steps to Water Street. Halfway between Tooton's and the Arcade she met Bertie Lane. He was staggering a little but didn't look as belligerent as he usually did after he'd been drinking. He stopped in the middle of the sidewalk, slipping to one side before he found his feet, and held his arms straight out from his sides so that Heather couldn't pass.

"Hedder, will you marry me?" he asked. His shabby parka hung open to reveal a fawn turtleneck sweater pulled down over his bulging stomach.

"I don't know, Bertie, I'll have to think about it." Heather shifted her parcels from one arm to the other. "I'll let you know later on, okay?"

Bertie leaned forward and gave her a wet kiss on the cheek. "Can I come over tonight to see your Christmas tree?"

"Yes, if you're not too drunk. I got to go now, Bertie. I got more shopping to do yet."

"Have you got either present for me?" His blue eyes had a hopeful glint in them. "I wouldn't mind havin' a flask of rum."

"Well, I'm not gettin' you that but I'll see what I can do. I really got to go now, Bertie. Merry Christmas."

"Merry Christmas." He lurched off in the opposite direction, singing *White Christmas*.

She bought the tinsel at the Arcade, waving to Shirley who was frantically busy in the toy department. When she was walking up the hill, Debbie caught up with her.

"How ya doin', girl?" Debbie sounded out of breath. "Haven't you got all your shopping done yet? I just bought a new pair of them velvet pants and a top down to Sally's." She opened the bag to show Heather.

"Oh, they're lovely, Debbie. Be careful you don't get them wet, now. You goin' somewhere special?"

"Chuck is comin' in tonight from Argentia; you know, that American fella I was tellin' you about? We're goin' to a house party at his buddy's girlfriend's place."

"That's nice. Were those pants expensive? I wouldn't mind havin' a pair like them."

"$19.98. They got 'em on special, Christmas Eve and all that, you know. Mom sent me some money and Ma gave me some, too. They don't know what to be buyin' me for Christmas any more."

They walked in silence for a few minutes. Then Debbie asked "How are you feelin' now, girl?" She had told Debbie about the abortion; it wasn't half as hard to tell her as she'd expected. She still hadn't told Linda.

"All right, I s'pose. I gets tired easy, though."

"Have you heard anything from Frank?"

"No, and I don't expect to." She didn't want to talk about Frank.

They spoke very little after that. When they got to Heather's house Debbie said, "Well, girl, have a nice Christmas, now."

"Same to you."

"I'll be over tonight, before I goes to the party. I got a little gift for you. I s'pose you'll give me my Christmas, will you?"

"Syrup and cake?"

"Syrup and cake, big deal. I'm sure your mother'll have something stronger than syrup over there." Debbie was still laughing as she ran across the street.

When Heather was unlocking the door she noticed that the cover of the mailbox was pushed up, with several white envelopes showing. She pulled out the letters and went inside.

The mail was mostly Christmas cards for Eileen but one, with an Iowa postmark, was addressed to Shirley and Heather Novak. She opened it; folded inside the card was an American twenty dollar bill, and a ten, "Buy yourselves something nice," read the handwritten words underneath the printed verse. "Have a nice Christmas. Love, Dad."

She was about to put the rest of the mail on top of the fridge when an envelope fell to the floor. It had an Alberta postmark on it, and a row of Santa Claus stickers just under the stamp. It was addressed to her. Her hands trembled as she opened it. Inside was a tall card with a chubby Santa Claus trying to squeeze down a chimney. The printed words read, "Hope you find something as fat as him in your stocking." Underneath Frank had written, "I hope you have a real good Christmas. It's a bit lonely here, but I'm making out okay. I'm planning to come home for a week or so in May. Will see you then."

Heather went into the living room and sat down on the chesterfield, her boots still on. She stayed there for several minutes, staring at the bare Christmas tree in the corner, a skinny spruce that didn't quite reach the ceiling. It looked forlorn. She reached into the plastic shopping bag for a package of tinsel, opened it and carefully hung three or four strands on one of the lower branches. She kicked off her boots and went to the mantelpiece where she propped her father's card and Frank's next to each other, against the old clock that no longer told the time. Then she walked slowly upstairs with her parcels.